T0162696

COMMUNISM:

A Love Story

FRED WEEKES

iUniverse, Inc.
New York   Bloomington

Communism: A Love Story

Copyright © 2009 Fred Weekes

All rights reserved. No part of this book may be used or reproduced by any means,
graphic, electronic, or mechanical, including photocopying, recording, taping or by any
information storage retrieval system without the written permission of the publisher
except in the case of brief quotations embodied in critical articles and reviews.

This is a work of fiction. All of the characters, names, incidents, organizations, and dialogue
in this novel are either the products of the author's imagination or are used fictitiously.

iUniverse books may be ordered through booksellers or by contacting:

iUniverse
1663 Liberty Drive
Bloomington, IN 47403
www.iuniverse.com
1-800-Authors (1-800-288-4677)

Because of the dynamic nature of the Internet, any Web addresses or links contained in this book
may have changed since publication and may no longer be valid. The views expressed in this work
are solely those of the author and do not necessarily reflect the views of the publisher, and the
publisher hereby disclaims any responsibility for them.

ISBN: 978-1-4401-9589-1 (pbk)
ISBN: 978-1-4401-9590-7 (ebook)

Printed in the United States of America

iUniverse rev. date: 12/10/2009

CONTENTS

THE NIELSENS, FATHER AND SON

PART 1

THE NIELSENS, FATHER AND SON

GERMANY DECLARED WAR on the United States on the tenth of December 1941. Carl Nielsen had finished four years of college in June of that year, during which time he had been enrolled in the Naval Reserve Officer Training Corps. The program was always known by its initials, NROTC. Upon graduation he was commissioned an ensign, a naval officer of the lowest rank. On the day of Pearl Harbor, Sunday the seventh of December, Carl Nielsen was completing his training in navigation, preparing for the duties of a deck officer, one who stood watch at sea as well as in port.

For two days, Monday and Tuesday, December eighth and ninth, Carl assumed he would be sent from his station, the Brooklyn Navy Yard, to San Francisco and from there by ship to Honolulu. He had hoped he would be assigned to duty on an aircraft carrier in the Pacific but when Germany declared war on Wednesday, he guessed that in all likelihood he would go to sea in the Atlantic.

A week later he received orders to become part of a crew of a newly-launched destroyer. She was a member of the Fletcher Class, the newest destroyers in the navy. She was being completed in the shipyard at Bath, Maine. The crew was to assemble at the Charleston Navy Yard in Boston and to make their maiden voyage into the North Atlantic, probably on a speeded-up schedule.

There was a Fletcher Class destroyer in the Brooklyn Navy Yard, in for routine maintenance. Carl inspected her from the dock. He guessed she was three hundred feet long. The guns were mounted in turrets fore and aft. The navy called the guns 'five inch thirty-eights.' The diameter of the shell was five inches; multiplying five inches by thirty-eight gave one hundred ninety inches, the length of the barrel. Amidships there were ten torpedo tubes and at the rear there were racks for depth charges.

Carl knew that Germany was not a threat on the ocean's surface. The Bismarck had been sunk in 1941 off Iceland where she was caught by three cruisers of the Royal Navy. Germany had two pocket battleships, heavy cruisers really, but it was doubtful that they would venture out from their home port of Brest. The crew on Carl's ship might see a German airplane from time to time, but Carl doubted they would be found by a squadron of dive bombers. The real threat, of course, consisted of the submarines whose bases were along the Atlantic coast of France.

As he stood examining the destroyer, Carl wondered where he might be stationed when it came time to go into battle. When General Quarters was sounded over the intercom, each crew member went to a particular part of the ship to do a specific job. The best place to be was on the bridge. The worst was out on an open deck exposed to the elements, particularly during the winter months. Among the men he met at the officers' club, the scuttlebutt was that if your ship was torpedoed during the cold months and you wound up floating in the North Atlantic you had thirty seconds to live.

Carl had not been east until the navy sent him. He had been to San Francisco and Los Angeles but admitted to himself that New York was larger, more important, more varied and more entertaining than the cities on the West Coast. One of the ensigns with whom Carl was completing his training had graduated from Cornell and was a member of a prosperous, well-connected family centered in Manhattan. Through him, Carl was introduced to several families living in either apartments or brownstones mid-town. The women were more sophisticated than those with whom he had grown up. They had been to Europe for summer trips. They spoke – he could not tell how proficiently – French or German. They talked casually of places, having made an acquaintance of museums in important cities. A few had spent a year or two at school in Switzerland.

Carl asked some of these women to go out with him. They were enthusiastic and curious about going to the officers club at the Brooklyn Navy Yard. It was not a world they knew although many of their male friends were in the service.

Most of the bigger hotels devoted part of the first floor to dining and dancing. Carl had heard, either on records or on the radio, the orchestras that played in these club rooms. He would go there with a date. Another attraction, besides dancing, was watching musicians perform whom he had known about all along.

Some of the officers he met at the navy yard were already serving at sea on convoy duty. Their stories varied. Some said they had escorted a convoy half-way across the Atlantic to be met by British warships. Others said they had been across the Atlantic and had pulled into Londonderry in Northern Ireland. Those who made that claim indicated that what they had to say was not intended for public consumption.

Ensign Carl Nielsen went to sea in the North Atlantic in late February 1942. At that time the ship's mission was anti-submarine patrol and convoy duty for ships carrying men and material to England. He held to the belief that his ship was the only American naval vessel to engage in surface warfare with a German submarine during the course of the war. It was late in 1942 and they were not too distant from the East Coast of the U.S. A U-Boat surfaced a half-mile off the starboard bow. Carl's ship trained her guns on the U-Boat but did not fire. German sailors came out of the conning tower and lined up on the deck, some with their arms up. The captain of Carl's ship maneuvered closer to the submarine as the commander of the task force was being asked for instructions. A life boat was lowered and Carl was added to the regular crew of three. "The sub is probably from one of the French ports on the Atlantic coast. Bring the captain over alone," the captain instructed Carl. A great deal of trust was involved. Carl carried a side arm, a Colt 45 that he had fired once, just a clip of six cartridges. The crew of three was unarmed. The captain of the submarine spoke fair English. He jumped into the life boat promptly and was delivered to Carl's captain. In the short trip, submarine to destroyer, the German officer explained that a depth charge had caused a leak in the hull that could not be repaired. As the German crew was being removed in three trips by the life boat, the submarine settled in the water. German and

American sailors watched from the after deck of the destroyer as the submarine's bow came up out of the water for a moment then the vessel disappeared. Coffee and sandwiches appeared from the ship's galley. The destroyer's orders were to sail to the nearest American port, Boston.

Carl's son Douglas would return to this story again and again as he was growing up. He could always think of more questions. "What happened to the German sailors?" Douglas might ask. "They were turned into gardeners at military posts in New England. Some of them went to work on farms. All the young American men had gone off to war."

In 1943 the routine changed. In June his ship transferred to the Mediterranean, where it accompanied landing craft for the invasion of Sicily the following month, and later, in September, for the landing of British and American forces at Solerno. His career started and ended on the same ship. He was promoted to lieutenant junior grade and then to lieutenant and finally became the executive officer. Other officers were transferred off the ship and replaced, but Carl Nielsen remained. He imagined that the Bureau of Personnel had forgotten about him, except for his two promotions.

Carl Nielsen's ship shelled the invasion beaches prior to landings in Sicily and at Salerno in Italy. Carl was sure to emphasize to Douglas that the real enemies were winter weather in the North Atlantic and boredom over the routine. Standing watch underway across the Atlantic for two weeks consisted of a repeated cycle of being on deck four hours followed by eight hours off. The best times were when their ship came in for routine maintenance in the Brooklyn Navy Yard. The hunt then was not for submarines but for the pleasures of civilian life, which abounded in New York.

When the war ended and his ship was put into mothballs, Carl returned to Seattle and the northwest country. He found work in a large lumber corporation that supplied materials for the building industry. Carl had no experience with lumber, but then neither did most young men returning from the war, all looking for work.

Carl married late, not until 1958, when he was almost forty. He met Amelia and made contact with her when she was eighteen, just after her graduation from a select girls' school. Amelia was part of the family that owned the lumber firm for which Carl worked. Carl had been invited to Amelia's graduation party in error. Amelia's father, Carl's supervisor at work, had placed Carl on the list of those to be invited from the company instead of another employee who was a much younger man. When the error was discovered after the invitations had been mailed, Amelia's parents agreed that it would be embarrassing for all concerned to withdraw Carl's invitation. Her father was one of the vice-presidents and not much older than Carl.

The seventeen-year disparity in age between Carl and Amelia became a subject much discussed, but they seemed to be meant for each other. He looked and acted young. She saw in him maturity and kindness. Having met Amelia, he never wandered during her college years. It never occurred to either of them that they wouldn't marry soon after her graduation.

At the start of her senior year Amelia gathered up all the opinions available to her on the subject of men. Of the young women she knew, a few had trended against sex until marriage. A few more had sampled intercourse and kept it at a minimum. The notion that a fair amount of activity cheapened one was still current, though dying out, and a few of her friends still responded to that point of view. These were the women who wanted to marry men with at least a little experience so that the wedding night would go well. Yet others of her friends thought that abstaining was a Victorian viewpoint and that sex was a normal bodily function for adult women to enjoy.

Carl did not move in Amelia's direction lightly. He appreciated that he was scheduled to die first and leave his wife to organize a new life for herself. If he made it to seventy, the children, if any, would be grown up. There would be no financial difficulties. It came down to loneliness versus companionship. When he died, would Amelia choose to live it out alone or would she find the best arrangement available and marry that man? Carl suspected that she would select the latter course. She was so desirable.

Amelia stood out from all the women he had met. He felt himself lucky not to have committed himself to any of the previous women in his life. He had found several traits lacking in each and had reached the point of wondering if he was being too selective. Then Amelia came along. He could not remember the first time he had seen her. Perhaps it was at a company picnic when she might have been ten years old. He remembered from those occasions that she played the picnic games well and with enthusiasm. He recalled that while standing with her mother and father she came up to chat about a game she had just played. In response to a question Carl had asked, she remarked that she did not like skiing. "It's way too cold," she had said, adding that her favorite activity was camping and hiking in the mountains. She liked long walks in the woods and sleeping outdoors and building a fire to cook dinner and starting a second to cook breakfast.

Carl didn't think of Amelia sexually in the few times they met during her high school years nor at her graduation party. The change occurred during an annual Christmas party at her home. Most of the adults worked at the company. The young people were their children. Amelia and Carl found themselves near a fireplace sipping eggnog. She was dressed simply, her curly brown hair arranged casually. Before Carl said anything he became conscious of her beautiful figure. He may not have noticed it before, but then they had not been standing close together. He loved her mouth. When she spoke to him, always softly, he was conscious of her full lips and perfect teeth. They talked about her courses during that first year at the university.

Carl anguished at being smitten by someone so young, and his boss' daughter at that. He knew he could either continue to agonize over the matter or deal with it directly. He telephoned her to ask her to dinner. She answered, "I'd love to, Carl. That's so nice."

When he brought her back to her house and led her up the stairs to the front door he said, "Amelia, I have to kiss you." She said nothing but he heard a trace of laughter. At the top of the stairs she turned to face him and leaned into him. Carl thought that if he had to tell someone about her kisses, he would say they were joyous. It didn't seem as though they were her first kisses, but he hoped that they were the first kisses from a man who understood and appreciated her and was on a path to loving her.

Amelia thought that her situation differed from the situations of all the women she knew. She had the undivided attention of a thirty-eight year-old man whom she planned to marry the following summer. Her reasons for starting to share his bed were the following: she was twenty-one; it would be enjoyable; Carl wanted her. She concluded that the time had come and announced her decision to him. She told Carl that it required no additional commitment from him. She simply moved their relationship one large step ahead.

They were married and started the unadorned life of a typical young couple except that they enjoyed social position and money. Amelia worked until the first child arrived, a son, when she converted to full-time mother. Her daughter was next, followed by a second son, the last child. Both parents found ample time for their children. They discussed the personality of each and did their best to provide the ingredients required to construct complete adults with guidance in ethics, intellectual stimulus and civilized behavior.

The results of Amelia's decision to be intimate with Carl before they married reverberated into the lives of their children. She told her daughter that she could be disappointed if she expected great amounts of romance and appreciation in return for the gift of her body. Better to treat sex as an item of limited value from which pleasure and satisfaction could result. The romance and appreciation parts could wait for marriage and the intention of having children. In the meantime it was not worth living with unmet desires.

To her sons she stressed that subterfuge to obtain sex was neither necessary nor desirable. "Don't force anything on anyone," she said. "Sex has greater value when volunteered in return for what you give honestly. How sweet such a gift can be." That's how she put it to them in conversation. She told them that at the present time the standards of behavior between the sexes were being relaxed and this included restrictions on sex between consenting adults. Amelia had two other pieces of advice for her sons: never discuss any sexual activity with a third party and respect the attitudes of women. It was important not to dismiss the woman's point of view. After all, women were the intellectual equals of men in all pursuits.

Rising executives in the firm, of which Carl was one, were sold shares in the company after they reached a certain level of responsibility. In most cases these young executives borrowed money from the firm to finance the acquisition. Repayment was made by permitting the docking of their monthly paychecks. The ownership of shares was an inducement to all executives to manage the company for growth in sales and profits. When an employee retired, in accordance with the employment contract, the firm repurchased the individual's shares. The employees paid capital gains taxes on the increased value and the remainder was invested. The firm's stated policy was to avoid dilution.

Amelia was a granddaughter of one of the two brothers who founded the company. Over the years the number of family members who reached a position of ownership increased. These third and fourth generations of the family understood the perils of dilution, that is, an increase in the number of dependants owning stock, the greatest of these being the difficulty of finding a chief executive who could manage the company while keeping most of the relatives at bay. Those relatives not working at the firm but owning a portion of it always wanted more money. As often acknowledged, it came down to money. The relative who rose to the top and became president found that as much time was spent placating relatives as managing the firm.

It was because Carl was buying his allotment of shares and was a valuable executive that Amelia's family objected less than they might have when she married him. He was already in the firm and performing well. The cousins agreed that Amelia and Carl's children would be of sound quality. There were three: boy, girl, boy; Walter, Marguerite, and Douglas, who came in 1964.

Carl continued to do well in the company. His interest was in managing the vast acreage of trees for the long term. He opposed clear-cutting, the practice of deforesting a fair amount of terrain. In this procedure new and old trees alike were felled. He advocated removing only the most mature trees, leaving the bulk of the growth standing. The intent was to prevent erosion of topsoil when the rains came. Carl made the careful harvesting of a crop of trees his field of expertise so that the firm's performance improved year after year.

Carl was a trim man of medium height. He moved quickly and gracefully. He was not arrestingly handsome but good-looking nonetheless. His hair was sandy and eventually turned gray. His features were nicely proportioned. Whenever Carl was in the company of Amelia he felt an extra dimension had entered his life. He had considered her a delicious morsel from that first kiss. It seemed that she was the complete woman at eighteen, a mature person devoid of all affectations.

Their life together was a model of simplicity, fortunately graced by ample money. Most people with money, they both noted, introduced complexity into their lives in the form of houses, cars, yachts and even planes. For Carl and Amelia the focus was a life of fewest diversions filled with the intellectual pursuits they both enjoyed. They had no interest in matters except for their life together, their children and their home. They valued activities that gave pleasure and left memories.

The children followed closely in their parents footsteps. The first-born, Walter, went into the family business. The second-born, Marguerite, did as her mother had done, married an executive in the firm. The third-born, Douglas, arrived in the first month of 1964. He was the image of his father and like him joined the navy on graduation from college and married late in life. As were his father and mother, he was an avid reader. In that area, his interests were two-fold: modern literature and history, not uncommon pursuits.

He enjoyed analyzing how a novel was constructed, how plots evolved, whether the characters were defined carefully, whether they grew or were static, and whether the ending was logical and satisfying. He read American authors as well as translations of authors from non-English speaking countries. For history he started with the Egyptians and moved to the Trojan War. He studied the Greek and Roman civilizations and was particularly impressed by the organization of the Roman Empire, as well as its longevity and its contributions to modern everyday life. He kept a notebook, which he had started at the age of fifteen when he finished reading *War and Peace.* In the notebook he listed the title, the author, and a few reflections on each book he had read.

Douglas attended the same college as did his father, in part for continuity, and for the rest to take part in the NROTC program. He was not fascinated by a career in the family business and was familiar with his father's experiences at sea during World War II. Photographs of that era were not on display in their home but Carl had assembled an album, which Douglas and others examined from time to time.

Douglas had contemplated attending the Naval Academy at Annapolis but he failed to see how the system there produced naval officers of a quality superior to those produced by the NROTC program.

Douglas's character did not develop by chance. His parents

recognized the difference between him and his older brother, Walter, and his older sister, Marguerite. Walter had realized early on that he could excel at a career in marketing. He thought the family firm did not realize the opportunities that existed for their raw material: logs. Export overseas was one possibility. Manufacturing plywood was another. As a very junior executive in the sales department he had started by pointing out what various markets offered in the way of profits for the firm. Many of his recommendations were accepted. When not yet thirty, Walter made the case for establishing a marketing department separate from the sales department. Of course he suggested that he should manage the new department. The effect over the years was to maximize profits for the company. Walter married his sweetheart from high school. From that time on he needed little guidance from his parents.

Marguerite was made from the same mold as Walter. The firm offered summer jobs for a few fortunate college students. She availed herself of secretarial positions in the company, all the while examining and evaluating the young males already employed. She was young, of course, but the males came around. It appeared that in the summer between her junior and senior year an accommodation had been reached. Her mother's early life experiences of courting and marrying young were repeated. Carl asked Amelia whether Marguerite had been led along such a path. Amelia told him that their daughter had always expressed a desire for a husband and children and that she, Amelia, had not been a guiding influence. "Well, she sure picked him off early," Carl had remarked to Amelia, who answered, "We're not certain who picked off whom."

Douglas' parents pondered how they might reconcile the difference between him, his older brother Walter, and his older sister Marguerite. In his teen years, Douglas lacked certainty, did not know what his career would be, and had only vague notions about a major in college. Concerning women, he had only expressed an interest in marriage later in life. He liked women and had listened to his parents' opinions, particularly those of his mother, to the effect that women need to be treated with care and respect. "In addition, people close to you need to be understood," Amelia had told him. "Love cannot develop between a man and a woman unless each party arrives at a deep understanding of the other." That's what Amelia had told him. The words and sentiments stayed with him all his life.

For his majors in college, Douglas chose French and Spanish, finding Spanish more practical because it was spoken south of the Rio Grande except in Brazil. He did acknowledge that many educated people world-wide spoke French and that with the combination of English and French one could be at home on most of the continent of Africa. In any event he selected Madrid over Paris for his junior year abroad. Deep down, he thought that too many people chose French over other languages on the basis of its attractiveness to people of the establishment.

Amelia and Carl's contribution to Douglas' life was to understand they could not direct it. They discussed between themselves what might be done. Amelia's position was that for balanced personalities with no particular direction, the greatest asset was curiosity. Douglas appeared to them to have a normal amount of curiosity; and to reinforce it the three of them discussed books he might read. Carl enjoyed history and literature. Amelia appreciated literature and poetry.

When Douglas finished *War and Peace* in his fifteenth year, the three of them took up an examination of Napoleon. Who was he, how had he installed himself as Emperor of the French, why would he find it necessary to invade Russia? Their discussions led to finding two biographies of Napoleon, not those written by sycophants but by objective authors. Because Douglas had had an interest in the Egyptians and ancient Anatolian civilizations, Douglas' parents bought the eleven volumes by Will and Ariel Durant, *The Story of Civilization.* Douglas read portions of these volumes while in high school and college. Many years later he would inherit them and proceed to read them through.

When opportunities arose, but not each time, Amelia and Carl recounted to Douglas the results of their own curiosity. As they discussed the history of Russia brought on by reading *War and Peace,* Carl moved on to the arrival of Communism in Russia. He had read several times about a sealed train that carried Lenin and others across Germany in 1917 from Switzerland to Petrograd. He was not certain of the details of the voyage. Carl did know that Germany wanted to end its war with Russia so that a great number of troops on that front could be moved west to gain superiority over British and French forces and perhaps win the war. Lenin's bargain with the German government was to the effect that if he and several others were given safe passage through Germany on the way to Petrograd, he would do all in his power to form a government which would end Russia's participation. Indeed Lenin was able to achieve his goals. There was a cost in money and Russian land, but Lenin held to his word.

After graduation from college in 1986, Douglas took two steps. The first was to state in writing that he wanted neither the cash distribution that young members of the family might receive from the firm if they decided against joining it, nor would he enter the firm at this moment. If he joined the navy and found it unsatisfactory, he wanted it left open that he could apply for a position in the firm. He knew that several years could have passed by and the pickings might be slim.

Douglas attended a navy school for new officers that continued his training in navigation, communications, gunnery, and ship handling. On completion he was assigned duty on a light cruiser. Within three months of coming aboard he joined the list of regular watch standers. His rotation differed from his father's in that there was an extra watch. One now stood four hours on and twelve hours off. Douglas had no idea how much difference the extra watch stander contributed. His father spoke of an accumulated shortage of sleep. Douglas felt he had a relaxed schedule with sufficient time to take care of his duties as the assistant navigator with a bit of time left over for reading.

In port, when he went ashore with other ensigns, he tended to stay close to the officers' club, particularly when in their home port of Norfolk. The night life in that city did not impress him. At sea he enjoyed the quiet that descended on the ship, in contrast to the constant noise at the Norfolk base produced by cranes, trucks, busses, bells and whistles, and internal combustion engines engaged in all manner of activities. At sea there didn't appear to be any extraneous expenditure of energy, either by the crew or the ship's machinery. His ship was in a task force with an aircraft carrier at the center. They sailed in a group of thirty ships in the Mediterranean and occasionally they broke off and went into ports of call singly.

At the very end of his time on the cruiser his father died. Carl was seventy. His heart gave out on a ski slope. He was taken down the mountain by the ski patrol in a sled and pronounced dead in the first aid station at the base. The person skiing with Carl when he died was a friend of many years, Andy. He went that evening to break the news to Amelia. She burst into tears at the door. "Oh my heavens, it was that fast, was it?" she asked.

"Yes, he was skiing well, as he usually does. He stopped and looked at me and then fell over. I got out of my skis and unzipped his parka to put my hand on his heart. There was no pulse. I planted my skis to make an X and the ski patrol was there in a minute with a sled. They took Carl down the hill."

"Stay with me for a little while, Andy. Come in and fix us a drink," Amelia said.

Amelia controlled her crying as they talked a bit. "Could you possibly call Marguerite, ask her if I can stay the night and then drive me over? I would rather you told her that Carl is dead. Can you do that?"

"Yes, I can do that," Andy said.

Andy guessed that there would be a rush for Amelia's hand. She was only fifty-three. A few months might pass and several bold males would make their moves. Douglas was notified and received a short leave to attend his father's funeral. He knew that he was slated for a transfer soon after his return. He had put in for the navy language school in California. If he continued his Spanish and French he might qualify for an embassy post as an assistant naval attaché. Paris and Madrid were the prizes. Other possibilities were the numerous capitals where Spanish or French was spoken. Realizing what was at stake he worked diligently for the duration of his stay and was rewarded with the second position at the embassy in Paris. At that time he was promoted to lieutenant junior grade.

Social functions found him. The embassy crowd needed young, unattached males. Women related to employees at the embassy, not necessarily by blood, would arrive to spend their vacation. There was a stream of young women who came to taste Paris. It was from these that Douglas learned without a doubt that women had a sex drive and when conditions were right would respond readily. When in Paris for two weeks, they might not expect to meet Mr. Right, but they wanted a good time and to be taken to famous places. They did not resist offers made by Douglas. He lived alone in a small apartment.

Most of these young women, when at home, were on a career path, socially and at work. In their twenties, they were searching for an arrangement with a man that would work satisfactorily for ten years or perhaps a lifetime, as the marriage contract suggests. As far as work was concerned, they were putting to use the elements of the education they had received, but for two weeks of their life they wanted to taste freedom from the restraints that society imposed. They wanted to be in bed with an attractive male. These moments would be the foundation of memories that lasted a long time in their lives.

Douglas met many women in this fashion. He would be invited to parties and affairs. He met French people during his work in Paris and during his visits to the naval bases at Toulon and Brest. He reflected that if he were to meet any of his female partners in their cities at home, normal social restrictions would be firmly in place. It was the first great lesson for Douglas, to the effect that under certain circumstances women could let go. It drove home the point to him that all people are formed by the circumstances they find themselves in. His behavior would be entirely different were he not a young naval officer stationed in Paris. The women he met on their vacations would act entirely differently at home.

From the embassy in Paris, Douglas was transferred to sea duty on a heavy cruiser, once again in the Mediterranean. There were several ports of call: Naples, Cannes, Piraeus (the port of Athens), Heraklion in Crete, Alexandria in Egypt, and others. Many ports once open to American ships were now closed, but their ship did anchor off Valletta, the capital city of Malta, and Bizerte in Tunisia. These were the final years of his twenties and he was now a lieutenant and with two one-inch stripes of gold braid on the sleeves of his blues. He felt he had arrived as a naval officer. The captain of his ship called on him for translations, oral and written, including what the press might be saying about the fleet and their ship in particular. There were incidents ashore in which members of the crew did no credit to the navy, being drunk and disorderly. Douglas would visit the local gendarmes to arrange the release of imprisoned crew members, promising the officials that time in the brig, and therefore justice, would be served aboard ship.

Having become aware of the actions of a few women under the proper circumstances, Douglas introduced himself to the world of prostitution. Because he was at sea much of the time, he found little opportunity to establish a personal, constant relationship with a woman who made sense to him for the long term. The first time his ship anchored off Cannes, he came ashore wearing civilian clothes and headed for one of the two large hotels on the Croisette, the street along the seashore. He went into the bar and ordered his favorite drink, a red vermouth and soda.

When his drink was served a woman came up and addressed him in fluent English. She asked, "Would you like some company?" Before answering, he glanced around the room and noticed that there were several unattached women waiting for an opportunity. He looked at the pretty woman in front of him and answered, "Yes, of course. Sit here. What would you like to drink?"

As he began talking with her he thought over what he knew about sexually transmitted diseases. It wasn't a great deal. People talked about syphilis and gonorrhea, both of which could be cured by a shot of penicillin. He knew that the act of being treated by a navy doctor would be entered into his record, a damaging matter. She gave her reasons for being on the Riviera. Her university classes were closed for the summer and she needed to earn her tuition for the following year. Douglas thought that of all the reasons a beautiful Nordic woman could come up with, hers was the best. He thought she would have made arrangements, sexual or monetary, with the manager of the bar and with management in general. Certainly the higher-ups would not allow these lovely women to have access to their hotel without recompense.

The evening moved from the bar to the dining room and eventually to the third floor. The routine had been established and there was no need to register the guest. No doubt the other women that Douglas had spotted in the bar were operating under similar circumstances.

She gave her name as Inga. Once in the room she asked Douglas the time he needed to be at dockside to catch the last boat to his ship. She set an alarm clock and called the front desk for a wake-up. Douglas admired her thoroughness. He fell in love with Inga's body and after seeing her dressed and undressed he felt that he could detect what was concealed under the clothes of most young women. Besides being on close terms with this desirable body, he experienced what he decided to call her professional attitude. There was nothing that she couldn't deliver for his pleasure so that he had three additional encounters with her over the next few months, twice during each of the two times his ship dropped anchor off Cannes. She demonstrated to him that she was free and able to give herself completely to a man. In exchange he parted with money and he guessed that to obtain the same response from another woman in his life he would have to come up with a complete commitment, and even that might not generate the response that Inga provided. Douglas was not so naïve as to think that only he could so stimulate Inga --she must do as well by other men -- but he had known a professional presentation and he now knew the difference between that and what the amateurs delivered.

Douglas had now experienced spirited moments when young women let down barriers (Paris). He had met a best-ever body and had love made to him by an expert (Cannes). There would be another lesson that Douglas would be introduced to over the next decade. It was that perfection, the obvious goal, was unattainable. Compromise ruled. Compromise would dominate his relationships with women.

Douglas was starting to think in European terms rather than strictly American ones. He had been in Europe, read some of its history, and asked himself why countries situated close to one another would have governments based on such different fundamentals. These governments did not resemble one another in the least even though neighboring populations were much the same. The question came down to: how are governments formed in various countries? He could see several types. The crudest existed among the under-developed countries. A strongman seized power and made plans to stay in power for the remainder of his life. In such countries only one political party was allowed and it was the property of the dictator. Elections, carefully rigged, were held and the dictator was re-elected on schedule. Dictators cannot hold power without a following to do their bidding. Followers at several layers accept largess to perpetuate the system. From among the elite, the objective was to become a minister or a sub-minister and take a substantial cut of whatever money flowed through the system in order to lead the good life while fattening a foreign bank account. The idea of bringing about improvements in the lives of the citizenry was a distraction to business at hand. Money taken from the taxpayers of industrialized nations served the purpose of assuaging the guilt built up among the elected officials of those donor nations. Never mind that precious little was accomplished beyond financing the life style of the ruling members of the receiving nations. Enough attention was paid to do-good projects to keep the money flowing year after year. The money not allocated to the various show-projects was divided according to plan. In effect, the regime was held in place by well-wishers and do-gooders living sufficiently far away that they could not monitor the rampant waste and corruption. Distance and layers of administration made scrutiny difficult.

A second form of government that Douglas recognized was similar to the first except that in addition to being driven by the usual greed that would be satisfied after gaining power, there was an ism , a doctrine, Communism for example, that had infected the minds of the leaders. Douglas placed the Soviet Union, China, North Korea and Cuba in this camp. He recognized what everyone knew, that these regimes had to be held in place with force. There had to be a top evil person who was willing to kill his countrymen by the millions. Communism provided so few of the needs of its people that it could only be held in place with a secret police and an army, both willing to kill citizens when asked to, even when there was no particular need.

With this unlimited power, the top men in the Soviet Union had apartments in the Kremlin, country houses for weekends, and limousines to take them from one to the other. No doubt they had available excellent liquor, food, and women should their appetites run in those directions. Of the entire group of communist leaders, Douglas felt that the top dog of North Korea was the most outlandish. His father had designed and ruled over a system that starved a tenth of its population, forcing wealthy nations to ship in food and oil. Father and son spent vast resources developing nuclear weapons, no doubt for the purpose of intimidating neighbors. The son had put great store in one-on-one negotiations with the United States as though that act would show the world how powerful he had become. Of course the son was reputed to have ample supplies of the best cognac and girls to taste. It annoyed Douglas to read about this demon-on-the-loose in the civilized world but as a naval officer he kept his opinions to himself. Several of his commanders-in-chief, after all, had negotiated with North Korea and it wouldn't do for Douglas to voice a contrary point of view.

A third style of government in Douglas' evaluation was Socialism, a form used to divide the wealth by soaking the rich in order to provide social services for the many. He recognized the need for a safety net for the very poor, as civilized societies had made available to the extent possible from the earliest times, but he understood as well that the bulk of people in any society became accustomed rapidly to handouts, whatever the source. He could not decide on the merits of the case: was it better to soak society in order to provide benefits or was it better to be stingy with other people's money and require a far greater number of citizens to rely on their own abilities to cope with challenges? This question would go unanswered in his mind for a long time. It would require the insights of his wife, when she appeared in his life.

Finally, there was democracy as it is practiced in countries around the world. Douglas thought that there were social programs in all of them to varying degrees. Nevertheless such characteristics as freedom of speech, freedom of peaceful assembly and regularly scheduled elections were taken for granted and were at the heart of the social contract. Douglas did not know which of the countries that thought of themselves as democracies offered the most personal liberty. It could be Luxembourg or the Principality of Monaco, or Norway or Sweden, in spite of social support systems practiced in the last two. These generous support systems took the will out of many of their citizens.

FRANK WEST

WHEN CARL NIELSEN died, many friends came to his service to listen to a select few relatives send him off to his new address. Among those in attendance was Franklin West, an attorney, a bachelor, and a fellow member with Amelia of the board of directors of an experimental theater. He had served four years on the board, all that time with Amelia, who had been on the board three years longer than Franklin.

Franklin had to be honest with himself. He did not know whether he came to the service out of respect for Carl, whom he knew at the margin, or to be close to Amelia. The day after the service, Franklin had sent a dozen and a half roses, divided equally between red, white and yellow, to Amelia with a card enclosed. The message on the card read as follows:

My Dear Amelia,

No matter how I look at it, these flowers and the sentiments they represent are too early. I should wait a while to express my feelings for you, but were I to wait, I might be lost in the crowd.

I know you only through our work together, but what I know encourages me to know more. I will telephone you in a couple of weeks to see how you are faring.

Yours,
Franklin

Amelia answered as follows:

Dear Franklin,

The woman doesn't exist who isn't moved by receiving roses, particularly the large bouquet in three colors that you sent.

About the crowd you mentioned, I have my doubts that it would assemble. I do appreciate your thoughtfulness, though.

Your note was dated the eleventh. In two weeks it should be the twenty-fifth. I've marked my calendar to expect your phone call between six and seven. You've suggesting that I should embark on a new life, perhaps the sooner the better.

Fondly,
Amelia

The telephone call came on schedule. Franklin was still in his office. The legal assistant and the secretary who made up his staff had left for the day. The important aspect of the conversation came when Franklin got around to asking Amelia when she might go out with him. She answered that she did not know and would tell him when she knew. In the meantime she asked him to her house for dinner.

He showed up with a bouquet whose contents he could not identify. As she arranged the flowers into a vase she commented on each. She said, "I'm calling you Frank. Is that alright?"

"Yes, of course. We're quite formal at board meetings."

They sat in the living room, in the corner with the best view of

Elliott Bay. There were two easy chairs and a small table for their wine glasses. They talked about his attraction to the law (something interesting to do) and his reason for selecting divorce and family law. He had finished law school and passed the bar. To be sworn in he chose to go to Olympia where the Supreme Court, assembled, administered the oath to a few who had passed the bar recently.

A woman acquaintance was obtaining a divorce and he was asked to represent her. Frank's point of view held that if divorce was inevitable, discord and expenses should be held to a minimum, with as little money as possible going to the two lawyers. Frank summed it up. "Work came to me. I never found myself in the position of having to apply to a large firm for a job. I specialize in protecting children and at the same time making certain that the adults involved get a fair deal. It varies. Once I had adult children attempt to commit their father in order to tap the old man's resources. You have to be vigilant against such mean impulses. Unfortunately there's plenty of work for a person with my qualifications. It's too bad, but we need lawyers."

For her part, Amelia discussed her family's history and Carl's accomplishments in his years at the firm. She gave a few details about each of her children, saying most about Douglas. "He may be the intellectual of the three. I wish he were here right now. You two could talk about the books you're reading."

"I'd like to meet him," Frank said.

After dinner they returned to these chairs for coffee and talked briefly.

Frank thanked Amelia for dinner and moved to the front door. "Would you mind if I held you in my arms?" Frank asked.

"I might like it," she said.

They held one another for a long moment and then Frank said, "I've heard that you need a dozen of these a day to stay balanced."

"Naturally I've fallen behind," Amelia said.

He turned his head and she hers and they kissed for a long time, long enough that each had to breathe. Frank broke off the kiss, moved to her cheek, kissed her, and slowly released his hold.

"We have to slow down, Frank. This pace is too fast for both of us."

"I suppose you're right."

"We'll make better progress, more certain progress, if we go slowly."

"You're delicious," he said.

She said nothing but smiled slightly because her husband had said that about her often.

The family gathered for Amelia's marriage to Frank. Carl had died a little over a year before the event. Walter and Marguerite had gotten to know the groom during his courtship of their mother. Douglas, however, had not been home during these months. Amelia and Frank did not vanish on a wedding trip immediately after the ceremony. Frank brought the first of his possessions from his apartment to Amelia's house. He would get rid of his furniture but he kept the clothes and books. It was on these cross-town trips that Douglas and Frank came to know one another. Frank was about twenty-five years older than Douglas.

One of the cardboard boxes of books that Douglas carried was heavier than the rest. Douglas remarked, "Frank, this box is overloaded." Frank peered into the box and said, "It has my stuff on and by Karl Marx. That might make it seem heavy." On the trip across town and up Queen Anne Hill, Douglas asked Frank if he had read *Das Kapital* "Yes, but it was a while ago. The *Communist Manifesto* is much shorter. I'll lend it to you if you wish. You sound interested."

"I'm trying to account for groups of human beings, seemingly much alike, living in adjoining countries yet under vastly different forms of government. On the surface that doesn't make sense."

Frank thought for a moment. "It might be that the forms of government are not as different from one another as you suspect."

"Well, compare the Nazis to the Canadian government of the same era."

"You might have me on that one," Frank said. "When the three of us are sipping wine before dinner, let's go over the whole business. There are reasons for the establishment of all these political movements and styles of government, and for their ultimate demise. They don't come and go by chance."

Frank and Douglas completed three round trips and had made a substantial dent in the goods that Frank would be taking to Amelia's house. Frank and Amelia placed his clothes in the recently emptied closets and dressers. Douglas took charge of removing books from cardboard boxes and arranging them into newly-arrived bookcases. Frank had measured the number of inches that he would need. They rested during the late afternoon and then gathered at the corner of the living room with a view for drinks before dinner. There was a third easy chair for Douglas. After filling the glasses, Frank turned to Douglas and asked, "Where did we leave off?"

Douglas bypassed Frank and turned to his mother. "Mother, I ran across Karl Marx's books among Frank's treasures and we thought we might listen to Frank for his recollections on *Das Kapital* and the *Communist Manifesto.*"

"Frank, angel, only thirty to forty minutes until dinner so stay on target," Amelia said.

"Can't we continue at the dinner table?" Frank asked.

"We'll need a new topic by then. I would guess that anything Marx wrote would be heavy going," Amelia answered. She was right. When they were at table the conversation shifted to Douglas' career. Shore duty in Honolulu was next for him.

Douglas prompted Frank. "As to where we left off, you were about to enter into the preliminaries."

"Right you are. I might try to summarize the Communist Manifesto for you but I always prefer to start with background. What was going on politically during Marx's productive years, how did events affect him? I'm convinced that the times make the man and not the other way around."

"I do know that he spent a couple of decades in England and is buried there," Amelia said.

"And that's correct," Frank answered. "To understand Marx you have to understand the Revolution of 1848 and the major currents of the times. He had the training required to write his stuff, having devoted his life to the social cause of the workers. He had been part of that movement for at least a decade, a long-time newspaperman, a writer and a publisher."

"You should be able to explain Marx and Marxism in one paragraph," Amelia said.

"You might be taunting me, but it is possible," Frank said. "I would have to leave out the details."

"Such as the Revolution of 1848, Mother."

Amelia didn't answer her son. She addressed Frank. "He hated the bourgeoisie, didn't he, and we certainly are bourgeois."

"No question, but your family firm's treatment of its workers is so advanced from Marx's times that he would consider you a new economic model, someone he couldn't imagine, let alone understand. You and your family are miles from being the robber barons and the captains of industry that he detested."

They were silent for a moment, reflecting. Frank said, "Amelia, you asked for a one-paragraph summary. I'd settle for two paragraphs, one on the times and the other on the man, but both in one paragraph would be difficult to come up with. I think that historians and biographers are intent on writing books, not highly condensed versions of events, with the result that you simply don't find the summaries that you are looking for. You can't blame the writers. As an example, I read a book on the Revolution of 1848 in which the author writes a chronology of the spring of that year in Paris. It's revealing but doesn't make condensing an easy job for me. After reading it, I was not certain of the parties that made up each of the two factions and exactly what they were fighting over."

"I think it would be a treat for us and a good exercise for you if you tried to do the condensing," Amelia said.

"Well, here goes. The Revolution of 1848 was piled on top of the French Revolution of 1789 that we know so well, the one that started with the destruction of the Bastille, went through the execution of Louis XVI and Marie Antoinette and ended with Napoleon. I suppose many French had thought they were through with monarchy after Louis XVI lost his head on the guillotine in 1793. The excesses of Louis XIV, Louis XV and Louis XVI were beyond endurance and the French population had every reason to hope for a new type of government. Louis XVI's son was spared being executed. Nonetheless he died at the age of ten in 1795. I recall that he had tuberculosis. He was called Louis XVII. But Louis XVI had two brothers who were destined to ascend the throne. I'm not certain, but I think that during the years of Napoleon, say 1796 to 1815, roughly, these monarchs-to-be were on the loose in Europe and perhaps in England. After Waterloo in 1815, when Napoleon had lost to Wellington, brother number one ruled as

Louis XVIII until 1824 and brother number two ruled as Charles X until 1830 when he abdicated. Neither had produced successors."

"Would you please put those Louis on a 5 X 8 card for me? I'll never remember them," Amelia asked. Frank answered, with mock seriousness, "Anything for you."

"Didn't Napoleon have one hundred days in there somewhere?" Amelia asked.

"Yes, he was forced to resign in the fall of 1814. They shipped him off to Elba. He escaped from that island, sailed to France, and came back for his hundred days. That led to Waterloo. Then he was off to St. Helena until his death in 1821."

"Mother's distracting you, Frank, with her hundred days," Douglas said.

"Well, she has every right to. Straight Marx is hard to take. But let me continue. The French, some of them, thought they were through with monarchy, but when Charles X abdicated in 1830 the royalists were able to come up with Louis Philippe who occupied the throne to 1848. He was a descendant of a brother of Louis XIII, who was the son of Henry IV and father of Louis XIV, so Louis Philippe had a legitimate claim to the throne even though he was not a direct descendant of the previous king. None of these kings was particularly evil but they were unwilling to meet the demands of the new groups of workers. Or, I should say, they didn't grasp that there were demands to understand and accommodate. Charles X was the most blind. He reversed some of the adjustments that his older brother had made, such as granting the vote to thousands of new voters. He held to the divine right of kings. Had these three kings understood the demands of this new class in society, there still could be a constitutional monarchy in France as there is in Great Britain."

Frank continued. "Many of the French wanted parliamentary rule; but before they got that in 1871 with the Third Republic, they had to live through Napoleon III and his Second Empire and they had to survive a war with Prussia, which they lost. They finally achieved their goals."

"That Revolution of 1848 must have been about more than getting rid of kings," Amelia said.

"If they had got rid of monarchy once and for all in 1789 with their first revolution there wouldn't have been a need for the second. But think of this. James Watt had invented the steam engine, which could run textile mills, railroads and ships. Working people -- factory workers -- were being created by the thousands. They wanted education, improved working conditions, standardized working hours and finally they wanted the right to vote. They saw the owners, the ones they called the bourgeoisie, enjoying these rewards and they wanted a portion for themselves. I think that Marx made his reputation by blasting these new owners of industry for not making enough of the new resources available to the workers. He put it in terms of class warfare, a term we still use."

"I think we have to break for dinner, Frank. Bottoms up or just bring your glass," Amelia announced.

When the food had been served, Amelia went to the topic of Douglas' new post. "I've been to Honolulu with your father. I'd call it the standard trip. We went to another island but I can't recall which one it was."

"I understand they are all beautiful so I'm looking forward to the assignment, two to three years."

"What will you be doing?" Frank asked.

"Personnel, getting the people with the correct qualifications on the ships and on the bases, taking care of promotions and training, that sort of thing," Douglas said.

"This will give you an opportunity to mix with the unmarried ladies. Perhaps you'll find one you like," Amelia said.

"It could happen," Douglas answered.

"Why haven't you found someone yet?" Frank asked. Before Douglas could answer Frank said, "I should talk. I married in my early fifties. Worth the wait, though."

"Two groups of women," Douglas said. "I didn't seem to be in one place long enough to spend the time required to single out a woman, or for a woman to evaluate me. The first group, those would be the women I met away from home. The second group consists of locally-grown women, some of them dug up by Mother. All that I can say is that they are political lefties. It's one thing to be a Democrat but quite another matter to be irrational."

"You're inferring that Democratic women are irrational, are you?" Amelia asked.

"No Mother. I'm saying that those I've met are in favor of the redistribution of wealth even in the few cases when they have ample money themselves. They want higher taxes and more government. Mostly they want higher taxes for other people and for corporations, not necessarily higher taxes for themselves. In their thinking, individual behavior and the performances of corporations are not influenced by the levels of taxation and the size of government. I would have to re-educate one of them and I doubt that's possible."

"Can't you live with a difference of opinion?" Amelia asked.

"Not with that one, Mother. It goes to the heart of my beliefs."

"If you read the Marx I'm about to lend you it might have some influence and get your thinking to line up with the thinking of these women," Frank said. He laughed at his own words.

"I'll guess reading Marx would solidify my right-wing, reactionary tendencies, but I can't tell yet. I'll read the Manifesto."

"Do you remember that lovely Beverly I introduced you to?" Amelia asked. Before Douglas answered she added, "Well, an enterprising man took her off the market. You have to move quickly to get one of these superior women."

"I'll say you have to move quickly. I didn't even have time to check into her politics."

On the day following, Frank and Douglas finished moving the clothes and boxes containing the possessions that Frank wished to keep. "How do you close down this apartment?" Douglas asked.

"A charitable organization comes to pick up the furniture. It's used, of course. They clean it up and sell it at their store, and something good happens with the money. And a cleaning company arrives here. That's it."

"I'm glad you're moving in with Mother. She couldn't break up that household. Too much stuff accumulated over the years."

"Yes, she loves the place. I'm planning to insist on additional help. She has Martha who's been with her for years, as you know, but the money I was spending on rent can go towards another person. And I'll add money to that. Your mother needs another person about three-quarter time."

"You might tell her that Marx would approve. There you are, two members of the bourgeoisie directing money to a member of the proletariat."

"I'll go there as a last resort. I hope my suggestion stands on its own merit without invoking class warfare."

"I'll start the Manifesto after lunch," Douglas said. Before picking up the slender volume, Douglas read two entries in the encyclopedia that his family had always kept. His father had been assiduous in replacing the edition in the house with the new edition whenever it was published. Concerning Marx he read that he was born in Prussia in 1818 and died in England in 1883 where he had moved permanently in 1849. He was educated, having received a doctorate from the University of Jena. He lived in Paris from 1841 to 1845 where he wrote for a radical newspaper. He was expelled from France over his approval of the attempt on the life of the King of Prussia. He settled in Belgium. In 1848 he was expelled from Belgium and invited to live in Paris. He was present for the revolution that spring and witnessed the uprising known as the Revolution of 1848, which failed in its attempt to form a permanent parliamentary government without monarchy. It had reverberations over Western Europe. Once again, Marx was unwelcome. He moved to England to stay for the remainder of his life. While in France, it should be noted, he met Engels. They remained friends and collaborators for all of Marx's remaining years.

Friedrich Engels was also born in Prussia. His dates are from 1820 to 1895. His father was a part-owner of a textile company in which Engels worked, eventually rising to partner in the British plant. Douglas thought it ironic that Engels would side with workers at the same time as he was part of management (the bourgeoisie), determined to earn money that he could share with Marx so that they could carry on their research and issue publications on the matters that interested them both. It was while they were in Belgium that they wrote the *Communist Manifesto*, publishing it in the spring of 1848.

Douglas was surprised at the thinness of the *Communist Manifesto*. The edition he was holding covered a scant forty-three pages (exclusive of the introduction) in a five-inch by seven-inch format. As he always did he debated whether to read the introduction, prepared in this instance by Eric Hobsbawm. Because Marx had written in German and

Douglas was holding a translation into English, he thought it prudent to read the introduction, all twenty-six pages of it, for the reason that it would contain valuable insights and important footnotes.

On the first page of the introduction it was written that the *Manifesto* had been commissioned by a group called the 'League of the Communists', and that the purpose was to establish a policy document. The fact that the author of the introduction placed the following quote on the first page indicated to Douglas that the sentences served as a summary of the *Manifesto.* Here is the quote:

> . . . drafted by Marx and Engels as a policy document . . . committed to the object of the "overthrow of the bourgeoisie, the rule of the proletariat, the ending of the old society which rests on class contradiction and the establishment of a new society without class or private property."

Douglas reread the sentence and decided that Marx and Engels would support violence to achieve their ends. How else can one 'overthrow the bourgeoisie' and eliminate 'private property' without violence on the part of a segment of society against the rest? He knew not to be surprised by anything he read in the pages that followed.

Douglas leafed through the short text and found that it was divided into four sections as follows:

I.   Bourgeois and Proletarians
II. Proletarians and Communists
III. Socialist and Communist Literature
IV. Position of the Communists in Relation to the Various Existing Opposition Parties

He recalled his mother's recent statement to the effect that Marx and Engels came down hard on the bourgeoisie. He wondered whether she had read the *Manifesto,* perhaps studied it at her university. What a sly fox she is, he thought, simply asking Frank a question on the matter rather than divulging her past. He would ask her about it.

Concerning the first section, the author of the introduction wrote an important footnote identifying the bourgeoisie as 'owners of the means of production' and the proletariat as those who have only their labor to sell to the owners. Douglas read the first section to determine what his mother meant by coming down hard on the bourgeoisie. He found nine topics, not all damning. Douglas hoped that his list was complete.

A. Society is splitting into two great camps, bourgeois and proletariat.
B. New means of production have pushed aside the guilds of feudal times.
C. The new bourgeoisie has become the dominant political force.
D. The bourgeoisie is driven by naked self-interest.
E. The bourgeoisie has set up free trade between nations.
F. The bourgeoisie encourages the constant change in the means of production.
G. The bourgeoisie has expanded its markets to cover the globe.
H. The bourgeoisie has increased the urban population at the expense of the rural.
I. The bourgeoisie has advocated free competition.

When Douglas finished his list, three failures of Marx and Engels came to him right away. If these failures were not recognized by the bulk of economists then these economists were derelict in their duties. The fact that these failures were not discussed by the authors indicated to Douglas that there was a fair amount of apologia going on. If he could put his finger on the failures of the *Manifesto,* then trained economists should be able to jump on them in an instant. Why hadn't Marx and Engels mentioned them? They knew them to exist, certainly. Perhaps it was inconvenient to acknowledge these failures in their views.

The first failure was that if the proletariat was to destroy the bourgeoisie, then the proletariat had to learn the vocations of the bourgeoisie. Industry and business do not run by themselves. The proletariat would need the skills required to invent new products, identify markets for them, devise a business plan, locate capital, persuade capitalists to invest their money, organize research, engineering, and manufacturing, and finally settle on a marketing plan that sets out the means of distribution. Each of these elements of industry requires specialized study and Marx and Engels wrote as though these specialties fell from trees.

The second omission found by Douglas was that Marx and Engels did not consider that the industrialists (finance people, researchers, engineers, manufacturing managers, marketing specialists and sales people) had their labor to sell as well. Douglas thought that all employees in a corporation had their labor to sell, irrespective of who they were, and that the cost of their labor was determined by the value of that labor to the corporation. Marx and Engels appear to think that those who work in industry but are not the proletariat are sponging off the factory workers while contributing nothing. Without a managing group in place, Douglas believed that any industry would grind to a halt in a week.

The third omission that Douglas found was one he could not prove, that as the proletariat replaced the bourgeoisie, the managers and leaders among the proletariat would become the new bourgeoisie. Douglas thought that it would be contrary to human nature to have former members of the proletariat rise to leadership positions and not ask for greater remuneration than they had received previously.

Douglas moved on to section II, Proletarians and Communists. Here he found six aims embedded in the text that he had to dig out to make his list, and a compilation of ten other goals which he summarized into a couple of sentences. Here are the six aims.

1. Common interest in the entire proletariat, independent of nationality
2. The Communists would represent the movement as a whole by:
    Formation of the proletariat into a class
    Overthrow of the bourgeois supremacy
    Conquest of political power by the proletariat
3. Abolition of private property
4. Abolition of the family
5. Abolition of countries and nationalities
6. Abolition of all religion and morality

These were the six measures that Douglas found listed. There were ten more, which he summarized in his mind as the state imposing heavy taxes with no right to inheritance; the state owning and managing transportation and communications; agriculture and manufacturing to be combined gradually; and free education to be provided for all children.

Douglas noted the use of the word 'free' interspersed in the text. He had concluded along with millions of other people that nothing is free. Every item and aspect of our lives has a cost. The few benefits that appear to be free are in fact paid for out of funds supplied by taxpayers.

Section III, Socialist and Communist Literature, did not hold Douglas' attention. He read the section once only. Section IV, Position of the Communists in Relation to the Various Existing Opposition Parties, was brief. One sentence seemed to summarize the goals of the party. It read as follows: "In short, the Communists everywhere support every revolutionary movement against the existing social and political order of things." With that as a credo, Douglas thought that Communists everywhere were up to no good.

That evening, before dinner, the three were gathered as usual in the corner with the best view of Elliott Bay and Seattle. Amelia was holding a spiral-bound notebook that had an air of antiquity about it.

"Mother," Douglas began, "I wonder if in your past you did read the Communist Manifesto?"

"I was about to get to that. Yes, I have. I went to the basement this afternoon and found the box with my class notes. This would be in my junior year. Course on Modern European History. Among other matters we looked into the origins of Communism so we covered Marx, Engels and their period, including the Revolution of 1848."

"What else do you have in the basement?" Frank asked.

"When my three children left home and that includes you, Douglas, they couldn't part with some of their junk so they abandoned it in the basement. I plan to die here so at the end my children will have to throw their stuff away, which they ought to do now. What else do I have, Frank? Well, most of my life. I haven't thrown much away either. Runs in the family."

"Could you open that notebook and tell us what you have on the Revolution of 1848, please," Frank asked.

"These are notes taken on the fly, during the lecture, as the professor was speaking. Here goes:

"Revolution started in France and spread. On kings. Louis XVIII best of lot. Gave citizens what they wanted. Universal suffrage. Ruled 1814-1824. Time out when Napoleon came back from Elba for his one hundred days. Napoleon out for keeps after Waterloo, 1815. Charles X, youngest brother of Louis XVI. A jerk. Ruled 1824-1830. Abdicated. Believed in Divine Right of Kings. Undid the good that Louis XVIII had done. Louis-Philippe, last king. Ruled 1830-1848. Abdicated. Republic started. Kings could not respond to public's wishes. But Revolution of 1848 failed to meet its goals anyway. On one side army and National Guard. The Guard made up of men from districts of Paris. On the other side workers. Paris was an industrial city. A few military men changed sides and gave weapons to workers.

"Louis Napoleon Bonaparte, nephew of Napoleon I, elected to the National Assembly fall of 1848. Then elected president of France with seventy-five percent of the vote in December '48. Coup d'état in 1852. Made himself emperor and ruled as Napoleon III."

"How well did you do in your classes, Mother?"

"I usually got Bs, good enough to graduate."

THE GARDNERS

PART 3:

DOUGLAS RETURNED TO his ship and stayed on her for five weeks until his orders came through. He flew commercial to San Diego and then in a military plane to Hawaii. He took two suitcases containing uniforms and a few civilian clothes. He packed the clothes that were not accompanying him and he filled a suitcase with his books. They were meant to catch up to him in fewer than ten days.

When they flew into Honolulu, Douglas, sitting in a window seat, had a view of Pearl Harbor. He could see the USS Arizona, now a memorial, still lying in the shallow water where she sank that Sunday morning. He thought about the 1,100 men who had perished with their ship, many of them still aboard below decks. Life went on in a normal fashion around them

He reported to the personnel department and was assigned a room in Bachelor Officer Quarters, known by its initials, BOQ. It would be six weeks before Douglas signed a lease on an apartment downtown. He had flown in on a Friday afternoon. That weekend he rented a car and drove over the Pali, the pass to the northern side of the island. There were houses where pineapples had grown. He had this information from a friend of his father who had served in the Pacific during the war. He drove around until he found access to a beach, got out and studied the breakers. They were substantial. He thought he might swim at Waikiki instead.

On his first Monday he reported to work where he expected that his supervisor would be a lieutenant commander or perhaps a commander. It turned out that he reported directly to a Lieutenant Commander Moran who had had much the same service experience as he did with the exception of the tour of duty in Paris, at the embassy, as an assistant naval attaché.

Moran, as Douglas had hoped, was deluged with work. He explained what he wanted from Douglas, handed him a stack of personnel folders and said, "Nielsen, you may be saving my fanny. Start with these. We'll review your work after lunch and I'll assign more files to you."

Douglas made a short list on a notepad. These were guides to himself, which he had thought about on the plane. The first was, "Men with wife and kids." The second was, "Married." The third was, "Could use training." The fourth was, "Out to sea." The fifth and last was, "Switch career path."

Douglas knew that the Bureau of Personnel in Washington made the assignments for officers. His contribution was to make a recommendation for each officer's next assignment. The higher-ups at BuPers were not bound in any fashion. Lieutenant Commander Moran had told him that he may get a note asking him to cease making suggestions and that they were perfectly able to move officers around unassisted.

Douglas made six recommendations during the first morning. The one that gave him the most pleasure was what he had found for a lieutenant from the Naval Academy who had graduated high in his class and had received outstanding fitness reports. He assigned him to the Naval Architecture program at MIT where he would earn a master's degree and in all likelihood move on to the Bureau of Ships where he would spend his days designing the new vessels the navy needed. This lieutenant was married and had a child. An apartment in Cambridge would suit the three of them just fine after his sea duty.

He questioned his judgment on one of that morning's recommendations. He would discuss it with Moran at lunch. A lieutenant junior grade seemed to be overdue for promotion. His fitness reports were satisfactory. He was unmarried and had been at sea too long, in Douglas' estimation. He had been a gunnery officer, which Douglas knew required mechanical aptitude. Douglas thought that he should be kept at Pearl Harbor, reporting to the captain who was in charge of maintenance in the yard and re-fitting ships that had been at sea for extended tours. Douglas thought that this officer could survey the women on the base and those among the civilian population. Perhaps he would find a wife among them.

During their conversation after lunch, Moran did not make any changes to Douglas' recommendations. He reviewed each one for about five minutes and added his initials. "I'll keep you on this until we work down the backlog. You have a knack for it. Then we'll move to a new training program the fleet wants." Douglas realized that he would be kept busy in the coming months.

On his third day, Moran suggested, "How about a swim after work? I can pick you up at the BOQ. I want you to meet my wife." Douglas accepted and then Moran said, "Plenty of unattached women at the pool. My advice would be to go slow. I think they're all buying items for their trousseaux."

Douglas could not help notice the navy women in the office. Some were enlisted and others were officers. Many of them were pretty and others had lovely figures. Some had both. Douglas recalled Moran's warning to go slowly. His mother had told him, several years ago, that she had a six-month rule to the effect that when two people meet they risk thinking that the other is perfect and six months have to pass by before they both realize the other is just a human being, not a deity. With that thought in mind, Douglas looked more selectively at the young navy women in his department.

Fall was coming around. Douglas wondered if he might find a course on European history at the university. He assumed that there would be an extension program consisting of evening classes aimed at the adults interested in continuing their education.

He found a course, one evening per week for fifteen weeks, taught by a certain Elizabeth Blair. She had her PhD and Douglas guessed that she was on the faculty and taught classes to undergraduates and graduate students. There were no prerequisites listed but there was a recommended text. Douglas repaired to the university's bookstore and purchased a copy. There might have been fifteen people in the classroom the first night. Elizabeth Blair strode in at precisely 6:30 and proceeded to check the attendance. Elizabeth Blair was older than Douglas by perhaps five years. Her hair was short and light brown and her skin tanned. Her arms were tanned as well. On her left hand she carried an engagement ring and wedding ring in the customary gold.

The title of the course was "History of 20th Century Europe." The teacher had made certain to have a map of Europe displayed on one wall. Douglas guessed by the frontiers that it was a map of Europe around 1936. The Polish Corridor was in place. There was such an area as East Prussia. Czechoslovakia was there as well as a separate Austria, not yet swallowed by Hitler.

Indeed Dr. Blair's first two lectures were on the treaties and events that precipitated the First World War, to be followed by two lectures on the war and one on the Treaty of Versailles and its consequences. Douglas was interested particularly in the next lecture on the arrival of Communism in Russia and the part played by Lenin and the Bolsheviks.

Douglas had been more vocal than most in the class, that is to say he responded when Dr. Blair posed a question to the class in general and he asked his own questions when he thought clarification was warranted. At the end of the sixth lecture, he approached the lectern and asked Dr. Blair what she knew about the sealed train that had taken Lenin from Switzerland to Russia in 1917.

"I only know of its existence, but no details," she answered. "You might like to meet my husband. He should know."

"And who is he?" Douglas asked.

"Dmitri Kutuzov, a former Russian, now a card-carrying American citizen."

"I note you didn't change your name."

"No one spells either of his names correctly."

About ten day later the invitation was issued to Douglas and another woman in the class, a person who without a question was the oldest member. Douglas thought that Dr. Blair had included her because she had lived through a fair part of the twentieth century and could add to the discussion. Her remarks in class gave evidence of a powerful memory spanning many decades.

Douglas arrived at dinner first and when he was introduced, he said, "I recall reading that a Kutuzov became head of the Russian army when Napoleon invaded."

"Yes, distant relative," Dmitri said. "Old Mikhail Kutuzov. He fought Napoleon at Borodino and lost half his army. What kind of a victory is that?"

"We call it a pyrrhic victory. That means you lose so many men in achieving your victory that another similar victory and you've lost the war."

"Kutuzov must have sensed that. He retreated through Moscow, but caught the French as they were leaving Russia. Six hundred thousand came in; twenty thousand made it home."

The elder lady from the class arrived for dinner. She was introduced as Mrs. Alice Gardner, Elizabeth's aunt. Douglas and she spoke to one another several times during the evening but Douglas found Dmitri's conversation more interesting than Mrs. Gardner's, with the result that they did not carry on exchanges.

Douglas thought it unusual to find a Russian citizen in Honolulu. Dmitri had been in the Russian navy, serving mostly at sea on nuclear submarines. He had been dispatched to Tokyo to serve as a high-level currier and therefore had diplomatic immunity.

"I walked out of the Russian embassy and walked into the American embassy. Very simple. Americans flew me to Hawaii. I was ready to tell my secrets if I could stay. Very simple. It turned out that I didn't know anything the American navy didn't already know. If you build nuclear submarines yourself you find out all the secrets as you go along. The Americans contacted the Russian officials -- they all know one another -- and said I was of no use. They asked what they would do with me if I was returned. The Russians said they would try me for treason and shoot me. The Americans said that if they killed me no one else would defect and if no one defects many of us will lose our jobs, on both sides."

"So you were allowed to stay," Douglas said.

"Yes, I'm a scuba diving instructor. I taught that in the Russian navy."

"Where did you meet your wife?"

"Underwater. She took classes from me."

There was a great deal more to Dmitri's story. Douglas was able to get it out of him over time. To be certain that he had access to Dmitri he signed up for scuba lessons at the end of his semester with Dr. Blair. Two significant aspects of his story had to do with his father and grandfather. In the Great Patriotic War, as Dmitri termed it, his father was a foot soldier who fought from 1943 to the end, arriving in the outskirts of Berlin in 1945. He was wounded twice, both times from shrapnel. He made fast friends with two sergeants to whom he spoke disrespectfully about Communism and the politicians at the top. It all came out during interrogations with the result that his father was sentenced to ten years of labor in Siberia. When Stalin died in 1953, his sentence was cut short and he was released. He met and married Dmitri's mother who gave birth to him and a sister. Dmitri's grandfather's story was bleaker. He was picked up by the authorities as a small bourgeois, a shop keeper in an agricultural community. "He was arrested in 1934. Nothing was ever heard from him. As we say, he was liquidated."

On one occasion, Dmitri went to the heart of the matter, at least as far as Douglas was concerned. "Two important parts to my story," he started. "What kind of a country doesn't allow you to leave? Isn't that saying that if you leave you might not come back? And I didn't trust the people at the top anymore. I didn't believe what they said, and that's because they couldn't believe it either. What kind of a country is it when the leaders lie all the time?"

Douglas and Dmitri's friendship deepened because of their common past in their respective navies and Douglas' interest in Russia's history during the twentieth century. Douglas realized that he had a source of information that went beyond what he might read in books. They would talk on weekends at the close of the scuba class. The others in the group would disperse while Douglas and Dmitri sat on the warm sand near the water's edge. Douglas steered the conversation while Dmitri searched his memory for the most thoughtful answer to questions.

One day Douglas asked Dmitri about his defection. "You would be the last person I'd select as a currier to be sent to a neutral capital. You know too much about nuclear submarines."

Dmitri reflected for a moment. "We were near to getting an American officer to sell us secrets, or so we thought. Maybe it was some sort of double agent business that we missed. I was there to evaluate what he had to sell. When he changed his mind I thought it was my moment. I had been thinking about changing sides. Not married. Only my sister alive. They wouldn't bother her. No, I was the logical person to send to Tokyo to complete the transaction."

Douglas wanted to know how Dmitri felt about the Soviet system, particularly about forming a classless society and the other claim, to the effect that this was to be a revolution by the proletariat. On the first topic, Dmitri made the point that in the military services there were officers and enlisted men, and grades within each group. He said, "More responsibility, higher rank, more pay. It's that simple. You cannot eliminate class. Some people are smarter than others. Some people work harder than others. The best come to the top. That's class, no matter what they say."

The idea that the Russian revolution was instigated by the proletariat annoyed Dmitri. "The proletariat is not smart enough to start a revolution. The people who made the Russian revolution are very smart, with Lenin at the top. He was a professional revolutionary. He knew how to push over the government and seize the power; and he knew what to do with the power once he got it. And most important he was a killer." Dmitri paused for a moment to allow the last sentence to sink in. He went on.

"When you put together a dictatorship, you need a killer at the top. He has to be a person who does not worry about blood. Take Napoleon. When he was on St. Helena dictating his memoirs, or in conversation, he asked, 'What are a million men to a man like me?' He was talking about all the young men of Europe who had been killed during his campaigns. It was three million, in fact. One million French and two million from other countries. Anyway, the dictator will need many more like him who will do the killing for him. There are plenty of men like that. They enjoy killing given the least excuse. Their life is dedicated to killing. They always need new lists of people to kill. The man at the top must believe in the revolution or the reasons for the dictatorship, but that next layer, the enforcers, they only need the prisons, the weapons and the lists. That's all they need. They do the rest."

"I knew Hitler killed gypsies, Jews, homosexuals, people mentally retarded, those who opposed him politically and so forth. I didn't know that Lenin and Stalin were that bad," Douglas said.

Dmitri shook his head. "Same thing. Dictatorship is not the normal way. If you start one you need force and enforcers. The story that tells about how the dictatorship worked in Russia is the story of the show trials, the purges of 1936, '37 and '38. All true. The judges were corrupt. They did what Stalin told them to do. The secret police did what it was told to do, which was to get confessions out of innocent people. After the trials when innocent people were found guilty, the secret police obeyed orders and put a bullet in the back of the head."

"Why do you call them show trials?" Douglas asked.

"Stalin wanted to get rid of the important people who came up with Lenin. They owed their position to Lenin, not to Stalin. That was enough to get a bullet in the back of the head. Stalin had the power to kill these men but he wanted to do it within the law. A joke. He put on trials and executed men who confessed to crimes they never committed. The most famous case for me is the case of Marshal Tukhachevshy. Do you want me to tell you about him?"

"Yes, of course I want you to tell me about him."

"The Stalin version is that he wanted real revolutionaries in important positions and the men he put on trial had betrayed the revolution. I don't think so. My theory is that these men he killed did not have loyalty to him. They had loyalty to the Party and to the idea of the revolution. Tukhachevshy was in the revolution from the beginning. In 1921 he took soldiers to a place where peasants were not cooperating with the new rules. He slaughtered most of them. No question he was on the side of Lenin and the Politburo. He became more and more important in the army and rose to the top. He was a marshal. When the King of England, Edward VIII, was to be crowned, in 1937, Stalin sent Tukhachevshy to represent the Soviet Union. He went through Germany to get there but never made it. He was called back from Germany. In 1937, at his trial, Tukhachevshy was accused of spying when he went through Germany. I never knew the details. Anyway he was shot in 1937. But he wasn't alone. Zinoviev, Bukharin, Kamenev and other old revolutionaries who came up with Lenin were shot as well. Not a pretty picture, as you say here."

"Is there more to the story?" Douglas asked.

"They say that the Nazis made up evidence that Stalin used to get at Tukhachevsky, and that's possible, but Stalin and the government, after killing Tukhachevsky, went on to get rid of half the officers in the army."

"Get rid of?" Douglas asked.

"Some were let go, other liquidated," Dmitri explained.

"Did you read all this somewhere?" Douglas asked.

"No, mostly from my father. He hated the system and we would talk in private. He had a question for me about Tukhachevshy and the other original revolutionaries as they sat in prison waiting to be executed. He wanted to know whether they had brought on their own downfall by helping to build a system that failed them in the end and whether they knew that to be the case."

"How did you answer your father?"

"I knew what he wanted me to say. It would make him pleased. So I said, of course, they came to realize that revolutions eat their young. That was a saying that was whispered around. It has a nice sound to it."

"What did your father do?"

"We are from Smolensk. When he came back from Siberia he went to work for the tram company. First he cleaned them at night. Then he became a conductor."

"He has died?"

"Yes. You add up the war, the years at labor in Siberia and the long hours at the tram company. But he was a wonderful father to me."

Douglas realized that the long talks he was having with Dmitri were not the result of study on Dmitri's part, but were personal reflections. Both were valuable, Douglas thought, but the study of several books would provide a more balanced view than would conversations. He would make himself read about the time elapsed from Marx's writings to Lenin's taking over the government of Russia. After all, Marx had died in 1883 and Lenin had not installed the Bolsheviks into power until 1917. Thirty-four years had passed between the first and second event.

With two lectures remaining in the semester, Douglas received a second invitation, this one not from Elizabeth Blair and Dmitri, but certainly promoted by them. Douglas interpreted the invitation as an effort on Elizabeth and Dmitri's part to include the navy in the social life of the island. They could only include a few of the people in the services but it would be their contribution. This invitation was from a Mrs. Ellen Devaney. Elizabeth had added a note in her hand, which instructed Douglas to be at her house at six on the Saturday following so that they could drive together to her sister's house. This would be a family affair, Douglas realized. Douglas was flattered that he had moved beyond the classroom relationship with Elizabeth and the conversations on the beach with Dmitri. These meetings were adequate but in this new fashion he would be able to enlarge his circle of friends.

He arrived at Elizabeth and Dmitri's house on the outskirts of Honolulu in his recently acquired automobile. The older lady, Mrs. Gardner, Elizabeth's aunt, who was in his class and whom he had met previously at dinner, came out of the house to get into Dmitri's car.

"Good evening, Mrs. Gardner," Douglas said.

"We're on our way to a superior view and a dramatic sunset," Mrs. Gardner said.

"It's my first excursion in the direction of Diamond Head," Douglas said, "and I'm looking forward to meeting Elizabeth's sister."

"My two nieces," Mrs. Gardner answered.

"I didn't catch that previously, Mrs. Gardner, that you had another niece besides Elizabeth."

"No, we didn't get around to that."

Douglas caught the slight reprimand for not conversing with Mrs. Gardner at the small dinner party when they met. He would make certain to right that wrong.

The Devaney establishment was substantial. There was a semicircular driveway that could accommodate a fair number of cars. Three were in evidence as they drove up. Douglas assumed they belonged to guests as the Devaney cars would be in the garage. His calculations were correct as there were twelve people in attendance. Ellen Devaney resembled her sister, Elizabeth. She was older, perhaps in her late forties. There would be no Mr. Devaney. They had divorced. Two of their three children were living on the mainland and only flew in for vacations. The third child had found more interesting companions for the evening. All this Douglas learned in the car. He wondered if there would be a single female member of the family to provide company for him. As he sized up the guests the only single people were Mrs. Gardner, a widow; Ellen Devaney, divorced; a handsome male Ellen's age who was solicitous

COMMUNISM: A LOVE STORY

about her drinks; and himself. If he was not invited to be looked over by a female, then the family could be placing him under observation to determine his acceptability. Yet again, being invited could just be an act of kindness, which the sisters extended from time to time to the newly-arrived.

The patio overlooked Waikiki Beach and on into the distance where the naval base was located. The top of the wall at the edge of the patio was wide and the distance from the top of the wall to the garden below was only four feet. It would be normal to set one's drink on the wall or sit or lean back on it. The cocktail hour took place outside and the dinner inside, although the windows connecting dining room to patio had been left open.

Douglas went out of his way to meet and talk to all the guests, couples around Ellen's age. He concentrated on Mrs. Gardner who told him that she had been to Russia four times. Two of the trips were to explore St. Petersburg and Moscow. On one trip she cruised along a portion of the Volga and on the fourth trip the purpose was to examine Estonia, Latvia, Lithuania and their capitals. Douglas wanted to ask whether these Baltic countries were Russian but he let it go as they only recently had left Soviet domination.

Douglas found out from Mrs. Gardner that Elizabeth had learned Russian from Dmitri. Indeed they had met on the beach. Yes, she did take lessons in scuba diving. But she was interested in learning the language and this formed the bond between them. Dmitri would not return to Russia, even after receiving his citizenship papers and new passport. "Too dangerous," he said. Elizabeth had made the four trips with her aunt. Perhaps, Douglas thought, Elizabeth had not changed her name for the same reason that her husband had refused to set foot in the Soviet Union, even after it had become Russia again. Mrs. Gardner's grasp of history was adequate although not profound. She had lived through a fair amount of the twentieth century. Concerning Russia, she told Douglas that her niece, Elizabeth, had made the trips enjoyable through her knowledge of the language. "She's way beyond ordering a meal," Mrs. Gardner assured Douglas. "The most disturbing site," as she put it, "was Lenin there in his mausoleum. I wish they would give him a decent burial. He's just a dead God, lying there."

Douglas persevered and asked Mrs. Gardner about Lenin. She

confessed to not having read a book on him and only knew that he was at the head of the band of Bolsheviks who had ousted the Kerensky government in 1917. She did add to Douglas' knowledge. "I have it from Dmitri that Bolshevik means having the majority while Menshevik means you are in the minority, or something like that. Trotsky, by the way, was the most famous Menshevik." Douglas decided that he should go to the library and take out several books on the Russian revolution to study. He could get titles from Elizabeth.

After the dinner party, the four of them talked books on the way to Elizabeth and Dmitri's house. Elizabeth asked Douglas in. "I'll lend you one book at a time. It wouldn't do to have you skip from one text to the other and then jump back." Douglas could feel the mind of the professor at work. The book that Elizabeth settled on was a biography of Lenin by a general in the Russian army who had been given access to the archives by President Yeltsin. The general's name was Volkogonov.

It had slipped Douglas' mind to ask Dmitri whether he knew about the sealed train that carried Lenin from Switzerland to Russia in 1917. When he asked Elizabeth in class she had suggested asking her husband. In all their times together Douglas had neglected to bring up the topic. The biography in his hand reminded him. He asked, "Do you suppose that the story of the sealed train is in this book?"

"I don't recall reading about it," Elizabeth answered. They both turned to Dmitri. He said, "Lenin arrived in Petrograd by train from Finland, I think. I don't know what is a sealed train."

As they were saying goodnight, Mrs. Gardner turned to Douglas. "I had hoped that Caroline would be with us. Same last name as mine. She's a granddaughter. We're a big family. But she's in California for the moment."

"How big a family is this?" Douglas asked.

"Difficult to tell. We've been here for a long time," Mrs. Gardner answered.

Driving home Douglas thought about Mrs. Gardner's closing remark. There is a Caroline two generations down that Mrs. Gardner will introduce to him. She must think they are meant for one another. Mrs. Gardner knew that Caroline would not be in attendance. Mentioning her was Mrs. Gardner's way of letting Douglas know that there was a relative in reserve. Matchmakers are not interested in having their subjects become friends. They want them to fall in love and marry. What did Mrs. Gardner mean when she said that her family had been here a long time?

The following Saturday morning Douglas drove to the bank where he had opened an account. Perhaps the manager of that branch would know about the Gardner family. It was worth exploring.

He walked into the building, which the bank shared with a brokerage firm. He entered the bank on the left and could see a woman in the glass-enclosed office who might be the manager. She was reading, perhaps a report. Douglas asked the receptionist if he could speak to the branch manager for a moment. "Shall I tell her what's it about?" the receptionist asked.

"Yes, of course. I have an account here but it's a non-banking question and it will only take a moment."

The receptionist walked to the manager's office. Douglas could see them chatting. The manager looked at him. She got up from her chair and came out to meet him. She was short and brown. Douglas guessed that she belonged to the stock of native Hawaiians. She gave Douglas a warm smile as she extended her hand. "Please come in," she said.

Douglas explained that he was a naval officer and had been stationed at Pearl Harbor for a few months and recently had met members of the Gardner family. "It's a nosy question," Douglas said, "but it would help to know who they are. I'm about to meet more of them."

"The Gardners," the manager answered, "if we are talking about the same ones, are a big family and they've been here a long time, if one hundred and fifty years means a long time. The best known of them might be Alice Gardner. She must be nearing eighty."

"I have met that lady."

"Very well positioned socially, I would say. Does a lot with the navy. Fine family. They appear to stick together. They've been in ranching on one of the islands and in banking here in Honolulu. Of course everybody is in real estate now."

"Are they with this bank?" Douglas asked.

"No, another, and as for the farming, I don't recall that it was pineapples. I think it was cattle."

Douglas got up and thanked the manager. As he walked to his car he wondered at his good fortune. He had been introduced to a family similar to his. There was a family business and there were several generations who had acted together for a common goal of creating an enterprise that produced fine products and at the same time a crop of employees who were assets to their communities. Only a few families resembled his and perhaps the Gardners were one such. And what of Caroline?

Douglas felt he would be stationed at Pearl Harbor for another two and a half years before being transferred. During that time he should be able to determine whether Caroline and he meant something to one another. She could calculate if there was a place for him in her life. Perhaps with the Gardners it was a decision in which several members discussed matters in order to achieve consensus.

Douglas knew the Blair sisters, Elizabeth, married to Dmitri, and Ellen, divorced from a Mr. Devaney. Both were very appealing women, in the obvious ways, and also in the quiet consistency they both had. He had only seen Ellen once but she had exhibited a warm attachment to her guests and calmness in moving them through the steps of a dinner party. She had adopted the technique of having glasses of water served at ten o'clock as a signal that guests could leave.

Elizabeth appeared to have a fine relationship with Dmitri. They were attentive to one another. It appeared to Douglas that Dmitri was mad about Elizabeth. He didn't gush but he was kind, pleasant and interested in her. She laughed when he talked. It was not humor that could be transported to other people and other situations. It was his ability to be amusing in his analysis of everyday matters. Douglas wondered whether Elizabeth had laughed much before Dmitri arrived. He imagined that they had an affectionate love life.

What would Caroline be like? Mrs. Gardner wouldn't bother introducing them if she could not detect possibilities. Douglas could excuse himself for not having found the correct woman at twenty-nine years of age. That's an aspect of navy life -- at sea part of the time, transferred to various corners of the globe every few years. Now he would be anchored for a decent while and the time had come for him to be serious. He sensed that.

MORE ON THE GARDNERS

THE TELEPHONE CALL on his answering machine was from Alice
Gardner. She referred to herself that way. Was Douglas free for dinner
a week from Friday? Would he please return the call? The directions to
her house were detailed. When he did talk to her she ended by saying,
"On those directions, the important part is how to manage the last
three turns. Did you write them down?"

It was clear to Douglas that people in large numbers had been lost
while attempting to reach Mrs. Gardner's house. "Caroline is back from
California. I want you to meet her," Mrs. Gardner added in a matter-
of-fact tone. It sounded to Douglas as though her mind was made up,
that he and Caroline had a future together.

Douglas dressed with particular care. He started with a blue shirt
and chose a green silk tie with a paisley design in several shades of green
and bits of red. A subdued yellow coat, gray trousers, black socks and
highly polished loafers completed the outfit. He looked in the mirror
and brushed his hair again.

Mrs. Gardner's house was on the scale of her niece's, Ellen Devaney's.
It was older and Douglas guessed that the rooms would be bigger and
the ceilings higher than in Ellen's house. He pushed the doorbell and
heard steps. A middle-aged woman in a maid's uniform opened the
door. "Good evening, Lieutenant Nielsen," she said. "Won't you come
in?" There was a pause as they turned into the house. "This way, please.
Miss Caroline is expecting you in the library."

Douglas moved through the double doors and even though he saw Caroline standing to his left he chose to say nothing and instead took in the presentation. He knew he was acting in a perverse manner but then Mrs. Gardner had decided to stay upstairs while Caroline met him. They would introduce themselves. At a glance he took in the art on the walls, the bookcases, the fireplace and the comfortable furniture placed about. He then turned to Caroline. She was standing next to a dark, wooden table with one hand on it. Douglas studied her. She was lovely. There was a silver vase in the middle of the table. It was filed with flowers. Douglas smiled and said in a quiet voice, "Hello, Caroline."

Caroline lifted the hand resting on the table and extended it to him. "Hello, Douglas. I'm glad to meet you."

Their hands stayed coupled longer than each had expected. Douglas thought first of that crafty Mrs. Gardner waiting upstairs so that the two young people could absorb one another. Then he thought of Caroline selecting a pale blue dress with no pattern so that it would not clash with the large bouquet of many colors in the silver vase.

As he asked, "Just back from California?" he imagined what her body was like. As she was telling him that she had spent a week in Los Angeles he noticed that her face was long, her mouth wide and her eyes set farther apart than most. "Handsome woman," he said to himself.

It came out promptly that the son of Mrs. Gardner who was Caroline's father lived and worked in Los Angeles. Caroline had always preferred the Islands and was the only sibling who felt that way. Her two brothers lived and worked in Los Angeles. Her father was in banking, but not at the family bank. "I work at the family bank," Caroline volunteered, "but it's not correct to call it that anymore. We are a public company now and the president isn't automatically a Gardner. My grandfather was the last Gardner president."

They moved across the room to a large window and looked out at the view. There was a sofa to one side into which they settled.

On the type of work she did, Caroline had this to say. "I style myself as an economist but I'm in the loan department. When I use the expression 'style myself as an economist' I mean that I don't have the doctorate yet. I'm back from UCLA, where we all went, to find out what's involved in obtaining that degree. It's making me pause."

"Meaning?"

"That even though I have the master's it looks like three years and a thesis."

"Well, that would certainly make me pause," Douglas said.

"Before you think to ask it, let me say that I have a job at this bank because I'm a Gardner. If I had a different last name I might have landed the job and yet I might not have. Perhaps at another bank."

Douglas liked the direct way she spoke. He liked her hair, pulled back to reveal her forehead and her ears and neck. Douglas had always been aware of what went on above the shoulders. Caroline had a lovely neck and her skin was light brown as though she held a tan year-round. Her hair was nearly black. He hadn't been close enough to tell the color of her eyes.

Mrs. Gardner came down the stairs. It was a slow, measured gait and Douglas guessed she was holding the banister. They stood up when she came into the library. She went first to Caroline, then to Douglas, and kissed them both on the cheek. "We'll go to the porch and see what there is to drink."

When they were seated the maid appeared holding a tray with three glasses of lemonade, which she served. Douglas knew that if he had been asked for his selection he would have suggested a glass of white wine but he was glad that he hadn't been given the choice.

"Caroline, did you tell Douglas why you were in Los Angeles?"

"Yes, I did, Grandmother. You arrived before he had a chance to talk so I don't know his reaction."

Douglas recognized this as his cue. "I'm impressed when I come face-to-face with a doctoral candidate. It's the intellectual equivalent of climbing Everest."

Mrs. Gardner said, "I hope they don't invent a degree on top of the doctorate. Young people will turn gray in school."

"I think I can get it done by time I'm thirty or thirty-one, Grandmother. Still time to get married and have a family."

They moved into the dining room. Douglas held Mrs. Gardner's chair but Caroline had seated herself before he could move in her direction. Douglas noticed glasses of water at each place setting and alongside an empty glass. Wine of some sort would be served.

Mrs. Gardner led off. "Douglas, you might wonder who is a

Californian and who comes from Hawaii. Over the years it has become difficult to tell. I was a Pasadena girl and graduated from a Catholic girl's school up in the hills run by the nuns. My husband, Eric, was from here, fourth generation. He had finished a year at his university when he joined the Army Air Corps. He was shot down over Germany and parachuted into the arms, or into the pitchforks, of four or five German farmers."

Douglas interrupted. "Eighth Air Force, I suppose. B-17 or a B-24?"

"It had four engines. My husband called it a Liberator."

"Well, that makes it a B-24."

Mrs. Gardner continued. "He spent almost a year in one of their prisons. But our army liberated that place and the prisoners were discharged very promptly. He started his sophomore year as I started in as a freshman. I can tell you he was starved for a woman and I must have been very cute. I became pregnant with Caroline's father and married in my sophomore year. You may wonder why I'm telling you this, Douglas."

"There could be several reasons, Mrs. Gardner. It may be that there are now more books and magazine articles on the subject of the sexual revolution than there ever were, making the phenomenon appear to be new. I suspect that your conclusion is correct, that it's been around for a while," Douglas said.

"My reason is to give you an opinion of this sexual revolution. As you say, it's been around for a long time. I wanted more than anything else to make Eric whole again. I supposed I could make up for those years he spent in the service. Since the time of Adam and Eve, it's my belief, when a woman wished to play a particular role in her man's life, the opportunity always availed itself."

Douglas looked at Caroline. She arched her eyebrows, smiled a bit and cocked her head to one side. To Douglas that signaled that Caroline was in accord with her grandmother and that she was not surprised at hearing that opinion from her. Douglas wondered whether Mrs. Gardner was suggesting, as she recounted her history, that he and Caroline were free to become lovers. As Caroline's guardian of sorts she was stating her ground rules. Douglas could not determine precisely why Mrs. Gardner had told him that her first child came early, and that she felt obliged to marry. No doubt she had told many people and the news had long since been discounted.

Mrs. Gardner went on to summarize. "We've had and continue to have Californians and Hawaiians. In my case I started there and ended here. Some come and go. A few leave here and never come back."

"Caroline," Douglas said, "I would like to pursue this doctorate business with you, if you don't mind."

"Not at all."

"Tell me what's behind it."

"Banking is a simple business. Depositors bring in their money. Let's say that in a checking account you earn no interest but the bank handles your checks and sends you a monthly statement. With a savings account you earn interest but the bank has no checks to handle. Let's say that the bank pays 4% on average for all its deposits. The bank would try to lend out its deposits at 7%. The difference provides the bank with income. The objective is to place the bank's deposits into performing loans. Banks that get into trouble make stupid loans. As a loan officer, a junior one, I see attempts at making stupid loans everyday. These are loans to individuals or groups or companies that may not be able to repay the money they've borrowed."

"Did you learn that from your grandfather?" Mrs. Gardner asked.

"I wish I had. It would convince me all the more," Caroline answered.

"All bankers must know this simple formula. Why does anyone make a non-performing loan?" Douglas asked.

"If banking was as simple as I said it was this would be a safe and happy planet. But we're talking about the income stream for the bank. The loan officers who can place a great deal of money into performing loans get promoted. Those that can't get left behind. The challenge is to know how much risk to accept with any loan. The successful loan officers have a nose for risky loans that will perform. It translates to more money for the bank and higher income for them."

"I don't see a need for the doctorate," Douglas said.

"When you have a doctorate you can advance from loan officer to economist. You can read reports from the Federal Reserve and their branches and you can read reports from the Congressional Budget Office. Of course anyone can do that, but with the doctorate you can digest all this material and write guidelines for your own bank. Very exhilarating stuff."

Neither Mrs. Gardner nor Douglas said anything. Douglas tried to think of a penetrating question. Caroline filled the void. "It's been my observation that having a doctorate opens horizons for you. Economic advisors to the president, members of the board of directors of the Federal Reserve, university professors, all these people have doctorates. With one of those sheepskins, the world is more accessible. It's friendlier."

Douglas and Mrs. Gardner must have realized that they were having dinner in the company of an ambitious person who wanted to make her mark. Douglas thought he could change the topic and include Mrs. Gardner at the same time.

"Have you been on any of the four trips to Russia with your grandmother? I thought you might have learned about Communism."

"No, I'm sorry to say. All their vacations have taken longer than the time available to me. I've been told that all you need is a few days in Russia to see that Communism doesn't work. What I do know about Marxism, Communism and Lenin comes from an economics course. I haven't read Marx. I've read the impressions made by Marx on others. You know the expression 'smart, smart, stupid'?"

"I think we've all heard the expression," Douglas said.

"It must have been invented for people like Marx and Lenin. They could analyze events and make plans for a new world order, but they were inordinately stupid in the execution. You realize that their doctrine was based on the redistribution of wealth. Let's eliminate the bourgeoisie where all the money is, they said, transfer their property to the state, and let the drones, the workers and the peasants, agree with the leadership or else get shot, hung or sent to a gulag. If there was ever a more stupid idea I haven't run across it. Lenin was worse than Marx because he had opportunities day after day during his six years in power to change the formula but he charged straight ahead, starving millions of his people in the process."

Douglas realized that he had changed the topic but that Caroline still had the floor. He wanted to give Mrs. Gardner an opportunity to talk even though Caroline's observations interested him. He knew there would be ample time to carry on this discussion with her.

Douglas knew that he was about to ask a simple question that would not lead anywhere but he didn't want Caroline to wear them out. "Mrs. Gardner, in your opinion, why would some members of your family settle in California and others in Hawaii when they had a choice?"

"I came here as a young bride after Eric finished his schooling. He went right into the bank. I had my first child, Caroline's father, in Los Angeles and the second and third here. I was ever so cordially received by all the Gardners and made wonderful friends. For others it's a matter of business opportunity. For yet others, they develop a case of island fever and need to get away, to return to a continent, to find space and variety."

They adjourned to the porch for coffee. At ten, the hour announced by a clock in another room, Mrs. Gardner excused herself. "My bed time. Please solve the problems that we haven't covered." With that, Caroline and Douglas stood up. Mrs. Gardner kissed each one on the cheek.

"Caroline, I'd like to go back to your use of the word 'stupid' to describe Marx and Lenin. That word is a pejorative. Some people say it's name-calling and in bad taste."

Caroline rode over his objection. "Distribution of wealth didn't work for Russia. It never has worked and never will work. If you want to inflict misery and poverty on your country just distribute wealth. What you need to do is put in place a climate that produces more wealth. Since 1991 the Russians have had a form of government other than Communism. Fear has largely gone from the system. But it will take a hundred years to heal the wounds and catch up."

Douglas knew he could branch out on the topic of redistribution of wealth but it could wait for another time. He had been hooked. Caroline had a fine mind. She spoke well, without hesitation. She made no apologies for her opinions.

"Are you staying here?" he asked

"When Grandmother invited me I asked if I could stay overnight. I think we enjoy one another's company. We'll have a leisurely breakfast. I have an apartment down the hill."

"Can you let me have your significant seven-digit number?"

"Would you like me to write it down?"

"No, I can remember it," Douglas said. It didn't surprise him that the first three digits were the same as his. Concerning the last four he said, "Last two digits of the date Andrew Jackson was sworn in for his first term, followed by the last two digits of the year Grant handed over control of the army to Sherman."

"Smarty pants," she said.

They stood up and walked toward the front door. He took her hand. He had decided long ago that when he wanted to kiss a woman it was likely that she wanted to be kissed by him.

"You're a lovely woman, Caroline." They kissed for a long time. Not one kiss, but several kisses. "You're a nice man, Douglas."

Douglas awakened late Saturday morning. He knew he was facing an empty weekend but he had planned it that way. If he wanted to see Caroline on Saturday or Sunday, and she him, the decks had to be clear. He waited until one o'clock to telephone by which time she would have returned from her grandmother's.

She was home and in the process of cleaning her apartment. "We might go swimming," he suggested.

"Locally?" she asked

"Yes. Perhaps it's not too crowded," he answered.

She paused for a moment then launched off in a preachy tone of voice. "Swimming has an important corollary in life. When it's crowded, the people are packed in where it's dry, up on the sand. A few will be in the shallow water and when you're twenty feet from shore you're all alone."

"You want me to ask you about risk and all that?" Douglas said.

"Yes. The risk is out in the deep. If you go out just a little bit, though, there isn't much risk and plenty of reward. A good deal."

"Have you told that to your loan officers?"

"Next time," Caroline said.

"Perhaps you have more to say on the subject. Shall I fetch you around three o'clock?"

She came to the door wearing a terrycloth robe and carrying a canvas bag that held a towel, and under it, maybe, lotion and swimming cap. He guessed she would be wearing a black bathing suit to match her hair. Douglas was carrying a towel and nothing else but his car keys. He had never cared for prolonged trips to the beach, which could require bringing reading material and a parasol.

"I hope you'll stay for supper," Caroline said.

"I'm living off the Gardners."

"I love dancing. Can you take me dancing some evening? I'd like that."

"Would you prefer the club at the base or one of the beach-side hotels?"

"I think a hotel. You can take off your shoes and walk on the beach before heading home."

He had guessed correctly on the color of the bathing suit. It was black with two straps on the back that crossed one another. There were spaces without material and the suit was cut way up around the hips. As they walked toward the water he thought about designers of bathing suits and how they decided where to remove material and how much. Caroline had taken good care of herself. There were no bulges. If anything she might be slightly underweight. She was a bit shorter than he, but not a great deal. Her feet were perfect, as though she never wore shoes that pinched the toes.

Over a cold meal that Caroline served on her porch they returned to the conversation of the prior evening. "Do you think you are carved out to be naval officer, Douglas?"

"It suits me as well as anything. Why do you ask?"

"As you can imagine I've been out with naval officers before. They talk about their ships, how radar works, what a boiler is, and all that. You prefer talking about economics, politics and history. Do you think you'll make admiral?"

"I'm hoping to make commander. So few make admiral that I don't dream about it any longer."

"You should dream about it, about the top. I guess, but I don't know, that's where the fun is, where the important decisions are made."

"I wouldn't know," Douglas admitted. "Plenty of heat up there, though."

Caroline went on a new tack. "If you find Communism absorbing you might want to read up on the Spanish Civil War. Lenin thought there would be a world revolution and that the old governments would all topple and Communism would replace them. Didn't happen in

Germany or France. But in Spain there seemed to be a chance. I have read that Hitler and Mussolini sent forces to Franco while Communists in general went to help the other side."

"I do know about the Lincoln Brigade and that it was made up of American volunteers who fought opposite Franco," Douglas said

"Plenty to read," Caroline said.

"Good idea," Douglas said. "I have Elizabeth and Dmitri to fall back on for guidance. They can point me in the right direction."

"I'll have to speculate," Caroline said, "that Franco could see Communist domination of Spain if he didn't step in. He knew all he needed to know about Communism from what was taking place in Russia. He didn't want that for Spain. We're talking 1936 and later, but don't take my word for it."

Douglas telephoned Elizabeth and Dmitri and made arrangements to stop by. As he suspected, Elizabeth had a better grasp of the history of Communism than did Dmitri. However, he knew that China under Mao Zedong had adopted that form of government after two decades of warfare, at first among Chinese followed by war against Japan. Stories about China were prominent in the Soviet press. And he knew that India had brushed up against Communism but not taken the plunge. Elizabeth discussed the Soviet Union's attempts to introduce Communism into the African Continent. She told Douglas that it had taken root in Ethiopia only to be rejected as unworkable. "After you study Spain, you might want to focus on Cuba and Fidel Castro," Elizabeth said. "I think he's been in power since 1959. If he wanted to help the Cuban people he certainly took a wrong turn."

"I suppose Batista was bad news," Douglas commented.

"Yes, but Castro is worse news than Batista. Castro had to put in secret police and fill his jails with political prisoners in order to install his agenda. It's such a sad comment on a regime when dissent is no longer allowed. I think you agree that when you limit free speech you've lost your legitimacy."

"No question in my mind," Douglas said. "It's interesting that Fidel has his followers. Would you guess that ten percent of the population goes along with him?"

"Perhaps ten percent. He had brother Raoul who I understand is more the enforcer than Fidel. He wears four stars on his shirts. His speeches are shorter, though." She paused for a moment then added, "There would have been much more bloodshed had Che Guevara lived longer. He prosecuted then executed plenty of the people from the previous regime. I think the Bolivian army got him. He was introducing revolution into that country."

"No enforcers, no Communism," Douglas said.

"True enough," Elizabeth said. "After Cuba you might look at Chile. I keep Spain and Chile in the same portion of my mind. Pinochet plays Franco's part while Salvador Allende represents the Communist threat."

"I may be able to find out if there is a parallel," Douglas said. "How about Nicaragua?" he asked.

"Another brother act. The older Ortega, Daniel, being the politician and Humberto, the younger, being in charge of the military. To Daniel's everlasting credit he allowed elections after his term in office as president and was defeated by Violeta Chamorro. You remember her husband had been assassinated earlier to settle a political matter. Anyway, she took the presidency away from Daniel."

"This is unusual," Douglas said. "We've all heard 'One man, one vote, one time' for the way dictators run elections. Apparently the Ortegas have a soft spot in their hearts or they were vastly overconfident."

"I don't have the details. There's another reading assignment for you," Elizabeth said. She added, "Don't count out Daniel Ortega. The fact that he allowed himself to be beat in an election tells me he could be spoiling for a rematch."

"By the way, what's Hugo Chavez up to?" Douglas asked.

"It's not certain yet. He has dictatorial leanings. He says he wants to model Venezuela after Cuba and that's a sign of danger. Why would any rational person wish to inflict all that pain on their population?"

"You've put your finger on it," Douglas answered. "These people aren't rational."

Douglas' next evening with Caroline involved taking her to a beachside hotel for dancing. "You pay off, taking me to dance at a hotel," she said at her door. She was wearing a white dress, about to the knees. Her shoulders were bare except for the straps.

When they were having their first dance, Caroline said, "I supposed you noticed, I hope you notice these things, that I'm wearing a padded bra."

"I did notice and had to conclude just that. You are not the same person in a dress as you are in a bathing suit," Douglas said. He was becoming accustomed to Caroline's direct statements.

"Well, you won't get any false advertising from me. Around thirteen and fourteen I used to pray to the Almighty to give me beautiful breasts so that there would be no shortage of men. That prayer wasn't answered."

"I think the prayers were heard. The Almighty determined that you would be well served with a clear mind, a challenging personality and plenty of ambition. And by the way, you look lovely tonight, Caroline."

"That's nice, Doug. You don't mind if I call you Doug?"

"No, of course not. Please don't call me Dougie, though. My parents started the Douglas business."

They danced and sat out a few numbers and chatted. Around eleven o'clock they walked on the beach, taking off their shoes to wade in a few inches of water.

Caroline invited Douglas into her apartment. She had opened a bottle of white wine and poured two glasses. They stayed on her porch, the chairs pulled together. She spoke quietly. "I think in a year and a half I'll be moving to Los Angeles to start the doctorate."

"It's firm in your mind?" Douglas asked.

"Yes. I would feel half-educated if I didn't give it a try."

"Is there any question that you wouldn't be successful?"

"They tell me the thesis is the test. The class work I can handle," Caroline said.

Douglas leaned close to her and said, "I'd like to stay over tonight, Caroline."

She kissed him lightly on the lips and said, "Sounds like the right thing to do."

COMMUNIST DICTATORS

PART 5:   COMMUNIST DICTATORS

DOUGLAS FELT HIS life stabilizing, both in his navy work and in his social life. For the latter he had the Gardner clan to thank, starting with Elizabeth Blair and Dmitri Kutuzov and Elizabeth's sister Ellen. The two sisters introduced him to Mrs. Alice Gardner who in turn had him meet Caroline. Douglas speculated that he could have reached Caroline on his own because Mrs. Gardner was enrolled with him in the class taught by Elizabeth. She might have decided that he and Caroline should meet but more than likely it was Elizabeth who wrote the script.

Douglas continued recommending junior officers to billets on ships and to shore bases. Lieutenant Commander Moran had remarked to Douglas on the importance of his sea duty. "Your six years in the fleet have paid off. I can see that. You have a feel for the job." Douglas thought he was doing acceptably well in placing young officers who were following his career path as a deck officer but he was uncertain about how well he was doing with engineering officers. He brought up the matter with Moran who said, "Well, you can't know all of it." As the caseload in dealing with officers fell off, Moran substituted additional duties in examining promotion rates among enlisted men. The very intelligent sailors seemed to be clustered around communications and they were present in the combat information center of any ship. Many of these specialists had high IQs and had passed the exams for promotion but within the Pacific fleet as a whole there were insufficient openings to accommodate this pool of manpower. One of Douglas' suggestions, which was acted upon by Moran and his superior officer, was to take the surplus of these very intelligent people and assign them to jobs in which brain power could solve difficult problems. The areas selected by Douglas were housing for dependents, delivering medical services, entertainment at sea, continuing education on ships, and supply. When a logjam materialized, a fresh face would show up to work on the problem with the willingness to take risks, not risks with lives but risks in bypassing standard procedures. The organization to which this new person was detailed would be won over beforehand so that the new face could be put to work with high hopes of success. Douglas' plan worked. Moran commended Douglas for originality.

Caroline represented a situation new to him. He did not ignore her question about making admiral. This was a remark from a competitive, determined woman. Whether it had leapt out of Caroline or it was normal for someone with her personality to ask such a question, he was left with the impression that she thought he was not applying himself sufficiently in life and in his career. She would earn a doctorate in economics. What would he be doing?

He had felt at ease with his progress though life. Perfecting his reading, writing and speaking of French and Spanish were accomplishments. He continued to read novels in both languages and to use the languages conversationally at every opportunity.

By Caroline's standards, apparently, past accomplishments were just that, trophies once earned but now residing on a shelf. Her question was a version of, "What have you done for me lately?" He would continue to ponder his situation. Not only had Caroline brought up the matter of his career in an attempt to put it on a firm track, but also she had organized his social life. As Douglas reviewed it, from that first night in bed with her, they became absorbed in one another. The unwritten and unspoken contract was that they would be together on weekends. She seemed to be dedicated to her work and did not need entertainment through Thursday night. Friday night they usually ended up together. He knew they both looked forward to Saturday nights and that held for most of Sunday. Sunday nights were not obligatory. Douglas did not want to start for the naval base on Monday mornings from her apartment. Caroline needed portions of Sunday night to plan for the coming week.

The sleeping arrangements were straightforward, as was most everything with Caroline. On any evening they were together they knew when the time had come for removing their clothes and showering together. They dried each other and went straight to bed. Caroline did not have fetishes and unusual demands. She knew precisely what she wanted and had no hesitation in ordering it up. She did not mind repeating herself when she said, "Sweetheart, the second time is often the good one for me."

As part of their contract to be together on weekends, Douglas would always escort Caroline to a Saturday night function on the base when one came along and she always included him in any family affair. Douglas thought that a casual observer would surmise they were headed for marriage. On one occasion, perhaps in their third month together, Douglas told Caroline that he loved her. She had answered, "That's so nice, darling, but don't forget about my appointment with the doctoral program."

Douglas recalled a story that had been told to him by a classmate when they were in college. A freshman woman sorted out the males from September until right after Christmas when she selected the one she wanted. To him she made sex available for the remainder of their time at college with the predictable result that their social needs were met. Upon graduation they went their separate ways. Douglas had not believed the story on the basis that this woman's behavior contradicted what he knew about women. Douglas did believe that attachment comes with time together, and that attachment over time leads to commitment. Commitment leads inevitably to time in bed. He knew there was no commitment of the deep, permanent kind from either him or Caroline. Even though Douglas had not believed this story told to him in college, there he was living through it. When Caroline said to her grandmother that upon graduation at age thirty-one there would be time for marriage and having babies, Douglas now understood that during the course of her studies she would have selected her husband, isolated him from the crowd, and made herself so indispensable to him that he would announce his love and propose marriage.

The arrangement with Caroline was satisfactory and more. Those delicious times in bed, two nights separated by five days, seemed to fit into nature's pattern. By Friday afternoon he was thinking of nothing but that lovely, trim body. He knew it was a miracle of nature that there was continued urge for the repeated act. Nothing else in life held such a strong grip on the mind of a human being.

Douglas was starting to feel the need to marry and have children. It was another of nature's schedules to allow for maturing followed quickly by the desire to procreate. After Caroline left for the university to start her doctoral program there might be a year or so remaining to him in Honolulu before he would be sent to sea again. In that time he could find a wife from among the ample supply of women at the base but with that schedule he would be off to sea soon after marriage. That would not be the way to start life with the person you loved. The negative aspect of Caroline's program was that he was being kept on ice for her convenience and both of their pleasure. Any medium-term objectives of his received no consideration.

With the Gardners came the opportunity to study Communism. Politics and history were one and the same in Douglas' mind. The answer to the question, how are political regimes chosen for this and that country, continued to interest him. Caroline's contribution was what he had come to expect from her. She wanted anything he tackled to be completed so that in this case he would be prepared to discuss the invention, application, failure and eradication of Communism. She would expect the same from herself. That mind of hers must be processing knowledge all the time.

Douglas reviewed what he had learned so far. There were those crazy bastards Marx and Engels who had come up with a scheme contrary to human nature that they assumed would be the new way of the world. A major sign of their inability to think straight was that they admitted that force would be required to implement their theory. What type of government is it that has to be forced down people's throats? What dim wits! What a formula for disaster, for death, for destruction of property and spreading of famine. From what he had read, Douglas was left to wonder at the attraction that meddling in other people's lives had for a fair slice of the world's population. These enforcers, as Douglas called them, many hundred of thousands of them, had closed ranks to oppress hundreds of millions of their own citizens.

These enforcers wore the uniforms, ran the prisons, applied torture and performed the executions so that other like-minded individuals could operate the ministries. Douglas viewed it as a bankrupt system. If a sufficient number of people could abandon the principles of civility and impose tyranny in the name of government, then you could have any dictatorship you wanted.

Lenin was another miserable bastard whose life Douglas wanted to study. He gave his working days to revolutionary activities, to toppling regimes that governed people in a civil manner and put in their place governments that forced on populations nothing that they wanted. Douglas thought that Lenin's eradication of the ownership of private property and its transfer to the state went against human acquisitiveness. People want to own a house and they want savings and they want investments. They want to pass on this property to their children so that the children might have a better time of it than the parents had. He would study this man Lenin.

Staying in the proper sequence, Douglas planned to read up on the Spanish Civil War and determine the extent it was waged to keep Communism off the Iberian Peninsula. China, Douglas guessed, was too great a challenge. He knew nothing about the language, had no time to visit the country, and therefore would be reduced to reading reactions and histories written by western observers. Perhaps it would be enough to identify the similarities between Stalin and Mao Zedong, both butchers of the first rank. He would read the most informative texts he could find.

The *Cultural Revolution* was a brainstorm of Mao. He maintained that constant revolution was a solution to China's ills. Tear up what you have in order to make it better. The idiocy of such a program on the face of it made Douglas curious. He would read up on it, ending with Mao's Little Red Book. There must be logic to Mao's program that would come clear upon study. He would not have led a billion people over a cliff for nothing. Douglas thought that his job in the case of Mao's *Cultural Revolution* was to spell out the intended objectives and compare them to the achievements realized.

Next in line would be Cuba. Douglas wanted to find out how Fidel Castro had been formed. What were the influences in his early life that made him conclude that the ten or so million Cubans on his island wanted or needed regimentation, subjugation, brutality and poverty? He would follow his study of Castro with a look at Salvador Allende and the three years of his presidency before his assassination at the hands of the military of Chile. What was all that about? In addition, there might be lessons to be learned by a study of the Ortega brothers of Nicaragua. There were rumblings that Daniel Ortega wanted to take back the presidency after his failure to provide his people what they wanted during his first term, 1985-1990.

And lastly, Douglas would have a look at this new political phenomenon, Hugo Chavez, the president of Venezuela, who has had strong leanings to the left and was tempting his legislature to alter the constitution so that he might run repeatedly for the presidency. Douglas thought it was a short distance between a constitutional provision that permitted endless reelection and a coup d'état that guaranteed holding power for life.

Caroline was a driving force. The way she led her life served as an example to him. She pushed herself to do well at work. She was making plans for continuing her education. Douglas had little doubt that she had plans extending a decade. He surmised that she was reluctant to discuss these plans on the basis that they could be viewed as so much smoke, thereby reducing the opinions of her held by others. Better to show results than discuss plans. Douglas acknowledged to himself that at the moment Caroline started working on the doctorate their life together would end.

Caroline and Douglas discussed the personalities of the men who formed the upper echelon in dictatorial regimes, Communist or not. They concluded that they had to be willing to kill those who did not fall in line with their thinking. This held particularly for those opponents who gave vent to their objections by speaking and writing publicly. Of course these leaders did not do the killing themselves. That was left to the specialists who would do that type of work as long as it was sanctioned by the government. Caroline thought that this element existed in all societies and that the difference between dictatorships and democracies was that in the democracies the killing element was kept subdued by a well-organized law enforcement system. As long as their interest in killing was not permitted by the government, and indeed if killing brought on the most severe penalty, then the section of the population that could commit these acts of violence would be restrained. Caroline made her point with this example, that if turned loose, the vigilantes would castrate gay men and spay lesbians, all of them.

Douglas did not know about the strongmen who came to power toward the end of the twentieth century. Allende, Chavez and Ortega could well have operated without repression. They could win an election and remain in office by creating an administration that provided sufficient services to the poor to continue winning elections at the ballot box. He would get to the bottom of it.

Douglas decided that in over a year he could learn what he wanted to know about Lenin, Stalin and Mao. These would be reading exercises. Elizabeth and Dmitri were there to direct him. To decipher the Spanish Civil War he was certain that he could find the appropriate histories and biographies.

It might be impossible to visit Cuba. Douglas had heard there was a federal law that prohibited U.S. citizens from spending time on the island. If that was the case, as a naval officer who had taken the oath to defend the constitution, he would not make that trip. Douglas knew that there were former Cubans by the thousands in Miami and he guessed he might connect with a political organization that was familiar with the entire history.

It occurred to Douglas that he was not owned by Caroline. The relationship, as she had constructed it, had a term limit. He would be a lame duck toward the end of her stay. If an irresistible woman at the naval base came over the horizon, he was not duty-bound to stay with Caroline to her last day on Oahu. He felt relieved by this new thought while looking forward as much as ever to Friday nights.

Douglas recounted to Caroline his early conclusions from reading. He knew from previous experience that she would not interrupt him, but the movement of the furrows on her brow, which he had become accustomed to, would signal that there would be a substantial rebuttal to anything she disagreed with. It was not in her nature to allow his views to pass unchallenged.

Caroline's first observation went back to something she had said previously to the effect that the evaluation of events in a century long past was dangerous because the evaluation would be wrong in most instances. "We can't relive those times. We have no idea how people who lived in those times reacted to conditions and events."

Douglas thought that her point was valid and said so. He came back with his observation that Marx and Engels should have anticipated what Communism would be like, that force in all its grizzly aspects would be necessary to impose it on a nation.

Caroline's answer was that Douglas was asking for a great deal. Reading the future had always proved hazardous and inaccurate, particularly if one attempted to look more than a couple of decades ahead.

Caroline injected a new concept. "We agree that looking ahead is nearly impossible but looking back is simple. Marx and Engels only needed to go back fifty years to see that revolution was possible. A king had been beheaded. The old order was finished. That French Revolution of 1789 didn't turn out the way they would have wanted, but they saw that destroying a form of government that didn't satisfy the people was a distinct possibility. They could see that."

Douglas had learned what many do not learn in their lifetime: that it was unproductive to argue. He tried limiting himself to stating his position. Knowing that there would be a response, he listened carefully and analyzed. He had told himself that when he spoke he learned nothing because he knew it to be difficult to reason out a new theory or proposition as he talked. The process of establishing a fair, lucid position required study and concentration. On the other hand, if he listened to the reactions of an intelligent person such as Caroline then it was assured that he would hear a conclusion or two that had not occurred to him.

Douglas had given Caroline his reactions to the *Communist Manifesto*. When he spoke to her of *Das Kapital* she was attentive but he could tell she was eager to express herself on the topic. Douglas mentioned a few of Marx's theories. One held that when commodities are turned into products and priced for sale, the portion going to the owners of the means of production represented ill-gotten gains that belonged to the workers (the proletariat) and not to the bourgeoisie. Another of Marx's theories held that there would be a concentration of the means of production among the owners, a concentration that would bring about intense competition and therefore a reduction in wages. This would produce poverty among workers. When Douglas stopped to gather his thoughts Caroline jumped in.

"I haven't read Marx, as I told you, but I hear he was wrong on many of his predictions. The concentration of the ownership of the means of production never came, and therefore the poverty he anticipated didn't come. And as far as abolishing the middle class, vast numbers of the proletariat made money and moved into the middle class. Capitalism made headway around the world while his system lost ground. I'll be required to take a course on the history of economic theory in those three years of the PhD program and I might have to read him in the original -- that would be in a translation from German to English. But history didn't go the way he predicted, so why bother?"

Douglas had no argument with Caroline's thoughts. He did have another observation on Marx, however. "His writings reflect the world as he saw it in the middle of the nineteenth century. The concepts he advanced were at the heart of Communism. They were important to the extent that the Soviet Union and China are important to the history of man in the twentieth century." Douglas realized that he and Caroline had reached an impasse. They were both silent for a moment and then Caroline, for the first time, revealed to Douglas the part of economics that interested her.

"Here's a retired person. His or her income consists of a Social Security check, rent from an apartment, interest from bonds and dividends from stocks. Easy enough to calculate. Now look at fifty million retirees and determine the sources of their income. Quite a task! I want to locate the income available for all retired people. Look at rent. Some of it goes to pay down the mortgage. Some goes to maintenance and another portion for insurance and taxes. It's complex."

"That's major sleuthing," Douglas said. "To what purpose?"

"If I can identify the totals in these categories, interest, dividends, rents, capital gains, then figure out how each is divided between retired and non-retired recipients then I'll be able to calculate the number of people that our society or our economy can afford to finance as retirees and at which level, that is, how much money does the average retiree get." Caroline paused to note the effect she was having on Douglas.

"You must have a purpose beyond that," Douglas said.

"Yes, it concerns me that our society as a whole will not be able to generate enough income for all retirees some time in the future. We who wish to retire may be required to work five years more than we had anticipated," Caroline said.

"Has anyone collected this data?" Douglas asked.

"I'll find out. If no one has I'll get to it and write my thesis on the topic."

Douglas read the best known writings of Marx and Engels, the *Communist Manifesto* and *Das Kapital*. Both these men wrote extensively for periodicals but Douglas could not avail himself of that material. He knew he would have no way of locating it. Then Douglas read biographical sketches of these men, and finally he reflected. What were the social conditions at the time they wrote? What did they envision would be improvements to countries in Europe if they could put their recommendations to work? How could these improvements be put into place? They did not live to see Communism at work because they both died before Lenin seized power in Russia, but their writings were the most influential of all such attempts in the twentieth century. At least Douglas thought so from what little he knew and by time his study was finished he hoped to understand the movement as completely as possible. The Soviet Union was operated along Communist lines from 1917 to 1991. China became a Communist country in 1949 and remained one at the end of the twentieth century in spite of the adoption of many economic practices of the capitalistic world.

As Marx and Engels were writing the *Manifesto* in 1848, they were able to examine the recent histories of Great Britain and France. Both were monarchies, with Great Britain retaining her monarch (Queen Victoria occupied the throne at the time). France was seeing the final days of the third king after Napoleon. In both countries the monarch had yielded some power to the Parliaments, more so in Great Britain than in France. In both countries the Industrial Revolution was creating a new class of owners and an assortment of factory workers, railroad construction crews, and merchants by the hundred of thousands. The invention of the steam engine made plentiful energy available at bargain prices and intelligent people put their initiative and inventiveness to work to take advantage of this supply.

Marx and Engels seized on the unequal distribution of power and wealth and devised a scheme for redistribution. Douglas concluded that the taking of private property -- in fact, ending the concept of private property -- and making the state the owner of the means of production accomplished all that Marx and Engels dreamed of. The remaining paragraphs of the *Manifesto* were mere details. As an example, the notion that the state would vanish after a while was pure nonsense. If anything, in order to have the state manage an economy down to the last shoelace, the state had to grow and it needed to be all powerful.

In both France and England, the right to vote was extended. If the authority is to reside in a parliament then extending suffrage makes sense. But Marx and Engels must have realized that in their scheme, power would be concentrated in the hands of a small group of Communists and that the matter of voting was inconsequential. And while they guessed that force would be required to carry out their program they could not have imagined that millions would need a bullet in the back of the head to keep their program in place. Douglas thought that these two writers could not be cynical to that extent.

So much for the founders of Communism. How about the followers? How could thousands of otherwise intelligent people adopt a system that would need armies of enforcers to keep it in place, and in the end produce far fewer results than a laissez-faire system?

Douglas could think of a few reasons. Some people love power. Many people hate those who have more wealth than they have. Still other people think that when wealth is taken away from the few and redistributed to the many that fairness is restored and the many will enjoy a new level of richness. This last group does not consider that in most instances wealth tends to accrue to the intelligent, educated and industrious individuals, and removing their wealth only makes them search for new opportunities, while those to whom this wealth is distributed are not made rich. It was Douglas' observation that the recipients of distributed wealth were stuck with the level of intelligence given them at birth and the success of any acquisition for wealth on their parts depended on whether they wished to further their education and apply it industriously to projects that would generate rewards. The handout of another person's wealth did not produce lasting positive results.

It worried Douglas that so many in all corners of the world could fall for the simple solution that taking from others was more advantageous than improving one's self. It was the easy way out. People came naturally to blaming others for their ills and shortcomings -- bring them down to our level, they said -- and avoided taking responsibilities for their own situations.

But it had happened. Men with driving ambition had installed the system of Communism, with all its horrors, and other leaders who came after Lenin installed the system of Communism in their own countries even though they could see what would be inflicted on their populations. The people in these other countries were not different from Russians. They would not have any better luck with this form of government than did the Soviet Union. Many who could leave their country after the advent of Communism would leave.

Douglas felt that Marx and Lenin had not organized a rational system for accomplishing the goals they intended mainly for the reasons that the proletariat, the common man, was not up to running an organization as complex as a nation, let alone the various pieces that constitute a national economy: education, manufacturing, transportation, medicine and other social services, and so on. If that was the case then Marx and Engels had constructed an irrational system based on their emotions. They wanted to take down the bourgeoisie and replace it with a few Communist administrators and a sprinkling from the proletariat. They may have guessed that their plans would fail, but what of it? If the bourgeoisie could be brought down, if those aristocrats, managers, land owners, bankers, and intellectuals could be crushed and either not replaced, or if replaced, replaced by someone from the bottom, well so much the better. Damn the consequences.

LENIN AND STALIN

THE TIME THAT Caroline and Douglas had left drew short. Knowing that their life together would end soon changed their relationship. They were as amorous as ever but there were additional tender moments. Each wanted the other to know what their partner meant to them. Both knew that when a relationship ceased to grow it collapsed and neither wanted that outcome. Caroline, in her blunt manner, would address the situation now and again. "Hold on a while longer, darling. I couldn't bear it if you were thinking about another woman." Douglas found the correct answer. "Trust me, sweetheart. Except for this higher calling of yours, I'm certain we could have reached the altar." He meant it. She had said, "Very poor timing on my part. You're quite a catch, Douglas."

Douglas had met Ann Culbertson at the Officers' Club. His boss' wife, Adele Moran, had introduced them. Ann was Douglas' age and therefore slightly older than Caroline. She was a lieutenant, as he was, and worked as an administrator at the large hospital on the base. They had danced a bit on that first evening, a Thursday night, and as Douglas held her he sensed she would fill a bathing suit in places where Caroline did not. She was intelligent and quick-witted and Douglas thought they might enjoy a chapter or two after Caroline left and before his next assignment.

Douglas continued his reading on Communism. He was engrossed in *Basic Communism: Its Rise, Spread and Decline in the 20th Century.* It was written by Clarence B. Carson. Before starting on page 1, Douglas skipped around to locate any paragraphs about the sealed train. He found a few details but not the complete story. To end the Russian participation in the First World War, the German government was interested in having Lenin return to Petrograd to assist the government of Russia in reaching a peaceful resolution. So that Lenin would not be considered a German agent he asked that the train car be sealed and that there be no contact between him and the German government. There were thirty-eight people in the sealed car including Zinoviev, an original and important Communist, who would be liquidated in the mid-thirties as a result of Stalin's purge.

It did not seem to Douglas that one car would suffice for thirty-eight people, nor did the author discuss the route taken. If there were no fighting on the German-Russian front then the train might be let through so it could travel Zurich-Berlin-Warsaw and continue through the Baltic countries to reach Petrograd. If the border was not open, the train could travel Zurich-Berlin-Danzig and then by ship to Sweden or Finland where the passengers could proceed by rail to Petrograd. The author did recount that the train finally arrived at the Finland station in Petrograd making the second routing more likely. Douglas was curious over his need to know these details about Lenin's train ride. There were far more important aspects to Lenin than this. When he expressed his frustration to Caroline over not knowing more, she had looked at him and said, "Ho, hum."

Lenin arrived in April 1917. The Czar had abdicated. A provisional government under Kerensky was in place. The thrust of the Bolsheviks was to take over the Petrograd Soviet, the name for the regional council, then take over other soviets until they controlled the country. With the control of a soviet of an important region, such as Petrograd or Moscow, which included the city and adjoining territory, came authority over the administration and the police, as well as over limited military functions. The Bolsheviks obtained a majority on the Petrograd Soviet in October 1917 and the Revolution was underway. By July 1918 the Bolsheviks and Lenin were in power and the provisional government was no longer. The measure of the power that the Bolsheviks enjoyed is that they were able to order the execution of the Czar and his family in that month. Douglas had read elsewhere that in 1887 -- Lenin would be seventeen that year -- Lenin's brother Alexander was hanged for his involvement in an unsuccessful attempt on the previous czar. Had it not been for that event, Douglas speculated, the Czar and his family might have been exiled or spared in some fashion. The fact that Lenin cared not one whit for his reputation as a head of state caused Douglas to question Lenin's sanity.

Douglas read on. He could not explain to himself several aspects of Communism. The poorest Russians, the peasants and the industrial workers, were meant to climb in status and wealth. They would not be able to own property but they might enjoy higher wages than they had previously. And if the government was meant to be run by the proletariat then a few among the poor would have a say in the new order of things. It turned out that putting together a new regime brought about civil war. The two sides were the Reds, and the Whites (anti-communists). The war lasted until December 1920.

Douglas had not realized that in order to install Communism the individual had to be reshaped. Gone was any belief in God. Churches were closed and used for other purposes. Priests were defrocked and many killed. Of course the church's property became the property of the state. All freedoms, such as freedom of speech, peaceful assembly, press and religion were abolished. In the doctrines of the Bolsheviks, these freedoms were put off until perfect democracy was reached, so in effect these freedoms were abolished. Farms were collectivized, producing in the act famine and misery. While enslavement and terrorizing of the populace were taking place, the higher-ups in the Communist Party were evolving into the new upper class. They were becoming the bourgeoisie that had been held responsible for society's ills. The perquisites that once belonged to Russia's aristocracy moved into the hands of the Communists. The party apparatus fell heir to the best houses, mansions, real estate, and means of transportation, medical attention, and food and vacation schedules.

Douglas wondered at the hypocrisy of it all. Didn't Lenin and the rest of them understand that as they attempted to create a new society for the unfortunate many, they clung to the old ways of privilege for themselves? Of course they did, he concluded. To the victors go the spoils, they might have said. Or inasmuch as they were responsible for the operation of the state they deserved luxurious accommodations.

Whatever their thinking they must have known of the repression that they were putting in place.

To stay out of trouble, any and all members of society had to abide by the teachings of Marx as interpreted by Lenin. That is, all had to be loyal to the Party. Anything less resulted in arrest, followed by trial or summary execution or deportation to a labor camp where one attempted to serve out a sentence amid starvation and disease.

Douglas was astounded that a small portion of the Russian population, those in charge, wanted the life of poverty and enslavement for the majority, a segment numbering in the millions. Douglas concluded that the leaders among the Communists, as well as being corrupt were also psychopathic. Sane, rational people, living under a code of ethics, would not bring wholesale death and destruction to their own people.

When discussing with Caroline what he had read, she remained an attentive listener. She knew about Khrushchev's denunciation of Stalin and the gradual relaxation under Brezhnev and those who came after him and the final undoing of the system as orchestrated by Gorbachev and Yeltsin. She did not know of the purges put in place by Stalin. Caroline had this to say to Douglas, "I admire your tenacity in reading this recent history and coming to grips with Communism, but what will you make of it?"

It was classic Caroline, Douglas thought. Ever practical, she wanted to know how he would put this information to use. "I don't think you need a reason to absorb another block of history; you feel enlarged by it," he answered. Knowing where she was headed, that he ought to be studying a topic of value to his naval career, he spoke defensively when he said, "It's not lost on me that you are reviewing a book on basic economics that you must have read as an undergraduate and I see a book on statistics on your desk."

"I know nothing about statistics," Caroline said, "but if I'm planning to review the data on the resources that support our retirees, then there's no question that I must be fluent in that language, in statistics." Douglas concluded that Caroline had absorbed all that she would on the subject of Communism and if he wanted to delve deeper he should have a lengthy conversation with Elizabeth Blair. After all, she taught history and at least she would be interested in the topic, if not fluent in it.

Douglas telephoned Elizabeth and arranged for a Sunday afternoon visit. Dmitri would be home as well. Douglas wanted to talk about the implantation of the Communist system the first time, that would be in Russia, and how it could possibly be seen as a desirable form of government for another country after the experiences of the Russian people with it. Douglas asked Elizabeth whether Caroline could be included, as they were spending their weekends together. Douglas had brought a book with him to Caroline's apartment Friday evening. It was titled, *The Rise and Fall of Stalin,* by Robert Payne. It was filled with excellent material, including additional information on the sealed train. The book contained the contents of the telegram from Lenin to his sister in Petrograd, dated April 1917, announcing that he was leaving from Torneo on the Swedish-Finish border and was headed for Petrograd. So he had to have crossed the Baltic Sea! Douglas was mystified and told Caroline so because Torneo is as far north as one can go on the body of water that separates Finland from Sweden, the Gulf of Bothnia. Lenin could have come by ship to Stockholm and then by rail north to Torneo on the Swedish side, and then continued south by rail on the Finnish side to Helsinki. When they were holding Caroline's atlas open to the appropriate page and Douglas was indicating possible routes, Caroline said, "You won't be satisfied until you go to the archives and come up with the stubs of their train tickets."

Douglas understood that Caroline could not fathom his interest in Lenin's route, but then neither could he. "I don't know why, but I think it's important," he said quietly. They closed the atlas and as Douglas held up the book on Stalin, he said, "I want Elizabeth and Dmitri to see this book Sunday afternoon."

When the four of them were assembled on Elizabeth and Dmitri's back porch, Dmitri spoke up. "Czar Peter the Great built the city and named it after his saint, really after himself. Around the time of the First War, the name was changed to Petrograd. That is Russian language. St. Petersburg is German. When Lenin died city became Leningrad. When Communism died, back to St. Petersburg. Round trip in three hundred years."

Elizabeth picked up the discussion. "Douglas, you wanted to know how Communism got started the first time. Then I think you asked why anyone would want to install it in yet another country after seeing how it failed in Russia. I think that those who are interested in planting the system must look for fertile ground. Lenin hoped for world revolution and he thought all of Europe was ripe, particularly his own country. You knew he lived abroad constantly from 1905 on, mostly for his health. That is to say it is healthier to live in Switzerland than it is to live in exile somewhere in Siberia. He couldn't wait to start a revolution in his country, with him at the head of it, of course."

"So it was fortuitous that he was Russian and thought that Russia was the best place to start. Is that the idea?" Douglas asked.

"You need only look for fertile ground. The Romanovs had been in power for three hundred years. Any autocratic government breeds revolutionaries who want desperately to change the way of doing things. So in Russia you had a history of revolutions over the years, peasant revolutions that failed only to be followed by repression. There was a history of failed revolutions. And the Czar resigned in the middle of a failed war. The Russian armies had lost to the Germans, peace was viewed as the answer to all problems, and the bulk of the people dreamed of universal suffrage, more land for the peasants, and better working conditions for the workers."

"All those sound like the correct things to do," Douglas interjected.

"You're right. So it was not a tough sell until after the Communists took power and the revolver had replaced the whip. By then it was too late. Terror became a way of life. Eventually wholesale killings and concentration camps, or gulags, had become so embarrassing to the leaders that they too revolted against the system. Good Communists such as Khrushchev had to denounce Stalin. From start to denunciation took forty years."

"Funny that Communism didn't get a start in Germany," Douglas said.

"Yes, but remember that no battles were fought in Germany during the First World War. The Germans knew hunger, but not necessarily despair. And back to Russia. The Czar represented the ownership of property. You could not become rich without property, be it in factories or land. So when the Communists promised to abolish private property they were promising to abolish the segment of the population that owned property, perhaps one or two percent of the people. Because it was obvious that one had to have property to generate riches, then if all the property was placed in the hands of the state all people would become equal and the former owners, whom the Communists referred to as the bourgeoisie, would be reduced to the same status as the working class, and that's always popular with the have-nots."

"That's what they mean by the dictatorship of the proletariat?" Douglas asked.

"I think that's the slogan, the myth, but the proletariat was represented by the Communist Party. Don't think for one moment that masses of workers and peasants ran the country. The Party became the government and the Party was always the instrument that belonged to the top Communists. They, the top dogs, stood on Lenin's mausoleum in Red Square while the peasants and laborers marched by. I'm certain the Party was reviewing the faithfulness of the peasants and laborers."

"To continue with fertile ground," Elizabeth went on, "Russia was making progress in spite of czarism. There had been an elected Duma since 1905. The important, industrialized countries of Europe had moved from absolute monarchy to constitutional monarchy or outright democracy. It was Russia's turn to take the step. The First World War marked the end of progress. Then Russia's army broke up and many soldiers left the front for their homes where they were able to occupy land belonging to the gentry. The provisional government dissolved between April and October 1917 and the Bolsheviks took over."

"Would you say it was a bloodless revolution?" Douglas asked,

"Not bloodless at all and more were killed in April than in October."

Caroline, who had been sitting quietly, looked at Elizabeth and said, "Tell me about Lenin. What sort of a man was he?"

"I would say he was beyond description," Elizabeth answered. "He was a professional revolutionary, a man with no other career. Even though he had a law degree, he never practiced. He had been completely captivated by Marx and was determined to install Communism and in the process destroy the upper and middle classes. I cannot relate his determination to destroy human beings with the actions of any other figure in history. In that respect he was a monster. Without him, no revolution. Trotsky, who might have succeeded him, was made of much softer stuff."

"Was it good or bad that he died so young in 1924?" Douglas asked.

"As savage as he was, he was replaced by Stalin who set new records in killing fellow countrymen. You might say that it was unfortunate for many Russians that he died young."

The four of them stayed on the porch and ate a light meal that Elizabeth and Dmitri had prepared. Elizabeth asked her cousin Caroline about her plans for moving to Los Angeles. She answered, "I won't have to study Marx. I think I've absorbed all I need to know from Douglas."

Caroline looked ahead. It would not be long before she would hand in her resignation at the bank. She reflected that had the idea of a doctorate not come up she and Douglas might have married. He intimated as much. One reason for deciding on additional education was that being a navy wife did not appeal to her. There would be those months when he would be at sea. She would need to make new sets of friends with each assignment. On the other hand, he might be made naval attaché in an interesting capital and he could be given shore duty in Naples at the headquarters of the Sixth Fleet. For the long term, though, the plan to obtain the doctorate made sense. She could be an economist at a bank, or perhaps launch a teaching career at a prestigious university. In either event, she would isolate a field of research and make herself one of the dominant persons in it.

Caroline debated whether upon arrival in Los Angeles she should live with her parents or strike out on her own immediately. She knew she had grown accustomed to her freedom and enjoyed the closeness that she and Douglas had experienced. Their relationship had grown so that they viewed it as beyond dating. They lived separately for the first part of the week and lived together on weekends. She felt she knew what a sound marriage would be like, minus the children.

Caroline's family must have wondered about the final disposition of her relationship with Douglas. No questions were leveled at her, not even by her grandmother, Alice Gardner, who was the most likely relative to conduct an oral examination, if not a grilling. It was she who gave a Saturday evening farewell party for Caroline, leaving her and Douglas to themselves on Sunday before her flight to Los Angeles on Monday.

Douglas had never given himself over completely to Caroline. Knowing that she would be leaving and that he came second after her education, he reciprocated if only in his attitude. His career, or his hobby of reading, or another woman, could come before Caroline. He thought it was a defense mechanism, a natural one that all men in his situation would adopt. Their final Sunday was set aside for packing. Douglas had a few items to put into a pile to be returned to his apartment. Caroline had left a fair amount to be done in order to fill the day. They took a final swim in the ocean and stayed in for their supper. Bed time came. They turned out the lights and settled on the sofa. They awakened after midnight and moved to the bedroom. They slept on until the alarm rang. Neither had suggested intimacy.

Caroline had given Douglas her parents' address and telephone number. He was to make contact any time he came to California. Suspecting that there would be a new man in her life he made no such plans.

Douglas had grown accustomed to all that Caroline offered. Her entertaining mind, that forceful personality, the affection for him, these were the elements that kept a man and a woman together. He knew he would seek out another woman very soon. He wanted to move slowly but he was so used to having Caroline in his life that he knew he might lunge at the first opportunity. He knew also that any woman that replaced Caroline needed the personality and brains that pleased and aroused him. The body of this new woman and the extent the body would be available to him would be second in importance. Douglas understood that he had been in the company of a remarkable person. She was superior in all ways. There were no missing pieces. With her, because of her, he was able to determine which aspect of a woman was the most important to him. There was no question that Caroline's brains were her most valuable gift. Brains were the aphrodisiac.

Douglas embarked on his new life. He felt embarrassed thinking about other women, as though he were inviting a new woman into his bed while the sheets were still warm. Yet it was not his doing that Caroline was driven to obtain a PhD in economics. He thought that one month without feminine companionship would strike the right balance. In one month, the effect of Caroline's presence would be reduced by half and she would no longer fill his thoughts on weekends. In one month he would ask one of the women he knew slightly to share an evening with him.

In this first month alone he would devote all his evenings to reading about Communism. Having learned about the seizing of power by the Bolsheviks and Lenin, he would learn how Stalin shouldered and elbowed the competition out of the way to become top dog. Lenin had given Stalin a head start by installing him as Party Secretary, a perch from which he could observe the important players and their actions. Douglas had read far enough into the life of Stalin to find that he was the son of a brutal man. When he presented this fact to Caroline in one of their last conversations, she remarked that Lenin had come from a stable, upper middle-class family yet Lenin had the same brutal streak that Stalin had. "You might entertain the notion that both were mad for power. That would be more important to their make-up than the ferocity of the beatings their fathers dished out." Of course Caroline was right and Douglas had to agree with her. He thought that in this month of celibacy he could get as far as the purges of the late 1930s. Why did Stalin think that he had to kill off the old Bolsheviks in order to hold on to power? Couldn't he have sent them into exile out of the country if they were a threat to his position?

On the matter of establishing a far-ranging system of gulags where people could be sent to work and die, Douglas wondered about a parallel between Lenin and Stalin. Lenin's older brother had been hanged over an attempt on the then czar. Lenin had ordered the execution of the royal family, perhaps in retribution. Stalin had been sent to Siberia into exile, not once but several times, for his revolutionary activities. Inasmuch as those then in power, the bourgeoisie, had been responsible for sending him off, wouldn't it be fair for him, in his turn, to send the bourgeois, millions of them, to work and die in Siberia? Couldn't they populate the gulags? Douglas knew he would never find the answers to these questions. It would be more likely that he found the stubs for those railroad tickets in an archive.

For his first social outing, Douglas asked Ann Culbertson when they might go for a swim, followed by dinner at a place to be decided on later. Ann said that meeting at the pool on the base was convenient for her, after work that Friday.

When he arrived, Ann was already in the pool, chatting with a few women. When Douglas joined them she separated from the group and swam a few lengths with him. She had the strokes mastered, Douglas thought, and she swam them alternately, even a length of butterfly. "My high school stroke," she said.

When they were out of the pool and sunning themselves, Douglas glanced at Ann's body but didn't study it. He did not want to be caught appearing interested. In the short time they were at the side of the pool, he gathered the impression that she was hard to talk to, limiting herself to activities at the hospital and descriptions of the hill country north of Atlanta, where she originated.

The second time they were out for the evening, they started with a swim on Waikiki followed by a walk along the beach, prior to dinner. At one point Douglas did remark that she had a pretty figure. Her rejoinder surprised him. She said, "The true beauty of it will be displayed to my husband on my wedding night." Douglas analyzed the sentence. Ann could have slept with one hundred men and be on a campaign to reclaim her virginity, or she might be one of those rare examples of a modern woman who abstains. He limited himself to saying, "That's old-fashioned, but I respect it." With the topic open, Ann explored the matter. "I could have all the men on the base. For openers I could use the linen closets for the doctors at the hospital and then I could use my apartment for some and their apartments for more, and finish off in the back seat of my car. But that isn't the point. It isn't want I want. I don't want any of it. I just want all of me to go to the right man."

Douglas said nothing for an instant. He wanted Ann to think that he was mulling over her serious declaration. After twenty seconds he said, "I hope you get your wish, and more than that, I hope you enjoy what you get."

They let it go at that. They went back to the beauties and advantages of the hill country north of Atlanta. "I wouldn't mind living there after finishing twenty years in the navy. Having a farm, raising animals, growing some things. As a nurse I love live things and making them grow."

"What would your husband do?" Douglas asked.

"He could be anything he wanted. A doctor with a practice, or a lawyer at the county courthouse, or even a farmer."

Douglas had it drilled into him that intelligence came in many forms. Ann, in his estimation, was as intelligent as Caroline, but her interests rested elsewhere. She liked her work and must have been good at it. She held a vision of her future clear in her mind down to its location in her native state. She was, however, limited in scope. She may not have read beyond the material important to her work. Certainly she did not introduce topics for discussion nor did she pick up on any of Douglas' excursions into history, literature and politics. She had a mind, a fine, quick, clear mind, but she did not lead a life of the mind. As for her unavailability, Douglas concluded that she did not have the longings for passion that most humans did and if they were awakened the resulting storm might be difficult to contain. Douglas decided to allow another male to explore that territory. He would read about Stalin and limit his discussions of that man and his times to occasional evenings with Elizabeth and Dmitri.

About then a letter from Caroline arrived. She gave her new address and telephone number. She outlined the courses she was taking. She gave her impressions of living once again in Los Angeles and she talked about the campus and how it had changed since her undergraduate days, not so long ago. Of course he would answer, but he would be as non-committal as she had been. She had closed her letter by telling him that she missed him and that they had had a wonderful relationship. He read into it that the affair was closed. It was no longer on-going.

Douglas went on in his reading. He was deep into Robert Payne's *The Rise and Fall of Stalin*. He found that the author didn't want to treat Lenin and Stalin as separate phenomena. He felt they were a continuum. Lenin, because of years of service to the ideals of a revolution was the undisputed leader. From his arrival from Switzerland in 1917 until his incapacity due to a series of strokes in 1922 and 1923, he held unquestioned authority. Whether in good health or bad, Lenin couldn't lead a country alone. He delegated power to others such as to Trotsky, Stalin, Zinoviev and Kamenev. Because Stalin pushed harder than the others, he was treated by Lenin as the best trouble shooter among his subordinates. He would be sent away from Moscow to solve problems in parts of the country that the Bolsheviks could not tame.

Stalin enjoyed some successes. He did originate the concept of political officers to serve alongside army officers who might have deviated from the Party line. He was ruthless in his dealings with the minority populations that did not accept Bolshevik rule. Lenin's most costly error, the one that cost the lives of so many Russians, was to give Stalin authority in the appointment of officials throughout the government. Stalin became the General Secretary of the Central Committee, replacing Molotov. Stalin understood, and perhaps Lenin did not, that people in lower echelons give lifelong allegiance to the individual who selected them for advancement. Stalin worked hand in glove with the secret police and the political commissioners of the army.

As Lenin lost power through illness, the contest for the position of leadership got underway. Russia under the Communists would not be ruled by a committee. It would become a dictatorship under one leader. Trotsky could have pressed for the job as he was the leader of the Red Army. Both Zinoviev and Kamenev were candidates. Stalin, however, appeared to be the person best organized, the one who knew what to do in order to consolidate power, a process involving the elimination of his competitors. Over the years, Stalin pulled together a cadre of people loyal to him, such men as Molotov, Malenkov, Zhdanov and Voroshilov. Others he froze out, tending to assign them to positions of reduced authority in places removed from Moscow. In that sense they were exiled. Trotsky, indeed, was sent in exile out of the country. He ended in Mexico City where Stalin had him murdered by a man wielding a pickaxe. The event took place in 1940, an indication of Stalin's persistence and willingness to engage in unnecessary murder to complete a task.

Before 1930, Stalin had gained absolute power yet he felt compelled to break those whom he had already neutralized. Most of the old Bolsheviks, who had attained power through Lenin, and not through Stalin, were arrested, tortured, forced to confess to crimes they had not committed, tried and executed. The confessions were duly recited in court where the prosecutor, Andrei Vyshinsky, orchestrated what became known as the show trials of 1936, 1937 and 1938. These trials were also referred to as Stalin's purge of the Party and the army. Thousands died. Perhaps hundreds of thousands.

In attempting to sort out his feelings after reading a fair amount about Lenin and Stalin, Douglas held two thoughts in the forefront of his memory. Their retention in his mind was as perplexing as the obsession with the sealed train. The first was that in 1923, on the occasion of Lenin's wish to make a visit from his rest home in Gorki to the Kremlin, he was taken in a chauffeur-driven Rolls-Royce. Perhaps the car had belonged to a Romanov prince who left it behind. The second was that often when Stalin wished to be driven from the Kremlin to his country estate to visit members of his family, he would be taken in a Hispano-Suiza. The Rolls-Royce and the Hispano-Suiza were among the finest cars made. Douglas could not reconcile these signs of the good life with the dictatorship of the proletariat.

JOANNE

DOUGLAS FELT HE had a good grasp of Lenin and Stalin. He had read several texts that described how Lenin introduced Communism into Russia, and how Lenin and Stalin had kept it installed as the ruling doctrine. It remained a mystery why both men were imbued with cruelty. They were impervious to the suffering of others. A greater mystery for Douglas concerned Lenin and Stalin's willingness to destroy the classes of society that had built Russia. The landed aristocracy, the intellectuals, the engineers, architects, doctors, lawyers, merchants and bankers were not evil. No doubt as a group they had not solved the problems of the poor, but destroying that upper tier, as the Communists did, accomplished nothing for the poor. The Communists did not hand to the poor the accomplishments of the rich and talented. Those accomplishments went to the state, to the Communist Party and to those members of the Party who had risen to the top. Douglas could not understand the rationale for those actions. The hypocrisy of it all overwhelmed him.

Douglas knew that the Scandinavian countries, perhaps Sweden more than the others, had attempted a portion of Communism, only to back off from it. The portion they tried had to do with very high taxes that provided cradle-to-grave care for the individual. This form of government they called Socialism and Douglas did not know whether the actions of the Swedish government should be described by that term on the basis that Socialism had many definitions. The Swedes kept in place the aspects of democracy that the Western world had come to expect. Voters sent to their parliament representatives who created Socialistic programs. Voters kept the right to remove these legislators if they, the voters, changed their minds. Swedes who did not care for any of the programs were free to migrate, a freedom not available in the Soviet Union.

The upshot was that the programs were popular at the onset but when too many citizens began taking advantage of them, a portion of the support was withdrawn. When it became advantageous to be unemployed compared to holding a job, some members of society found ways to remain unemployed as wards of the state. Similar behavior greeted the system that provided unlimited health care.

Was not Sweden's experiment, Douglas asked himself, a legitimate experiment of introducing the social aspects of Communism without force, without the stated purpose of destroying the bourgeoisie? Had Lenin introduced this style of government his experiment might have been received as it was in Sweden: yes for the principal aspects, no for the excesses. Lenin could have accomplished what he sought without brutality and the attendant killings.

Caroline was no longer available to discuss these tentative conclusions. He relied on Elizabeth and Dmitri to an extent but they were not right there by his side. Douglas continued swimming at the beach on weekends. He had started the practice with Caroline and continued alone. It did not surprise him that he met a fine woman through her two ambassadors, her children aged five and three, a girl and a boy in that order. Waikiki was crowded this Sunday afternoon. Douglas had come for a brief swim, as was his habit. He had walked from his apartment and wore his swimming trunks under a pair of shorts. He had on a T-shirt and carried a towel around his neck. He settled on an empty spot on the sand and immediately the five-year old girl came up to him and said, "You look like my Daddy." Her brother was in tow, carrying a pail and shovel. Douglas looked around to find parents and settled on a mother a short distance away. There was no question that the five-year old would grow up in the image of this woman. He lifted a hand in a sign of recognition and started talking and playing with the children. The Dad the little girl referred to was at sea. She and her brother went to school and played. Their

Mom worked in an office. They had come by car. Would he take them swimming, not in deep but just so they could run in and out?

Douglas got up and walked toward the mother. She put down her magazine and looked at him and smiled. "I've been asked to take my new friends for a swim," Douglas said. She smiled again and stood up. "Are you coming?" he asked.

They exchanged names. Hers was Joanne. They moved toward the water. The five-year old took Douglas' hand. The three-year old boy stayed unattached, picking his way past people on the sand.

When they had reached the water's edge, the children dipped into the water. Douglas asked, "Joanne, when is your husband due back?"

"There's no due date. He's lost his enthusiasm for marriage but I know he'll come back to see the children. I'm no longer important to him."

"Another woman?" Douglas asked.

"No, I'm enough woman for him or most any man. He's made chief petty officer but thinks he should be a commissioned officer. He says he ought to be a lieutenant by now. He's depressed, feels sorry for himself, and thinks he's been dealt a few bad cards."

"How do you view it?" Douglas asked.

"He missed the years between eighteen and twenty-two, the years he should have been in college. I missed them too. That might be the reason we're married. Two damaged souls."

"What did you do in those years?" Douglas asked.

"Played around. Took any old job. Drank, danced, and went out a lot. Very stupid. When the children came I changed altogether. Gave up everything."

"They are dear," Douglas said.

"They're the reason I behave myself."

Joanne and Douglas took turns swimming and watching the children. When she came out of the water, he studied her and saw what she meant when she claimed that she was enough woman for most any man. She came up to him and asked him whether he was in the service.

"Yes, in personnel at Pearl Harbor. I'm a lieutenant by the way. In a few months it'll be back to sea for me. If not that, a transfer of sorts. He paused for a moment and then added, "Perhaps we can see something of one another."

"I'd like that, Douglas, but I suspect there will be children underfoot all the time. Would that bother you?"

"No, they are such nice kids. No problem at all."

Douglas knew that the little girl was headed straight for his heart. He thought the children should be Caroline's and his. By some miracle, Caroline and he should have met, married and become parents. He didn't know the term psychologists used to describe these moments, these moments of appropriating another's situation and making it your own without any effort. He liked the little boy but it was the girl he would find easy to love. She wanted and needed a father. He imagined that he might do.

Douglas concluded that he had read sufficiently about the lives of Lenin and Stalin to understand them. He thought Communism to be the epitome of the planned economy in which hair-brained schemes lived side by side with the best practices of government. Russia was probably a confused country in which market forces played no part and the success of government-run programs, needed or not, well-thought through or not, depended largely on chance.

The Show Trials that Stalin put on were more a commentary on his personality than an indication of how Communism functioned. These purges, in which Stalin eliminated the old Bolsheviks whose rise through the party ranks could be traced to Lenin and Trotsky, were a mark of how a dictatorship works when in the hands of an insane person. That was Douglas' conclusion.

Douglas knew, not in great detail, the military history of Russia in the years 1936 to 1941. He understood the game that Hitler and Stalin played. One of Hitler's declared objectives was to annex the Ukraine to the Third Reich and populate it with Germans. Stalin would have known this as Hitler included this goal in his Mien Kampf. In 1939 The Soviet Union and Germany signed a non-aggression pact and the two countries proceeded to divide Poland after it fell to the German invasion in September of that year. This study told him how nations play power politics, but it did not reveal how Communist governments acted beyond their boundaries. In 1940, Germany, Italy and Japan signed a treaty in which they declared that they would fight together to achieve world domination. More power politics.

Stalin must have realized that when he was not asked to be a signatory to the treaty, he would be a victim. And indeed Germany attacked the Soviet Union in June 1941.

Douglas decided that the events that took place in Spain were a fruitful study for learning about the operations of the Communist system. Spain had been a kingdom for centuries. The end of the line came in 1931 when Alphonse XIII abdicated and moved to Portugal. It appears that the government at the time, having lived under royalty for many years, was no longer responsive to the needs of the Spanish population, and had to give way to a republic and a popularly-elected Cortes, or parliament. The old aristocracy could not make the sacrifices necessary to come to the aid of the poor. Indeed, they might not have known what to do. Spain, an agricultural country, had allowed a significant portion of its population to slip into poverty and even despair. The new departure of 1931 consisted of a republic and its constitution, which replaced the government of the king. In the elections that followed, the division that would bring about the Civil War was evident. The new government, while freely elected, was left-leaning and consisted of Socialists and Communists. The opposition, in the minority, was made up of Royalists and Fascists.

Stalin saw this as fertile ground. Lenin had predicted world revolution, which had not taken place in Germany, Austria, France, nor in any other European country. But in this new division in Spain, perhaps there was opportunity.

*   *   *

Joanne was cleverer than Douglas had bargained for. She did nothing to advance their relationship. Douglas enjoyed coming to her apartment on weekends so that he might play with the children. There seemed to be two sets of games for the kids. The girl, Shirley, was more advanced than her younger brother, Brian. She enjoyed jig-saw puzzles and had a gift for identifying the small differences that distinguished the various pieces. She was quicker than Douglas, which annoyed him. Brian preferred mechanical toys, any object with wheels. Douglas would read to the children, sometimes from the same book.

It interested him that they had their favorites and wanted them read again and again. It was certain that Shirley would be reading within a year. The three of them would sit on the couch while he read. Shirley often anticipated the outcome of the story and would have the proper emotion ready for the end.

His relationship to the children changed the night that Shirley called out from her bed and asked him to come in and say goodnight. He went into the bedroom and kissed both children on the forehead. This would be the children's doing, not Joanne's. He now had made an emotional attachment to them.

Douglas thought about resigning from the navy, waiting for Joanne and her husband to divorce, and then reconstituting a family by marrying Joanne. The fact that they were not his children did not enter into his calculations. Douglas realized that he had started three relationships, one with each member of the family. Joanne did not foster any arrangement between Shirley, Brian and Douglas. It was up to them to fashion what they pleased.

Joanne played herself. She was uncomplicated, eager to please, and warm. Their evenings together found a pattern. Their card game was gin rummy at which they broke even. Their conversations were centered on their work. Douglas would describe personnel problems he was attempting to solve. Joanne, who was a legal secretary, enjoyed discussing the cases that came to her. She typed briefs and therefore knew the defense that was being mounted for the clients of the firm. Douglas, who knew nothing of the law, was impressed that Joanne understood the issues well enough to explain them in such a fashion that the legal principles were spelled out. On other matters, they were silent, as Joanne had stored away nothing of general interest. There were no repositories of data on any major topic that she could turn to in order to form an opinion based on material absorbed previously. In short, Joanne didn't read. Douglas couldn't tally the score: why would Joanne be certain to have the correct reading material in front of her children when she didn't continue the practice of reading herself? Douglas understood that she had a fine mind, limited to the experiences of work and family. She spoke beautiful English, clear, concise and grammatical. She had and used a large vocabulary, no doubt defined and stretched by working in the legal profession. Her mind, however, had not been made to explore the world around her.

There was a television set placed in front of the sofa. If played at minimum volume it would not disturb the children sleeping in their own beds behind a closed door. Joanne knew the time when her favorite programs came on. She subscribed to the cable network that brought her enormous variety.

When Douglas and Joanne sat on the sofa, their bodies touched. Joanne could be casual in the way she draped herself on Douglas. He would respond by kissing her and caressing her body, not going under the clothes. He knew it would be permitted but he also knew that it would represent a declaration of sorts, to the effect that he wanted a complete relationship. He was held back by the children, by Shirley more than by Brian. Shirley had started running to the front door to greet him when he came. She would throw her arms in the air so that Douglas would pick her up and kiss her. He would do this, realizing that he would be leaving Hawaii soon and that in Shirley's mind it would be impressed that mature men came into her life only to leave when she had started to count on them as permanent fixtures. He had made no secret of his coming reassignment but he knew that to Shirley it would seem that he was abandoning her. One result was that Douglas did not become intimate with Joanne. He was certain that she seized up the situation the way he had.

Douglas wondered about people and their minds. Did they fill them to any plan? The minds of Einstein, Newton and Galileo could have been full. When a new fact arrived that they wished to store, an old fact, no longer of any use, would be discarded and the new fact stored in its place. Other minds, such as his, were not yet full. In his case, spaces were taken up with history, and his three languages, English, French and Spanish. There must be a section of his brain that contained many of the experiences of his life. Certainly there were portions of his mind that contained nothing, awaiting the events and thoughts of the future.

Joanne's mind could be only half-full, if that. At the core there was English, then her experiences at work followed by all she knew to get by in life: how to function at the office; how to manage her household; how to drive. Another portion must be devoted to her relationships, those with her children, her husband, previous men in her life and lately with him. Finally, there was an allocation of space for her personality, her character and her feelings. She was thoughtful, sensitive and generous. There were other admirable traits such as kindness and attentiveness. These must all have been stored together in a quadrant of her mind. In these traits of character, she outshone Caroline. The missing element in Joanne was that she did not have a storehouse of interesting information. While he and Caroline could discuss several topics in depth, Joanne and he could not explore any area of knowledge beyond a few sentences. In addition, Caroline, with her finely-wired, nearly-full mind could draw from topics far afield and introduce them into a current discussion. That was a significant difference between the two women. If he wanted to, Douglas thought he could melt into the warmth and sweet womanliness of Joanne. They could fuse. Caroline, even though he might be married to her, would remain an individual, reachable in all aspects but separate from him. He couldn't explain the difference between these two women in greater detail beyond that. Were he married to Joanne he might end up bored, perhaps to desperation. Were he married to Caroline, there would be rough patches certainly, but they would get through them because both knew that they had entered into marriage without reservation. Douglas had this fear about Joanne's mind, that it had ceased to expand. He was curious that she did not sense the curtain this brought down between them. If she did, she did nothing about it.

Whoever had planned the arrival of human beings on Earth decided that matching up men and women into couples would not be a simple matter. Douglas knew that.

*   *   *

Before starting his study of the Civil War in Spain that spanned the years 1936 to 1939, Douglas took inventory of what he knew from past reading. He recalled that King Alphonse XIII had abdicated and that a new government, parliamentary in nature, was elected by the people to replace the old kingdom. He didn't recall the year and may never have known it. It turned out to be 1931. The king and his sons moved to Portugal. The grandson of the king, Juan Carlos, is the current king of Spain. Douglas knew neither the date of his birth nor the date he ascended the throne. It turned out that he was born in 1938 and came to the throne around the time of Franco's death, 1975. Douglas knew the names of the two camps that fought the Civil War. The side supporting the newly-elected government was called interchangeably Republican or Loyalist. In opposition, ultimately the victors, were the Nationalists or Franco's forces. Douglas knew that Germany and Italy helped Franco's side while the Soviet Union aided the Loyalists.

Douglas had to speculate on the following, although he suspected that if he were fluent in German and Italian he could find his answers in the appropriate archives.

Hitler, by 1936, had retaken the Saar Basin, a small piece of real estate on the French-German border. This was in violation of the Versailles Treaty and the first of Hitler's aggressive acts. The other acts were swallowing Austria (1938), occupying the portions of Czechoslovakia containing people of German origin (1939), and finally taking Poland by force, starting World War II (1939). By 1936, Hitler must have decided that Germany and Italy would go to war against Great Britain and France. It would be to his advantage for Spain, Germany or Italy to take Gibraltar and close the Straight to the Royal Navy. Other British possessions such as Malta, Rhodes and Cyprus should be set free or more likely become part of Italy's Empire. As for the Soviet Union, what part did it play? Tanks and planes were sent, and technical advisers came to assist the Loyalist forces. Douglas wanted to know whether General Franco and the politicians in his circle had originated the Civil War because of their fear that the Communists in the Republican government would, in time, take over Spain and install a Bolshevik government. That was his question. Any person paying attention knew the results of allowing the Communists to come to power. Their trademark consisted of a planned economy and the dictatorship of one man, which could only be kept in place through force. Again, Douglas would be at the mercy of the authors whose books he read. Some of these authors may have run across the answer to his question and not found a place for it in their telling of the story. Other authors may not have thought the question sufficiently important to research. To yet other authors the question, what the Spanish Civil War was meant to accomplish, may not have occurred. Douglas' reading led him to conclude that the rebellion staged by the higher-ups of the army, and therefore Franco, was indeed intended to block the arrival and installation of Communism into Spain.

Douglas started with a thin book, *Spain's Civil War: The Last Great Cause*. The author was Daniel S. Davis.

Spain of the twentieth century, the first third of that century, seemed to operate as a slightly modernized feudal system. The land was still owned in vast tracts. The land could be used for crops, or for grazing, or it could be allowed to lie fallow. The peasants who worked the land were poor and uneducated. They were ripe for rebellion and receptive to any political party that would give them hope. They wished to escape the poverty in which they were trapped. Because two-thirds of Spain's jobs were in agriculture, the number of impoverished peasants was large indeed. One of the popular movements advocated anarchy, and there were a political party and a union that called themselves Anarchists. Their belief was that the organizations of the government and the Church suppressed their ability to improve themselves. They wished to be let alone so that they might establish agricultural communes throughout the country. It sounded to Douglas as a repeat of the Revolution of 1848, when the new wave of industrial workers could not be accommodated by the upper class. There arrived neither a division of wealth nor access to the voting booth. Those would not come for twenty-three years after 1848, in 1871 in the case of France. In the case of Spain, the upper class could not assume the leadership of a movement that would recognize the legitimate needs of the poor. Leadership had to come from below. People from that class and those few from above who agreed with them were forced to take on much of the army in a bloody contest that lasted nearly four years. The population of Spain in 1931 was twenty-five million souls. A million of these would die in the coming decade because of the conflict.

The Communists were not a potent force. The conditions under which the poor lived were those in which Communists do well but they were not present in force. In their places were Anarchists, Socialists and other people of the Left.

The parliamentary elections went back and forth from 1931 through February 1936 when the Left, made up of various factions who grouped themselves into the Popular Front, won with 10% more votes than the Right. It became clear that Spain was divided into two camps that would be unable to reconcile their differences.

The Right and the higher-up officers of the army began organizing a plot for a military takeover of the country. The important man in the army was Francisco Franco. He occupied the position among Spaniards that General George Patton would occupy in the minds of Americans after World War II – a successful soldier who brought home the victories. For the biographical details that Douglas wanted, he turned to *Franco,* by Paul Preston. This book, meticulously researched, gave Douglas many answers. Franco was born in 1892 in the northwest corner of Spain. He entered the military academy for infantrymen at the age of fourteen and graduated on schedule as a second lieutenant. Spain, along with other European powers, was in the process of finishing the job of carving up Africa. The northern portion of Morocco, that portion opposite Gibraltar, would be known as Spanish Morocco for a few decades but presently is once again part of Morocco proper. In the early part of the twentieth century the Spanish army conquered local tribes and occupied an area of over 8,000 square miles, about the size of New Jersey. One earned a military reputation while serving with the army in Africa or while serving in the Spanish Foreign Legion. Franco did both and came up through the ranks at great speed. He became the youngest general in the army. He was fearless in combat, believing that officers should be out front, leading their men against he enemy. Through all his adventures he escaped with only a bullet wound to his mid-section.

Having become a general, he no longer served in the field. One of his assignments was to organize and be the commandant of the new military academy, which combined the four academies that had served previously to produce junior officers. These would be in the years 1928 to 1931.

Politics were not stable in Spain. The sides were drawn along classical lines with peasants and workers forming the Left and the middle class and wealthier segments of the population, along with most of the officer corps of the army, represented the Right. The King, although out of office and living in Portugal, was the leader of the Right.

These two factions, Left and Right, which found means of compromising their differences in most countries, were not able to reconcile them in Spain. A parliamentary election that produced a new majority for the opposite party would vote out the programs voted in by the previous government. The result was that the needs of the poor were never met.

The army in Spain at the time was not apolitical. Many officers, Franco included, viewed the army as the final arbiter of the direction that the government took, and therefore the direction that the country as a whole was taking. As an example, the leaders of the army would draw the line at a Communist government. The army would use its forces to overthrow such a government and replace it with a dictatorship. In the mid-thirties, various officers, thinking that the time had come, would approach Franco on the subject. He always preached caution, telling conspirators that the time was not yet ripe. Franco must have been measuring the mood of the people as well as that of the army.

After his term as head of the military academy, Franco was given other posts in the army such as military commander of a district in the country. There were eight such districts on the Iberian Peninsula. Although he was not the senior general in the army, he had held the position of chief of the general staff for a while. He was sent from this post to be military commander of the Canary Islands, where he was stationed when the Civil War started.

Douglas gathered from his reading that Franco would use the army to prevent the arrival in Spain of a Communist-led government. That's where he would draw the line. The election of 1936, won by the Left, led to several political assassinations and the stage was set for warfare between the two sides. The army's uprising started in Morocco and spread to the mainland. Franco joined the rebels on the condition that he would command the troops in Africa and the Foreign Legion. These forces were duly transferred to the region around Seville in the south of Spain, mostly by airlift provided by Germany. Germany supplied tanks, artillery and aircraft. The Italian government went one better by supplying infantry to fight alongside the Spanish army. The Soviet Union acted as Germany did, sending equipment but no soldiers from the Red Army.

Adding up the numbers of planes listed in Paul Preston's *Franco*, it appeared to Douglas that no more than fifty planes total were made available by Germany and Italy in the summer of 1936. With these planes an airlift was established and the Spanish army in Morocco and the Spanish Foreign Legion were flown to the south of Spain. The Germans and Italians provided pilots as well.

In the first three months of the Civil War, the Nationalists (Franco) consolidated their grip on the western part of Spain, that portion of the country with its back to Portugal. The Republican forces held on to the eastern portion of the country bordering the Mediterranean. Madrid, the prize, was to remain in the hands of the Republicans (the elected, leftist government) until near the end of the war.

In the autumn of 1936, it became necessary to appoint a supreme commander on the Nationalist side from among the several generals who had inaugurated the revolt. The foremost candidate had died in a plane crash. Other generals were tarnished in some fashion, or felt themselves under-qualified. The generals assembled and decided on Franco. He was made commander-in-chief as well as head of state. The emergence of one person to be in charge of affairs was also the wish of the governments of Germany and Italy.

The Spanish army in Morocco and the Spanish Foreign Legion consisted of battle-hardened veterans who had grown accustomed to killing their prisoners. This was the practice in their battles against the local tribes in North Africa. In was only a step to pillaging the cities and villages they took in Spain and raping women and killing anyone who could be identified with the Left. It appeared that in Franco's conduct of the war his principal interest was in killing the members of Leftist movements. This objective came before capturing major cities, even Madrid. It seems that a prolonged war, victorious in the end, which provided opportunities for killing opponents, political and military, was more advantageous than a fast war that would leave intact pockets of the opposition.

The war proceeded along those lines, with Franco more inclined to wear down his opponents than to take strategic targets to end the war quickly. Germany and Italy continued to help Franco, principally by supplying tanks and artillery, and by making certain that his forces enjoyed superiority in the air. The war went as Franco wished it would despite pressure form Hitler and Mussolini to speed up matters. In 1938, Franco's forces drove to the Mediterranean, near Valencia, splitting in half the Republican area. By April 1939 the war had ended.

Franco was left to examine his position, balancing his dislike for Britain and France with the debts owed his partners, Germany and Italy. To the partners, he claimed that Spain had been too weakened by the Civil War to engage in additional combat. He thought that five years would be required for Spain to regain her strength. Franco did repay Germany by granting it preferential treatment throughout World War II. He did assist Germany's submarine fleet from his ports on the Atlantic Coast. He could monitor the traffic through the Straight of Gibraltar – it is only seven miles at its narrowest point. He could allow German planes to land at Spanish airports for refueling His government was able to pass on strategic military information for analysis in Berlin.

Franco avoided entering World War II, keeping his country neutral. He succeeded politically by eliminating the Left. His methods did not differ from those used by other dictators, be they of the Left or Right: prisons, brief trials, followed by executions. He used a form of the gulag, converting prisoners of war into forced labor for public works. He held on to power to the end of his life, which came in 1975, at the age of eighty-three. Juan Carlos, the grandson of Alphonso XIII, was designated his successor in 1969. The implication is that Franco thought of himself as king during his time in power.

There had to come a last day, a last evening for Joanne and Douglas. She prepared a going-away meal and the four of them took their customary places at table. Joanne explained to her children that Douglas was being transferred to his new post and that it would be a while before they saw him again. Douglas had requested a transfer to sea duty, hoping to be assigned to a nuclear aircraft carrier, preferably in the Persian Gulf or the Mediterranean. When his orders came he was disappointed to see that he was being assigned to the Seventh Naval District in Miami. His immediate thought was that if he was transferred to a ship he might be promoted to lieutenant-commander during that assignment. Now he thought that he had been sidelined and that while he might be promoted again, he would never make commander. Other officers had been selected to serve on the navy's great ships. Perhaps he was as qualified as they but they might have graduated from the Naval Academy and were being given the best assignments. He didn't know what the top brass did in these matters. Douglas could see both sides. The captains and admirals would want to take care of their own and yet they needed to be fair. Douglas expected that he might be assigned to personnel work but had no notion how his services would be used. His second thought on digesting the news of his new assignment was that Miami was headquarters for the displaced Cubans and through some of them he could learn what he needed to know about Fidel Castro and his brand of Communism.

When the dinner was over and the children had been read to and put to bed, Joanne emptied the bottle of white wine into their glasses. Douglas asked, "How can we say goodbye and not inflict too much pain?" He thought he detected a mischievous smile on her face. In a little while, she got up and walked around, turning off all the lights. She came back to him, knelt on the sofa in front of him, and said, "I have a present for you. Something of me to take with you. Why don't you come with me?" She took his hand.

SPANISH CIVIL WAR

PART 8:

DOUGLAS HAD BEEN to a store in search of another book on the Spanish Civil War. Different author, different point of view, he knew. He would compare the two texts for emphasis. No doubt this second author would attach more significance to one part of the story than would the previous author. He noticed a change right away. In the biography of Franco, the author, Paul Preston, started at the beginning with Franco's birth, childhood, and details about the lives of his parents. In this second book, *The Passionate War: The Narrative History of the Spanish Civil War,* the author, Peter Wyden, started with the arrival of Americans, men climbing the Pyrénées to get from France to Spain, so that they might join the Abraham Lincoln Brigade to fight on the Republican side. The author then moved on to the activities in Madrid during the first days of the war, in July 1936.

Douglas tried to concentrate on his new book but found it difficult. He was occupying an aisle seat in the tourist section of a jet on a flight to Seattle. He had put in for a one-week leave between the end of his duties in Pearl Harbor and the start of his assignment in Miami.

Rather than read the book on his lap, Douglas' mind went back to the previous evening, when Joanne and he had said their farewell. Foremost in his mind was that she was a lover with everything of herself to give. Douglas was made to wonder whether she should be in his future. How to keep this alive? He asked himself whether they should have been lovers from the start. He was painfully aware of what they had missed, and yet as their romance progressed he had kept on the brakes for the good reasons that his time was short, that Joanne was married, and that the relationship was not all that he wanted it to be. Douglas had learned to trust his instincts at the moment over his reflections looking back on the event. His instincts on a week-by-week basis had been to keep in check his commitment to Joanne. His reflection was that he had missed many wonderful nights in bed with her. The decisions he made week to week were the important ones. The looking back, as he flew north at 37,000 feet, was a diversion. It's what you do at the time, at the moment of decision, that counts. Douglas told himself that mature people trust their instincts at the moment. The looking back business was for dreamers.

Douglas knew that Joanne was a lovely, wonderful woman. Among many things, she had said to him, "Come back, will you? It will be better between you and me. The kids will have grown. I'll be able to spend more time on our relationship than I have."

"How would it be different?" Douglas asked.

"I didn't appreciate the concentration required to raise two children. They absorb three-quarters of my life. That fraction's bound to go down. I'd like a relationship with you and me at the center. I'd like to think that we could construct a life that's interesting for both of us. That's what I sense you want and need, an interesting life. I haven't been able to contribute to that."

Douglas was dumbfounded by the thoughts she expressed. He did say, "That's perceptive of you. I think we would be good together." He had wanted to explore the matter but realized they would be speculating.

There were many air miles to go before the plane touched down at the airport between Seattle and Tacoma and Douglas tried to concentrate on his book. Because it spanned the war years and did not concentrate on the life of Franco, there was ample space for many detailed vignettes about the war.

Douglas thought about his mother and Frank, her new husband, and whether the Amelia-Frank duo was working out as well as the long love affair between his mother and father. He knew that Carl had been crazy about his mother. Douglas had overheard his father saying that more than once. Frank, as well, seemed to be devoted to

Amelia. Douglas would try to get a sense of how well they were doing together.

As he said he would be, Frank was waiting for him in Baggage Claim. His mother had not come. "Busy with the theater," Frank reported. His mother came in after they had returned to the house. "It always seems like half a life time that you've been gone," she said at the end of a long hug.

The pre-dinner wine-and-chat session took place in the same corner of the living room that it had always occupied. Frank had waited for the three of them to be together before asking Douglas about his study of Communism. Douglas told them that he had finished with Marx, Engels, Lenin and Stalin and was about done with the Spanish Civil War. "I bought my last book on the topic in order to read it on the plane. I should finish it while I'm here. Moving along chronologically, the next person will be Mao Zedong."

"I have some books on Mao," Frank said. "Why don't you plan on leaving for me the one you'll finish here and I'll lend you the ones I have. Promise to mail them back."

"That's very nice of you, Frank. Miami, by the way, is the correct place to be to launch an investigation of Castro."

Amelia changed the topic. "What have you heard from Caroline? I had my hopes up with her."

"We have exchanged one letter. That's it. You might have thought we would write more but it's as though Caroline had asked for a three-year leave of absence."

"Any replacements?" his mother asked.

"A nice lady here and there but nothing serious." Douglas had written his mother about Caroline but had not brought up the recent times with Joanne.

"I hope you come to church with us Sunday. There's a new member who sits near us and attends regularly. Lovely looking woman. I think you should meet her."

"What's her name?" Douglas asked.

"It's Elena. I forget the last name."

"And what does she do?"

"I recall something in science," Amelia answered.

Amelia brought the conversation back to Communism. "Do you

recall, Douglas, that I went to the basement in search of a few sentences out of my notebook on the Revolution of 1848?"

"Yes, of course, it's fresh in my mind."

"After you left I read more in that notebook and came across, in my handwriting, something like 'for origins of Communism read Edmund Wilson's To the Finland Station.' I didn't read the book and perhaps no one in the class did but it sounds as though you should."

"It's terrible that I don't recognize Edmund Wilson's name," Douglas said.

"Primarily a critic but he wrote fiction and poetry as well."

"I like the title, To the Finland Station. It might tell me the itinerary that Lenin followed in the sealed train."

"Don't get your hopes up on any train trips. The fact that our professor brought it up at the time means he wanted to trace the origins, find the roots of these social movements, and that's what must be in the book," Amelia answered

"I remember reading something on that," Frank said. I can come up with two names. Both were Frenchmen living toward the end of the Revolution and before Napoleon. The first name was Babeuf who thought that society should be organized so that most everybody had about the same amount. He went to the guillotine. The other was Saint-Simon who thought society should be a meritocracy. He kept his head because he came after Babeuf and the Revolution was losing its venom."

"You remember the darnedest things," Amelia said.

"I read and then remember about the one-hundredth part. Those names caught my attention."

"I don't believe that Marx and Engels sat at a table one day, and came up with Communism," Douglas said. "I would guess they had been thinking over the contributions that the peasants and workers were making to society and compared them to the obstacles they faced in improving their lot. It would be straight forward for them to conclude that the top echelon of society, the nobility, was contributing next to nothing and yet consuming a great deal."

"I don't think the nobility of France paid taxes," Frank said. "That could account for the plank in the Communists' platform that called for very high taxes and eliminated the right to inherit."

"It would be wonderful if you found the traces from the original idea, up through several economists of the time, to an article by the both of them that would identify exactly where their program originated." His mother was nothing if not persistent, Douglas thought. When she spoke as she had just done, Douglas was reminded that Caroline would have said the same thing. Frank broke in, "We must acknowledge that Marx and Engels had earned a reputation in this field. How else to account for their being commissioned to write the Communist Manifesto?"

"Those bourgeois materialists," Douglas said. "They probably accepted money in return for writing the Manifesto."

Sunday rolled around. Amelia and her family had attended services at the cathedral on Broadway over the years. It was really Tenth Avenue but Broadway breaks right there. Douglas had come along occasionally over the years. Frank drove, Amelia sat next to him and Douglas was in the rear. He tried to guess what Elena would be all about. They came off Tenth Avenue into the parking lot and then through an archway into a second parking lot for latecomers.

When they walked into the cathedral the choir was assembled. They went around it and into the fourth pew from the rear on the right side of the nave. Elena was seated there, waiting for them. There was only time for hurried introductions. They remained standing for the processional hymn.

Amelia arranged it that Douglas sat between Elena and her. The two young people shared a hymnal and were able to say hello again at the Peace. When the service ended they moved to the other side of the cathedral, in the rear, for coffee and cookies. Douglas studied her hair. It was black and there was a great deal of it. She wore it parted in the middle with the strands placed loosely around her face. He was not certain that he liked that her ears, neck and part of her forehead were covered. No doubt with that much hair she could wear it several ways to create different impressions. Her white blouse, made of a heavy material, was not meant to be tucked in. It came a few inches below her waist. The skirt was pleated and made of a navy blue material, probably flannel. It came to her knees. She was taller than the average woman and shorter than he. He couldn't decide on her age but it seemed that she might be a few years younger than he was. Her face was lively. She seemed on the verge of breaking into a smile. Perhaps she was waiting for the phrase from him that would make her laugh. He looked at her lips. They were thin. She had applied the lipstick perfectly. He enjoyed watching her when she talked.

Douglas was still holding the bulletin in his hands when he reached for his pen. He asked Elena for her telephone number. She opened her purse and pulled out a business card and said, "Let me have your pen, please. I'll write it on the back."

"I hope we can have dinner before I go," Douglas said. He studied the card. Her name was Elena R. Kelly. She had put PhD after her name. "I was expecting a Russian last name after Elena," he said.

"My great-grandmother was born in Russia. She came with her parents, I would say in the 1880s. Family name was Rokossovsky. You know that the system of serfdom was abandoned around 1860. 1861, I recall. I have no idea where the money came from for the crossing. They may have owned a small plot of land and sold it."

"Your great-grandmother mother was an only child?"

"Yes, so Rokossovsky disappeared when she married an O'Neil. Her daughter married a Monahan and her daughter, my mother, married a Kelly. So I'm more Irish by far than anything else."

"The American dream is spelled out on your business card. Three generations produce a young woman with a PhD."

Elena turned away, perhaps in shyness. She was smiling and Douglas guessed that she had struggled with putting PhD after her name, understanding that it was an academic degree and not a salutation, not part of her name.

He studied her hands as she wrote her phone number and again as she was holding her cup of coffee and handling her cookie on a paper plate. The hands could be the only part of her body not to receive the treatment that the life of the mind provides. Her great-grandmother may have come right off the fields, her hands witnesses to generations of manual labor. Elena's fingers were shorter than Douglas expected and the strength in her hands was evident. The fingernail polish had been applied with care but it did not change the impression that her hands made. Douglas wondered how the fingers of a daughter of theirs would be shaped.

On the way home, Amelia turned to her son. "If all else fails, bring Elena to the house. I'll just set another place at the table."

"Thank you, Mother. I'll find a restaurant with white tablecloths and candles, and a small bouquet of real flowers on the table as they do at those ritzy places."

The dinner went off as planned on Tuesday evening. Elena had put on a dress that showed off her figure. She wore a jacket against the autumn chill. Douglas thought that she was as attractive a woman as he had ever taken to dinner. She had pulled away from her face the mass of black hair and fastened it in the back in an arrangement that he did not understand. Her forehead and ears and neck were there to examine. She wore simple earrings and in the early part of the evening he could detect a musky perfume that he knew from before from another woman.

Her PhD was in microbiology and her responsibilities at the company were to follow research and identify fields in which instrumentation could be designed to take advantage of new developments. She knew aspects of mechanical and electronic engineering. Douglas was impressed. He would leave to another time delving into interests that had little to do with work.

Douglas thought they were pleased to be together. She directed him from the restaurant to her apartment building on the two occasions he was ready to make a wrong turn. She invited him in and without asking went to the kitchen and started a pot of coffee. He went to the end of the living room and said, "The Cascades must be spectacular on a clear day."

She answered, "They're the reason I took the place. The view is extraordinary when it's spring here and the peaks still have snow on them. I would guess they're sixty miles away."

Elena adjusted the lights and put on music by a French composer who must have written at the end of the nineteenth century. They installed themselves on the sofa. She asked him about his naval career. He started by describing the chance to work in the family firm and his reasons for rejecting the opportunity. Then he spoke of his father's few years in the navy during the war and how important that experience had been to him and how he, Douglas, absorbed the elements of that life and determined that it would satisfy him. Douglas was pleased that she did not ask him how long he planned to stay in the service. For her part she told him that her father and two brothers were engineers. Her father was a mechanical engineer and one brother an electrical and the other a civil engineer who worked for the city. "Science was around the house. Technical journals were on the coffee table. Mother allowed that. I did well in science courses."

Douglas interrupted her, "You did well in all your courses, I would guess."

"Well, yes, now that you mention it. I was a National Merit Scholar and microbiology was all the rage and it encompasses everything: biology, physics, engineering, chemistry and mathematics, all of them in one enormous field that is infinitely bigger than I'll ever be. I'm fascinated by tackling anything that's infinite in scope. It gives you the best chance of making a contribution because the frontier is not only limitless but also expanding."

"I'm glad we're sitting down, Elena."

She laughed and said that she may have gone on a bit and overstated the case. "I suppose it excites me," she said.

"Have you made that first contribution?" he asked.

"I've had a hand in several of the medical instruments our company manufactures and I suggested one on my own. Those are my proudest achievements." After catching her breath, she continued, "Those were contributions at the low level but you get a firmer grasp as you go along. Maybe someday I'll be able to see how several fields of knowledge are connected and make a large contribution. X-ray machines were one such, but look at CAT scans and MRI – phenomenal breakthroughs in applying knowledge from several fields to produce astounding results."

As Elena spoke, Douglas went back to Joanne's husband, the chief petty officer presently at sea for whom marriage had lost its magic. Douglas wanted what that chief petty officer had: a wife with the femininity of Joanne and two children of the quality of Shirley and Brian. Perhaps creating the family unit was more important than having in your life a woman with whom he could exchange thoughts on history and literature.

They talked about skiing and the resorts they had been to. They talked about Seattle's cultural life and the abundance of theater. They moved on to the politics of the state and finally to the revolution that strong coffee was bringing to much of the world. "We single people needed places to congregate and didn't know it," she concluded.

It was past midnight and they had finished the coffee. "When do you leave?" she asked.

"Thursday morning. A non-stop to Miami."

"And when do you come back? That may be more important."

"I'm not certain. I have plenty of leave accumulated so I'll plan to come back soon."

They moved across the living room. He put one arm around her back and when they reached the front door they embraced. She let her body come against his. He reached up with his free hand and touched her hair. "I've wanted to do this all evening."

He could feel the warmth of her body. With as much reason as Joanne had, Elena could tell him that she was all the woman any man could handle.

"It's wonderful to know you, Elena."

"I've met a significant person, Douglas. My life will never be the same and I'm not explaining that statement."

They laughed and kissed. Douglas didn't want to let go of her. She made no effort to move away. Finally, he let his arms drop. "I'll write you," he said. "It's not the same as being with you, but I'll write."

On his drive home he realized that she was correct, it had been a significant evening. She showed herself to be an accomplished conversationalist who would convey meaning with details, or humor, or an original choice of words. In conversation, she was willing to share with him the time available. At an early age -- she was not close to being a middle-aged person -- she had managed breadth and depth. Douglas admitted to himself that he was not yet mature enough to measure those aspects of anyone's makeup. As he had right away with Caroline and at the end with Joanne, he felt the first pangs of love. He knew that was an accurate description because he was familiar with the mild contraction in the chest that cannot be caused any other way and is not unpleasant.

He slept a little late the following morning and when he came downstairs he could hear his mother and Frank. They were finishing breakfast, reading the paper and gossiping.

"What time did you get in last night?" Amelia asked after good mornings were exchanged.

"Must have been around one o'clock," Douglas answered.

"Have a good time?"

"Yes, Mother. It could have been a notch or two above good," Douglas said.

"Would you like to ask her over for this evening?"

"Too soon," Douglas answered. "She would sense she was on display for the family."

"You're probably right," Amelia said. "We have this evening then Thursday morning you're on the plane. Don't let her slip away, Douglas."

"I told her that I would write. That could work against me if I composed uninteresting letters."

"I've always enjoyed your letters. And by the way, no one writes letters any more so if she receives first class mail from you, you'll stand out from the crowd."

"Mother, we gather here at six this evening. Is that right?"

"Yes, an early evening. My grandchildren have homework to finish. Tomorrow's a school day."

Douglas suggested to his mother the ways that he could help her put on the party. Frank begged off for the good reason that he was headed for his office.

Ever interested in having her youngest child marry, Amelia said, "Douglas, you can always invite Elena to Miami for a few days in the winter when you're having a warm spell."

"Good idea but it brings up sleeping arrangements and I think it's too soon for that."

"Right again," his mother said.

The family gathered at six and Douglas could talk with his nieces and nephews and the four adults who had brought them. He thought the kids were doing well. It pleased him that they, brother and sister, and in-laws, and cousins, liked one another. They chatted and laughed and refrained from arguments.

Douglas and his older brother, Walter, enjoyed swapping yarns about the work they were engaged in. Douglas kept up with the progress being made by various relatives in the family firm. Walter always asked

Douglas about his naval career, was it interesting and challenging, was he on track for the next promotion, and how long did he plan to stay in the service?

Walter addressed that last question by asking "Well, you've finished ten years. Are you staying for twenty or thirty?"

"I haven't had any luck finding a mate and I'm starting to get that domestic urge. I may not last too long."

"You realize that all of us know each other's business. Mother gets the news around. What do you make of Elena?"

"Superior woman. So much so that I plan to write her."

"The ultimate sacrifice," Walter said. "Miami could be loaded with fascinating ladies, though."

They were silent for a moment when Walter said, "If you decide to wrap it up in the navy, we'll find gainful employment for you around here. No need to worry."

"That takes a load off my mind," Douglas said in jest. He had packed earlier and finished reading his second book on the Spanish Civil War. He had examined the two volumes that Frank was lending him on Mao Zedong. One was a heavy book; it could be 700 pages long. The second was much shorter, a biography called *Mao Zedong*, by Jonathan Spence. Given a choice, Douglas usually started with the shorter of two texts. He would assimilate the main points in the first and catch the details in the second. In that fashion he would find familiar material in the second book, made familiar by having read the shorter one first. Finishing a short book gave him the energy required to read on and complete the lengthy work.

Douglas settled in the rear of the plane. It would be at least five hours in the air and he would be losing three hours flying west to east. He removed *Mao Zedong* from his carryon bag and started reading. There were fewer that 200 pages so he should be finished by time they landed in Miami. Before he got very far into the book, Douglas was distracted by the thought that he should take inventory and note in a section of his mind what he knew about China from reading and conversation. He wanted to situate Mao Zedong properly in the history of China. Surely Mao was a product of the times in which he grew up, and as in the case with many Chinese, he was the product of the country's culture, which Douglas thought was formed to a large extent by the influences of Confucius, who lived around 500 BC. China and Egypt were the two oldest civilizations in the world, which was the older being a well-kept secret. The language was written in characters, works of art themselves. To read a newspaper, a person needed to know the meaning of 3,000 characters. To be considered educated, one should recognize 9,000 characters. Douglas thought he had read that there were 50,000 characters and that the Japanese, to construct their language, had taken China's set and assigned heir own meanings and pronunciations. A Chinese scholar visiting Japan would see characters that, while familiar, had no meaning to him.

His father had told him that the Emperor Kublai Khan had tried to invade Japan with a navy built for that purpose, around 1280. This fleet had been dispersed by a divine wind, which the Japanese called kamikaze.

The European powers, through their missionaries, had started bringing Christianity to China around 1600 with limited success, although by the early 1900s several sects from Europe and the United States had established themselves.

There had been many dynasties over the centuries. A group led by a powerful war lord would topple a decaying regime and establish itself to be known as a dynasty until it exhausted itself and in turn was overthrown. The last dynasty of China went by the name of Manchu. It was replaced in 1911 by a republic whose first president was Sun Yat-sen.

Douglas had read of the Opium Wars, the first in 1842, in which European powers wished to consolidate their rights to sell opium, principally in the region of Canton. Hong Kong became a British colony that year. Japan went to war with China in 1894 and took the island of Taiwan. The name was changed to Formosa, which it remained until the island was returned to China at the end of World War II. European countries nibbled at China and established trading centers here and there, and about that time, 1904, there was a war between Japan and Russia, a war in which the Asian country defeated the European one. Douglas reflected that the Japanese had the advantage with short lines of communication. The Japanese took Manchuria in 1931 and captured China's sea coast in 1937. The Chinese army, led by Chiang Kai-shek, fought the Japanese until 1945. In 1949, when the Red Army prevailed against the Nationalist forces, as Chiang's army was known, Chiang left the mainland and transported the remnants of his army to Taiwan, where the descendents of that group remain.

Concerning Mao, Douglas knew that he had been part of the Long March, starting in 1934, in which the Red Army went west across China and turned north to settle out of the reach of Chiang Kai-shek's army. The survivors of the Long March remained in the North until the end of the war in 1945, when they set about establishing themselves in all China. Mao declared that the People's Republic of China had come into being in 1949.

Douglas wanted to know about Mao, his origins, the forces that formed him, why he launched the Great Leap Forward and the Cultural Revolution, and finally what was the extent to which he felt compelled to kill his own people?

Douglas' final reflection was about the Soong sisters. One had married Sun Yat-sen. Another was the wife of Chiang Kai-shek. The third married H.H. Kung, a rich man who became the minister of finance in Chiang's government. There were a few brothers, the best known being T.V. Soong, who, his father had told him, was Chiang Kai-shek's ambassador to the United States during the war. Madame Chiang Kai-shek was a graduate of Wellesley College and because of that, well connected in the Eastern Establishment. Douglas had always wondered how a family, Chinese or not, could achieve such power and success. Their father was a missionary.

Douglas could not recall much else. He settled back in his seat and started reading.

MAO

HALFWAY THROUGH THE flight to Miami, Douglas' reading was interrupted by the arrival of the drinks cart. An attractive flight attendant provided coffee and pretzels. He had finished a good part of Mao's biography, the one by Jonathan Spence, and was pleased that the couple sitting next to him had not dragged him into conversation. He wondered whether he could understand Mao's life. Douglas had not visited Asia, knew little of the history and nothing of the languages. He didn't think there was any relationship between Mao's years from six to thirteen and his own as a boy. Douglas came from an upper-middle class family. He had attended private schools and by his thirteenth year could read, do mathematics and write grammatical sentences. He had started learning literature, science, history and Spanish. Mao, between the ages of six and thirteen, had been to the schools his father could afford. Mao had memorized a few Chinese classics and learned the characters required to read texts suitable for people his age. He was skilled in using the abacus.

At thirteen, Douglas had nine years of schooling to look forward to. He would graduate from college at the age of twenty-two. At thirteen, Mao entered the work force because he was approaching maturity on the Chinese schedule. Women and marriage came into his life soon after. The first years of his professional life were devoted to teaching the high school curriculum. Later on, as a young man, Mao became a writer of significance. His opinions appeared as editorials in newspapers of the Left. It would be an overstatement to say that Mao became a nationally-known person through his writings as he wrote only political treatises. It would be acceptable to say that he became a familiar name in political and literary circles, particularly among people who were playing a part in the revolutionary struggle that was taking place in much of China from 1920 on.

Douglas did not think there was any connection between the life of a young man born to a peasant family in China and the life of a young male born into an American family at the same time, the day after Christmas, 1893 (his grandfather, for instance). The disparities were so large that Douglas doubted he could digest Mao's life.

Douglas thought from reading this biography that Mao was unusually sensitive to the plight of the average person living in his province. Douglas knew that he himself had not lived in the midst of poverty. He had not known what life would be like without medical care, without entertainment, without substantive nutrition, without personal transportation, and perhaps as important as all these together, without the hope for change and improvement in his life. Peasants in China knew that their life was presently what it always had been. It appeared to Douglas that Mao wanted to change an entire country, change the lives of about half a billion people, the population of China at the time. If indeed that was Mao's goal, then Douglas could not connect Mao's actions with the results, but Mao did achieve his goal. Douglas thought that Mao or another leader could have changed the Chinese people into a successful, democratic, industrialized society without all the Communist trappings, and could have managed the changes rapidly with far less carnage than was inflicted.

Mao seemed to have found the wish for change before having heard of the doctrines of Karl Marx. He did see on his own that redistribution of land could alleviate poverty and that the terms imposed by landlords on tenant farmers were unjust. While millions of Chinese lived in conditions of poverty, and millions of these understood the significance of the conditions, only a few, Mao among them, decided to dedicate their lives to changing what they saw around them.

Lenin and other Bolsheviks hoped that world-wide revolution was just around the corner. To make their prophecy come true, they established the Communist International (Comintern) in Moscow, an organization that would expedite and manage the coming revolutions, country by country. The Soviet Union made available money and training and sent agents abroad to assist nascent groups. Mao met and worked with some of these. He grew adept at forming peasant groups who worked together to improve their lot. He organized workers and managed their strikes for improved wages and conditions. These efforts were successful but Mao and others faced two daunting challenges. The first consisted of warlords spread across China, a country as large as the United States, the lower forty-eight and Alaska combined, in which transportation and communication facilities were meager. Warlords did not advance a political point of view except to seize control of a region for their own benefit. They were not agents of change. The second challenge consisted of the Kuomintang (the Nationalist Party) with General Chiang Kai-shek at its head. Sun Yat-sen, the founder of the party, and China's first president, elected in 1911, died in 1925 and Chiang became his heir (they were married to sisters). Chiang had been in charge of a military school and moved up to be in command of the Nationalist army. He was earnest about conquering China with himself at the head of both the army and the party.

The Kuomintang that Chiang Kai-shek was to lead had two main branches, established early on. One was conservative and the other left-leaning. Sun Yat-sen had been a reformer, but not one with a Marxist outlook. He may not have heard of Marx until the Bolshevik Revolution in 1917, or later. The left-leaning branch of the Kuomintang wanted reform in China consisting of changes in the society that would modernize the country. Needed were systems of education, transportation and communications, among others. The Communists, Mao included, understood the value of associating themselves with the left-leaning branch, and indeed the Communist Party merged with the Kuomintang around 1923. Mao joined as well. Stalin and the Soviet hierarchy thought highly of the union. It would come as no surprise that both sides thought they could get the better of the other, but because the Kuomintang party had one hundred times the membership of the Chinese Communist Party at the time, the Kuomintang might not have felt threatened.

The situation between the two parties remained more or less peaceful from the start of integration in 1923 until 1927 when a complete reversal took place and the Kuomintang determined to eliminate the Communists. Mao had long suspected that he would need an army to achieve his political purposes and it was in the year 1927 that he became convinced.

Mao and Chiang Kai-shek had the same aim: conquer and rule China. The Communist China that Mao hoped for was different in many aspects from the modernized but traditional China that Chiang wanted to lead. Armed conflict between Nationalist and Communist forces in 1927 resulted in severe losses among the Communists. It was not until 1934, however, that the Communists decided that they would move their operations west, and then north, to a sanctuary in the northwest corner of China, far removed from danger. This movement, this 6,000 mile trek, became known as the Long March. It was not completed until 1935, a year after its inception. Mao and Chiang did make accommodations during World War II and to a limited extent before that time: they would fight the Japanese rather than fight one another. This negotiated truce lasted until 1945 when Japan was defeated. There ensued a race to collect the arms left by the Japanese army in Manchuria as this army disbanded and returned to Japan. The Communists won that race with the help of the Soviet Union.

The years that Mao spent in his lair in the northwest of China were fruitful. He established himself as the uncontested leader among Communists in China and he mastered the science of Marx and Lenin so that he could apply it to China's problems. He became a theorist.

Douglas finished reading the biography by Jonathan Spence while in flight over central Florida. To fill the time, he studied the cities and beaches as the plane made its approach to the Miami airport. As Douglas had hoped, the short biography provided many details about Mao. In the next text he would read, *Mao, A Life*, by Philip Short, Douglas would be on the lookout for two pieces of information, if indeed they were to be found in the material. The first would discuss Mao's adoption of Marxism as the solution to the problems of life in China as he perceived them. It must be said, Douglas reminded himself, that the horrors associated with saddling a country with Communism did not become known immediately. That is, in 1920, the brutality associated with a Communist regime had not yet been demonstrated completely. Lenin, however, had shown little compunction over killing those who obstructed his revolution. Mao could have guessed or hoped that the Communist system of government was no more dictatorial, cruel and rapacious than the governments the Chinese people had been used to.

The second piece of information would contain the data on the number of Chinese that were killed in the process of converting the country to Communism. Douglas had heard that Mao was different from Stalin. He had a romantic and poetic streak in his makeup, a feature missing in Stalin. How could it be that a man with this softness in his personality could sacrifice the lives of millions of countrymen? As his plane landed and taxied to its gate, Douglas decided to get clear in his mind what he had learned from his reading so far.

In answer to his first question, Douglas understood that Mao had not had a conversion as Paul had on the road to Damascus, when all came clear at once. In Mao's case, it was a matter of evaluating the strategies available that could be used effectively in overturning Chinese society. He examined anarchy, as an example, and turned it down. Perhaps his eventual adoption of Marxism was based on the success Lenin appeared to be having in Russia. Mao wanted to unite peasants and workers; he wanted the proletariat to come into authority and it appeared to him that this goal was being met in the Soviet Union. As Douglas recognized from being able to look back over seventy years of history, it was the Communist Party and not the proletariat to whom power devolved.

Mao's following the direction of Marx, Lenin and Communism may have been influenced by the effect on him exerted by the Comintern. It was not as though Mao was free early on to decide his fate and the fate of his country. There were Chinese Communists active in other cities, notably in Shanghai; there were delegations of Russians dispatched from Moscow; and there did exist a Chinese Communist Party from whom Mao took orders, and when he didn't accept the orders, he was required to plead his case and attempt to get his way.

In the 1920s, Mao was a fair distance from the top of the Chinese Communist Party apparatus. He might have been the twelfth-ranking person, although that position changed as the emphasis in the party line changed. Mao, however, developed considerable abilities, both political and military, over the decade 1920 to 1930. In his native district, Mao assembled several small regiments of infantry, which were used in combat against Chiang Kai-shek's army. Mao had victories and suffered defeats but he was able to capture sufficient weaponry from the Nationalist forces to arm his troops with riffles, machine guns, ammunition, and radio equipment. Through trial and error, Mao developed a winning strategy: allow his opponents to invade deeply into his territory, thinning out the opponents' fighting force; attack the opponents' weakest positions with significant fire power; and enter only into battles that could be won. By using these tactics, Mao became one of the most experienced and successful revolutionaries.

On the second question, when did the killing start and how severe did it become, Douglas thought that Mao instigated purges when he thought he needed them to keep discipline.

At first, Mao's compassionate side held sway. His own soldiers could leave his army if they wished. Their transportation home would be paid. As time went on, when discipline was administered too severely by some of Mao's officers, Mao would step in to restore civility. But a willingness to let blood flow began to show itself. Some leaders among the Communists suspected that there were legions of counter-revolutionaries and anti-Bolsheviks, as they were called, who were at work in small cells within the Communist Party and the army, whose purpose it was to thwart the revolution. It was required that these people be eliminated. The techniques used by the leaders consisted of accusation, torture, confession, followed by execution. Once accused there was little hope of escaping execution. The two intermediate steps, torture and confession, were used to extract from the accused the names of additional suspects. The refusal to confess was viewed as an admission of guilt. The Communists turned against their own army. The number of innocent people shot or beheaded rose above one hundred thousand.

As the plane came to a stop at its gate at the airport in Miami, Douglas reflected that it had been proven beyond doubt that a person under torture will confess to anything. Chinese Communists had proven it. Soviet Communists had proven it, but higher-ups in so-called civilized countries were still extracting confessions under torture and treating the information as valid. How many millennia, Douglas asked himself, must pass so that it would be seen that confessions obtained from people under torture had no value?

Before Douglas had started the biography of Mao by Philip Short, he made himself think through the differences that existed between the Russian and Chinese societies. These differences would have a telling effect on how Lenin, followed by Stalin, would introduce Communism into Russia and how Mao would do the same in China.

In 1917, Germany and Russia were at war and had been since August 1914. Lenin knew that he had to end the war to institute his program. This he did in 1918 with the Treaty of Brest-Litovsk. Lenin's principal objective was to organize industrial workers into Communist blocks so that they could form the backbone of a Communist government, which he succeeded in doing. He held Russia's peasants in low repute and had no need for them to institute Communism into Russia. He would assemble them into collectives and do away with the private ownership of land.

In Mao's case, China and Japan were not fighting a declared war until 1937, but Japan invaded and captured Manchuria in 1931 and extended its influence over the Chinese by its demand for concessions. Japan, more industrialized than China, was in need of the natural resources in China's possession. Mao had no idea of ending the war with Japan by treaty. He wanted the return of all Chinese land, and that included the island of Taiwan, which the Japanese took in 1895 and renamed Formosa. Mao would accomplish this retaking by force and he built an army equal to the task. Chiang Kai-shek, on the other hand, would be more accommodating than Mao and might accede to Japan's demands in order to avoid fighting. Mao's shorthand for his own policy was anti-imperialism.

China was not as industrialized as Russia and as a consequence had a far higher percentage of peasants. It was this element of the population that Mao would use to create his army that, along with the Nationalists and the Allies, would destroy the Japanese forces. Mao always maintained that the Japanese attack on China paved the way for the final victory of the Communists over all of China.

Douglas was in the habit of looking at his wrist watch to count the minutes from landing to emptying the plane. If the gate was available for the plane, the time averaged fifteen minutes. Douglas usually sat in the back of the plane. He made his way through the airport to Baggage

Claim and from there to the taxi stand. Not knowing where the headquarters of the 7th Naval District were, he decided against public transportation in favor of a taxi, whose driver, Douglas established in the first mile, had crossed the straight from Cuba. Ten years had gone by. He still described the trip as very dangerous.

Douglas was delivered to his destination and ushered into a reception area. There were greetings from a yeoman second class, and even though it was approaching the close of the working day, Douglas went into an office to meet a Lieutenant Peterson who asked him to take a seat

"Housing is taken care of," Peterson said. "You probably want to have details on your assignment." Peterson opened a file folder on which Douglas could see his name and rank written out.

"It's a new assignment. The admiral wanted a Spanish-speaking officer who could keep abreast of the political activity in the Caribbean, as far south as and including Venezuela and Columbia."

"That's a vast territory," Douglas said.

"Yes. You'll be traveling, visiting Mexico and the countries that border the Gulf of Mexico. That would appear to be all the Central American countries except El Salvador."

"It should leave out Cuba," Douglas added.

"Right you are. We're not welcome there. You'll travel in civilian clothes with a diplomatic passport. Your arrival will be announced to the military and civilian authorities and the purpose of your visit made clear. No covert operations. The emphasis will be on uncovering new routes for the movement of drugs. I'm told we know most of them but as we discover the established routes, new ones surface."

"And to whom do I report?" Douglas asked.

"To a commander, who reports to a captain, who reports to the admiral. He's the commandant, a rear admiral, new to the district. Your promotion to lieutenant commander should come through promptly. The expression we hear a lot is that Miami has become the capital of South America. True or not, the admiral wants you to be his eyes, ears, and perhaps mouth."

"I take it he does not speak Spanish."

"That's right. The commander and the captain are not fluent either. The admiral told me that he expected to be assigned to Philadelphia but was very pleased to draw this post as he plays tennis," Peterson said.

As Peterson spoke, Douglas felt his naval career slowing, perhaps ending. This would be two shore-based jobs in a row. He had requested duty aboard a carrier. Another senior lieutenant or junior lieutenant commander had edged him out. The way it appeared to Douglas, he could stay in for twenty years before retiring but never be promoted above lieutenant commander. It was a dim prospect for any ambitious person. He would write his mother and Frank about it. They should be aware of his feelings on the matter. He wanted to write Elena this evening, but for the moment he thought he would give her his job description and leave out the editorial comment. Why not write her his appraisal in two or three months? He would know more about his prospects and have taken a reading on the admiral.

Peterson told Douglas to report at eight the following morning wearing his khaki uniform. He would be assigned his office and would meet his superior officers. He was taken to the Bachelor Officer Quarters in a navy vehicle and shown his room. The driver indicated the location of the Officers Club where he could have his meals. Douglas wanted to unpack and start his letter to Elena. He wondered at the salutation and the closing. Perhaps it would come clear to him as he wrote.

Dear Elena,

Wonderful evening with you on Tuesday. The family gathered at Mother's on Wednesday. You might have felt uncomfortable being put on display as Douglas' new find. That was my reason for not asking you to attend. I hope I guessed right. You are a remarkably lovely person. Mother has a good eye for women of top quality. I like your approach to life and everything else.

"Can you send me a photograph of yourself? If you send me the photo you like, I'll take care of the framing. There is a place on this desk for it.

"It was an easy flight. My neighbors did not engage me in conversation. They were busy with each other. There was no food on the flight except for a bag of pretzels. We all lost weight and are much the better for it.

"My expertise in Spanish got me this job. As you know, I had asked to be sent to sea on a carrier, but no such luck. I report to others who report to the rear admiral who is in charge of this Naval District. I'll meet them tomorrow morning, Friday. They need access to the Spanish community in Miami and I'll keep them abreast of politics in the Caribbean area. That will mean travel and I guess that I'll visit ten countries or so. If you want we can talk once a week to stay close.

Affectionately,
Douglas

His father had always signed his letters 'Affectionately' and Douglas had received many of them over the years. It seemed about right, less demonstrative than 'Love' and more personal than 'Fondly.' Douglas had wanted to make the letter longer but he would have to add personal remarks, amplifying his views of her, as he had nothing yet to say about the beaches or life in Miami. Soon enough he might be able to tell her that he had taken the bus to Key West for the weekend, or gone to Palm Beach to explore.

Friday morning, a few minutes before eight, Douglas arrived at the building housing the offices of his superiors. He made the rounds and then was ushered into Admiral Stevens' office. He saluted smartly. The admiral returned the salute and then got out of his chair and came around the desk to shake Douglas' hand.

"Welcome to the Seventh District, Nielsen," the admiral said. "We will be seeing one another a fair amount. I asked for you particularly, not by name, but I asked for a Spanish-speaking officer who either was a lieutenant commander or would become one soon. Sit down, Nielsen."

Douglas thought that his career had been derailed by an admiral who assumed he would be more effective on the job by having a person with language skills than if he used the staff that the Bureau of Personnel assigned him. Was this why he had been denied the transfer to sea to serve on a nuclear-powered carrier? You get dealt funny hands of cards as you go through life, Douglas knew. He also thought that this could be the making of him. Politics, warfare, and the purposes of the navy were changing all the time. He might come off this three-year posting within sight of being promoted to commander, and be given a fine position in Naval Intelligence.

The admiral was back in his chair. "We must keep track of everything that's going on in the Gulf of Mexico. No surprises allowed. I know that the CIA and Naval Intelligence have people at work in the region but we have planes and ships at our disposal and they don't. When a ship we are not accustomed to turns up on a sea lane it's never sailed on then we want to report it. No boarding parties but it gets reported to Washington. If there's a change in military disposition in any neighboring country we want to know the details and report them. The drug business is our business. I would guess that plenty of those beautiful yachts have fifty pounds of heroine acting as ballast. Why would a particular pleasure vessel make the same trip several times, say from a port in Columbia to a particular island?"

The admiral paused for a moment and Douglas asked, "Where would you like me to start, sir?"

"A good place would be the important Cuban-American organizations centered here in Miami that keep up the anti-Castro pressure. You could meet their leadership and ask them what we might do to assist. Of course we can't do much, nor do we want to involve ourselves, but you'll need a reason for making contact."

Douglas noted that the conversation with Admiral Stevens had lasted thirty-five minutes. He made his way to his office, stopping for coffee. He was pleased to see that his office was completely equipped with supplies, telephone and computer. He asked a female civilian employee to instruct him on the electronics apparatus. She showed him how to log onto the Internet.

In mid-morning, Douglas telephoned the offices of the *Miami Herald* and asked for the city desk. A woman with a clear voice came on and Douglas asked her for the names of two or three organizations that specialized in Cuban-American affairs. When she told him that there must be one hundred organizations that met his description, Douglas asked for the first two that came to mind. There was silence on the line, then she said, "Sure, here are a couple and I have their phone numbers right here." Douglas thanked her for her kindness.

In both cases when he telephoned the organizations, he asked for a public affairs officer. He requested information on that group's stated purpose, and asked for any papers or studies published recently. He thought he would digest the material before asking for an interview. When the packets arrived three or four days later he was impressed that these two groups resembled one another closely. It would take study to find significant differences between them.

The published papers contained two topics in the broadest sense. The first outlined what the United States could do to help the cause of liberating Cuba from the Castro regime and the second topic spoke about the efforts that Cubans could make on their own behalf.

In the first topic it was noted that the U.S. could improve its program of awarding visas, particularly to reunite families that were split, part in the U.S. and the rest in Cuba. There were suggestions on improving radio and television transmission to Cuba. And there were calls for releasing political prisoners and holding elections. For the second topic, it was noted that the Cuban government might not survive in its present form much longer. Individuals were starting to object to the lack of political freedoms and small organizations were being formed, all this without the expected reactions from the government. Could the government of Cuba be relaxing its long-held position against discord?

It was also stated that the government could not outlast Fidel. Factions were forming that would pull apart the government. Only a person with Fidel's authority could hold the government together. As Douglas read the papers, he noted that American taxpayers were being asked to foot the bill for most of the programs and the American people were being asked to be hosts for many thousands of Cubans who might prefer living in freedom over living in Castro's island-jail.

Douglas had a stray thought, that Castro's long speeches would be his undoing. Perhaps Cubans were still listening only to be polite. What could Fidel find new to talk about after four decades of harangues? Douglas would study the rise to power of Castro. The Cuban government had a large army but insignificant navy and air force. As the Admiral said, "We do not want to be caught off guard." The Cubans were not a powerful nation yet they had almost destabilized the Western Hemisphere when Khrushchev was ready to install nuclear-tipped missiles on the island. But that was 1962.

MORE ON MAO

PART 10:   MORE ON MAO

As DOUGLAS STARTED reading *Mao, a Life,* by Philip Short, it appeared to him that Mao was being attacked by the germ of infallibility, a condition always self-inflicted. His power among the Communist leaders of China rose, and theirs diminished, as Mao forced them to recognize that his edicts in military and political matters had proven correct and theirs questionable. There was no purge as Stalin would conduct from 1935 to 1938 but important Communists were made to confess their faults and admit that their judgments had been erroneous. Mao wanted unanimity, with important Communists renouncing any positions held earlier that were contrary to Mao's. After the Civil War ended in 1949, with the Communists installed in power all over China, Mao waited a few years and then encouraged criticism of Communism as it was being applied to the country. He termed this program, which got under way in 1956, *One Hundred Flowers,* suggesting that minor variations on Communism were admissible. Mao had said, "Let a hundred flowers bloom; let a hundred schools of thought contend." He must have felt that the system he had in place was strong enough to withstand criticisms leveled at it. Mao proved to have a thin skin and in short order revoked the privilege. Not only did he revoke the privilege but also he went after those who had volunteered their points of view. There were a few executions, many went to prison and many more were sent to the countryside to live and work with peasants so that they might receive adjustments to their attitudes. In all, half a million people were affected. Douglas thought that Mao's conduct, that of eliciting criticism and then punishing those who criticized, left out the concept of fair play. Perhaps fair play was learned only on the playing fields of Eton, as Douglas adapted Wellington's words on the matter. Perhaps fair play was not a concept known outside the Western world.

After reacting poorly to the invitation to all Chinese to criticize the regime, Mao attempted a program, which he termed the *Great Leap Forward*, whose purposes it was to increase production of iron and steel as well as the supply of grain. The program was inaugurated in 1958. Douglas knew that the conversion of iron ore to iron and steel was not a trivial matter and that the implementation of demanding technology was required to produce products of high quality. Douglas guessed that Mao dismissed the notion that capital investment in the technology of manufacturing was required. Mao must have assumed that small ovens operated by inexperienced people in the countryside could achieve the same results as were achieved by experts operating time-proven equipment designed especially for the task. Because so many Chinese had been punished for criticizing the Chairman at his invitation a few years back, no one had the courage to tell him that his iron and steel program would fail. Fail it did, with attendant disasters such as the loss of great deal of wood from forests to feed the furnaces and the misuse of millions of man hours of valuable labor.

Improving the supply of grains, the second portion of the *Great Leap Forward*, required capital investment, additional fertilizer, new land, vastly more seed to plant, and new machinery along with its maintenance and training in its use. This part of the program failed as well, but in this case there was no residue such as abandoned steel fabricating equipment spread out over China. The residue was famine. Some say as many as twenty million died. Mao was bent on rapid industrialization. He wanted to catch up to Great Britain, for example, in the annual production of steel. To pay for the importation of technology and raw materials, he increased the estimates of the grain crops that would be for sale. When they failed to materialize, he cut the consumption of food allowed per person, which brought on the famines. He kept the level of exportation of grains at the levels contracted for in spite of shortages. Many important members of his government advised going slow, but Mao would not hear of it.

When the Great Leap Forward had run its course by 1960, Douglas would have expected that Mao would be replaced. Advocating a program so costly in lives and treasure should have been marked in the end by his retirement. It appears, though, that Mao's grip on power was stronger than was Khrushchev's, who was forced out by the Soviet Politburo in 1964, to be replaced by Brezhnev for lesser sins than Mao's.

Not satisfied with the disastrous Great Leap Forward, Mao bided his time for approximately six years before he put in motion another program, this one called the Cultural Revolution. The exact title was the Great Revolution to Establish Proletarian Culture. The timing is inexact because Mao spent several years laying plans for this program and launched it gradually.

Douglas thought he sensed that Mao trusted only the peasantry to be the arbiter of all activity in his society. He thought the masses should rule, and that the masses could do little wrong. In the political arrangements that he knew something about, Douglas was at ease with a distribution of power: some power to the judges; some to the legislators; some to the police departments; some to people in business; and the rest to the people. He wanted power to be distributed to the many segments of society because he guessed that a concentration of power produced abuses. Douglas and citizens of the Western World had grown accustomed to laws that were written down and that only violations of existing laws could result in the appropriate punishment He believed as well that if no law existed governing a certain matter, then no crime could be committed.

When Mao launched the Cultural Revolution he acted in an uncivilized manner on several fronts. People with no authority (the masses) were encouraged to accuse, interrogate and punish people who they thought had committed a crime. Out with the written code of laws! Out with the courts! Students attacked teachers and administrators. Young people attacked party functionaries, and in one case, a highly-placed administrator in Beijing, the capital. Valuable books and works of art were burned. Personal possessions, money and jewels were simply taken.

Translating this rampage to activities in his own state, Douglas envisaged crowds taking over the Seattle City Council, or the King County Council, or the Legislature in Olympia. These crowds would proceed to question their elected officials, disparage their work, and then violate them physically resulting frequently in manslaughter. All this vandalism, as Douglas viewed it, would be accomplished without any interference on the part of the local police. Let the masses rule, Mao had said. Of course there will be excesses, he said also, but those things happen.

Mao did not favor intellectuals nor did he value the advancement of successful people, irrespective of the class they were born into. If you made your way up in life, then you would tend toward capitalism and become a right-winger. You could even become anti-communist. You could be accused of being a spy or a traitor. You were fair game for punishment if it was said of you that you were counter-revolutionary or anti-Bolshevik. You could also be excessively left-wing. It could go against you if you were accused of being pro-Khrushchev – after all it was he who had ended the economic and cultural ties between the Soviet Union and China. None of these so-called crimes were part of the code but they were against the expectations of the day. Deviations that had been acceptable in previous decades were viewed as crimes at present.

While Mao did expect that rule by the masses would be uneven, he did nothing to prevent this disturbing, damaging behavior. As the author Philip Short pointed out, it may have been acceptable for Mao to permit many of the working functions of society to be destroyed, but only if he had something to replace them. It turned out that Mao had no substitutes for those elements of Chinese society that he had permitted to be destroyed. To make matters worse, in the time of the Cultural Revolution train travel was made free of charge so that young people who wished could travel to places where they could sow their brand of chaos. Mao knew what he was doing. He was advocating perpetual revolution.

Mao did not permit the Cultural Revolution to invade the armed forces of the country. He might have thought his army would break into factions only to go to war one with another. After three years or so, The Cultural Revolution came to an end. Perhaps even by Mao's standards there had been a sufficiently high price to pay with little accomplished.

Douglas had grown accustomed to the American navy's practice of changing the assignments of its personnel. Not only did those in the military services need the additional training that varied assignments brought, but also with change they did not grow lax from too great familiarity with any position. He noticed that presidents of universities, heads of corporations and all manner of people at lower levels changed jobs after ten years or so. As well, many jurisdictions had term limits for their elected officials. In dictatorships, however, the concept of changing the top executives after ten years did not apply. These individuals tended to stay for life, even after visiting on their countrymen such disasters as the Great Leap Forward and the Cultural Revolution. Much less costly errors would bring down an admiral, an elected official or an executive in the private sector. Douglas knew that to be the case.

Douglas admitted that he did not know Mao after reading what he had about him. The reason, he thought, was that he had never known anyone, or read about anyone who even vaguely resembled Mao Zedong. The Chinese culture differed from his at home and the political arena that the Chinese operated in was nearly incomprehensible.

When at the height of his powers, Mao could be satisfied that he was the undisputed leader of a quarter of the world's population. He had been able to install Communism as the form of government in his country. The important measuring stick, Douglas thought, was whether anything would remain of the changes he had made. When Mao died in 1976, at the age of eighty-three, there was a brief, perhaps bloodless, tussle over his succession. The four men he had selected to succeed him had failed him during his lifetime, one after the other, or so he claimed. The close associate who did come into power was Deng Xiaoping (one of the four, it turned out) who had been on the Long March and had held several important posts during his long tenure. He became the country's leader in 1978 and stayed in that position until his death in 1997. Perhaps in one of the oddities of history, Mao's Communism proved so unpopular that when Deng introduced a toned-down version of Capitalism the Chinese people were more than ready to accept it. Apparently Mao had awakened his people so that they would shake off feudalism and lethargy and rouse themselves to become an economic powerhouse. Mao could not have intended to achieve the results that came about. He stood for perpetual revolution and government by the masses. When he was no longer around to have his way, the Chinese people found that economic freedom and more political freedom than they had ever been accorded suited them fine.

If Mao was attempting to rid his country of the philosophy of Confucius, if Confucius' teachings stood in the way of progress, then Douglas knew he would require of himself to read up on the life of that sage because he knew next to nothing about him.

On the question of how many people died as the result of Mao's saddling China with Communism, Philip Short estimated that it would be more people than Hitler or Stalin had done in, but fewer than were killed on all fronts during World War II. On the existence of a state police to enforce Mao's will, the author was silent.

Mao was interesting. Douglas would continue reading about him. There was no shortage of material. On a Saturday morning, he entered the nearby branch of the Miami Public Library and moved in the direction of the reference desk. The lady librarian on duty wore a name tag bearing her first name, Helen. Douglas guessed that she was a young wife, aged between thirty-five and forty, in whom still resided many of the elements of her youth. She spoke quietly, as one does in a library, and fielded his questions easily. Her desk was equipped with a computer. She listened to his request, typed a message into the keyboard and examined the results on the flat screen. After absorbing the message, the librarian pivoted the screen in Douglas' direction and said, "You might start with these two by Edgar Snow. He was the first Western reporter to reach Mao Zedong and the Communists after the Long March. *Red Star Over China* was the first result. Many years later, many books later, I should add, he died and his widow put together *Edgar Snow's China* from notes and photographs he had collected. It's more of a picture book, but you know what they say about pictures."

Douglas thanked Helen, using her name as the name tag suggested. He found the two books on the shelves and knew he would have to apply for a library card at the circulation desk. He was required to use his powers of persuasion to convince the librarian to grant him a card. After a short discussion, she believed his papers to the effect that he was reporting for duty in the Seventh Naval District whose headquarters were not distant from the library. Douglas knew that he wanted to assemble data on Mao in chronological order, but the books he was reading did not accommodate him. The two biographies that he had read covered Mao's life in its entirety, in varying amounts of detail. He didn't know how Mao would be presented in the two books he had just taken out of the library. His interest was in the brand of Communism that Mao and others had installed in China, before and after their victory in 1949.

When home, Douglas examined the two volumes. The picture book, *Edgar Snow's China,* assembled by his widow Lois Wheeler Snow, would be the easier of the two books to read. He leafed through it, reading the captions under the photographs. The final photograph in the book is of Mao flanked by Edgar and Lois Snow. The caption reads, "Edgar and Lois Snow with Mao Tse-tung on the Tien An Men, October 1, 1970." Douglas reflected immediately that Snow in his writing would emphasize the positive aspects of recent history, Mao's and that of the Chinese people. Snow was the first Western reporter to reach Mao in 1936. He could and did bring Mao's story to the outside world. Snow recognized Mao to be a valuable source. Mao knew Snow to be a valuable conduit. They needed one another. It would not be an arrangement that sensible men would disturb. Reporting in detail portions of Mao's saga could meet with disapproval on the part of many Western readers. Having finished with the captions, Douglas started to read the text. Snow was most flattering of Mao and Communism and the Red Army. He compared them to the activities of Chiang Kai-shek and the Kuomintang and found the latter wanting in all aspects of the contest between the two factions. There was little doubt in Douglas' mind that Snow was reporting the truth. He suspected that it was not the whole truth. It's one thing to itemize the executions and atrocities performed by the followers of Chiang Kai-shek. It's another matter to do that without alluding to the equivalent behavior on the part of the Communists. Douglas wanted a balanced presentation. Douglas was convinced that Snow did not discuss the activities of both sides in an even-handed manner. Douglas turned to *Red Star Over China* and found that he was holding the 1968 edition. Inasmuch as Snow died in 1970, he could have brought his manuscript up to date, adding discussions of events that took place long after the material covered in the first edition, which came out in 1938. Here are the data that Douglas thought to be important, all taken from *Red Star Over China*.

In one of Snow's interviews of Mao, Mao emphasized that he could work with Chiang Kai-shek in improving the situation for the Chinese if the Kuomintang would do all possible to repel Japan in its attempt to conquer China. Mao labeled this a policy of "anti-imperialism." His second demand was that the Kuomintang would assist in ending the reign of warlords and the power of landlords. Chiang Kai-shek never adopted these two policies in full with the result that Mao and Chiang could never join forces. This appeared to Douglas to be the obvious development as both leaders were aiming for the top job in China.

In another interview, Mao expressed his disapproval of the arranged or forced marriage. His first marriage was one of these, being arranged by his father with a twenty-year old woman, he being fourteen. Further, Mao was ahead of his time in advancing equality between the sexes, not only in marriage, but also in social and educational matters, which included equal pay for men and women, and the right to vote.

In another departure from practice, the Red Army had been organized to respect the peasants and their possessions. Normally an army passing through a rural district would take what it needed without bothering to pay the owners. The new Red Army was taught to respect property rights and the well-being of the peasants they encountered. The landlords, however, did not fare so well. Snow quotes Mao on the issue: "Revolution is not a tea party." Snow then follows with his view: "That Red terror methods were widely used against landlords and other class enemies – who were arrested, deprived of land, condemned in 'mass trials,' and often executed – was undoubtedly true, as indeed the Communists' own reports confirmed."

As Snow writes about it, idealism is at the root of Communism's appeal. The gift of one's labor and fighting ability is for the benefit of the country. If the effort is directed against the Japanese it is for the benefit of the Chinese people. If the effort is directed against landlords, warlords, bankers, and vast commercial enterprises, then it is for the benefit of the peasantry, landless or not. The peasants have been abused over the centuries. They have been overtaxed and oppressed. When a regime arrives that distributes land and farm animals, and takes away from the landlords all but the land they are able to cultivate, and when taxes are reduced or eliminated, and when crops are no longer stolen, then the peasantry can be filled with hope and aspire to a better life for the first time. The natural response for the dispossessed is to work with this new regime and the new Red Army. Douglas understood the appeal that this force would have among the peasants but he wondered how this new regime would act when the two challenges, the Japanese and the Nationalist Army, had been defeated. Mao would be required to find new uses for Communism's zeal. It was that force which he tapped for his Great Leap Forward and particularly for the Cultural Revolution. But the enemies had been disposed of. The Chinese people may no longer have wanted nor needed revolution. It was Mao and a few others who felt that more revolution was necessary even after the revolution had been won. The Chinese people might have wished to savor their victory after 1949. They might have enjoyed peace, quiet, and a few luxuries.

Douglas reflected on the status of the Chinese people. The Manchu dynasty had been overthrown in 1911 when Sun Yat-sen became the first president of the new republic. Civil war of sorts had pitted Communists against Nationalists from 1920 on. There was peace from 1924 until 1927 but for the following twenty-two years warfare existed between the factions. The Communists did establish themselves in the Northwest after the Long March, which lasted a year, ending in 1935. The Nationalists, however, did not occupy the balance of the country because the Communists held several sizable pockets in which they held sway.

The Japanese arrived in 1931 to take Manchuria. Their industries needed raw materials. They started a war against China by attacking Shanghai in 1937. They managed to conquer the Chinese coast in the next few years. When World War II started, the Japanese took Hong Kong from the British and full scale war was waged by Communists, Nationalists, the Allies, and Japan over Southeast Asia until Japan surrendered in August 1945. The Communists and Nationalists kept at it until 1949 when Mao Zedong declared the birth of the People's Republic of China, speaking from Beijing. Chiang Kai-shek and the remains of the Kuomintang retreated to the island of Formosa, now renamed Taiwan. Douglas thought that the Chinese would be exhausted and that they would need a couple of decades to build their economy by resuscitating the systems that define a modern state: agriculture, education, health, manufacturing, transportation, communication, commerce, judiciary and so on. Douglas thought that while Mao tended to such matters he could not get over the notion that his country would slide slowly into complacency, which to Mao would bring on the habits practiced by the bourgeoisie. He could not allow landlords to reappear. The farms must be collectivized. There would be no rest, no sliding back to levels of comfort so that the Chinese people could engage in the activities that all people aspire to: after completing education, reach maturity; seek gainful employment; start a family; feed, house and educate the offspring; engage in activities of interest, be they educational, political, or cultural; for the rest of it, be left alone to one's own devices. That's what Douglas thought were the aims of most people on the planet. But Mao would not leave the Chinese people alone. There needed to be turmoil and continual revolution. When he vanished, how quickly the Chinese people reverted to what is considered normal behavior!

For himself, Mao concluded that he needed a less strenuous life. Never mind the people. He occupied sumptuous quarters in Beijing. He traveled in a private train. In the car containing his living space he had built an extra large bed on which he placed a great number of books because he would read, on frequent occasions, late into the night. Perhaps he ordered an extra large bed because on evenings when he did not read he might take two or three sweet young things to bed with him to while away what otherwise might have been lonely hours. Douglas had read this account elsewhere, not in the books by Edgar Snow.

On a return visit to his branch library, Douglas greeted Helen who had located material for him describing the cost in lives that the Chinese paid for the introduction of Communism as their form of government. She had located a text titled, *Mao: The Unknown Story*, by Jon Halliday and Jung Chang. "Read with care," Helen said. "The total deaths reported are controversial. Something to do with mathematics."

Douglas read the book to the end, all six hundred thirty pages. The authors were required to make assumptions to reach the numbers killed by the Communists. Douglas' reaction was that a humane, sympathetic leader, faced with famine in his country, would move mountains to alleviate the condition. Mao and his government could have spared millions of their countrymen. For those who died in labor camps, Douglas felt that there was no excuse. How do rational people determine that holding an unpopular belief is cause for incarceration and most likely death? As for the torture and executions in prisons, Douglas questioned the sanity of dictators who had to turn to murder to keep their regimes in power. The authors, Halliday and Chang, arrived at a figure of seventy-one million dead. Perhaps the estimate by Philip Short given in his biography of Mao was sufficiently accurate. He had written that the total deaths attributed to Mao were more than could be charged up to Hitler or Stalin but fewer than were killed on all fronts during World War II.

Douglas had found his balanced view. The authors, Halliday and Chang, covered the other side of the story. While Snow did not elaborate on the existence of a secret police, Halliday and Chang discussed the founding of the Political Security Bureau and gave the name of the first director. They also provide the details of Russia's and Stalin's control over the Chinese Communist Party. A surprising element dealt with Stalin's fear of having to contend with Japan in the east and Germany in the west. Because of this fear of encirclement, Stalin went to lengths in preventing the demise of Chiang Kai-shek and his Nationalist army. Stalin viewed them as a more effective force in keeping the Japanese occupied than Mao's Red Army.

An important aspect of the Long March is omitted by Edgar Snow in his account. According to Halliday and Chang, Chiang Kai-shek wanted to include in his conquered portions of China territories in the Northwest that were in the hands of warlords. His technique was to place his troops on three sides of the Red Army (roughly) so that it could move only to the north. This the Red Army did, to be followed by the Nationalists, accomplishing Chiang's goal of occupying provinces that had been denied to him previously. In the account, the Red Army came through, causing chaos in a province; the Nationalists followed and restored a semblance of order.

The authors, intermittently but in detail, analyzed the triangle consisting of Stalin, Chiang Kai-shek and Mao. Each had his own objectives. Stalin wanted the Japanese to be kept at bay, if not defeated, in order to safeguard Siberia. To accomplish this, Chiang Kai-shek and Mao must cooperate in the fight against Japan and not fight one another. Stalin's power came from his ability to deliver arms and cash to Mao. Stalin also wanted Communism to be the victorious form of government in China. In spite of that, Stalin signed accords with Chiang Kai-shek on two occasions. The first, in 1935, was anti-Japanese in nature. The second, in 1945, regained territorial rights that the Soviet Union were forced to give up when the Japanese invaded Manchuria.

Chiang Kai-shek wished to emerge as the unopposed leader in China, with the Kuomintang in charge. The threat that the Japanese posed was important but Chiang needed to keep an eye peeled for Mao, even though his forces were larger than the Red Army.

Mao was eager to have Communism the surviving form of government in all China, particularly with him at the head of the party and the government. He paid attention to Stalin's wishes because Stalin had many followers in the Chinese Communist Party. Mao's best chance of success rested with the Nationalist and the Japanese wearing down one another, with the Communists remaining the victors. Mao concentrated on the conquest of area, hoping that the Nationalists would do most of the fighting against the Japanese. The Communists, Nationalists, Allies and the Japanese were engaged in continuous warfare. Mao banked on the Allies defeating the Japanese in the Pacific so that he would be the survivor on the mainland. His cause would be furthered if at the end of hostilities he had a stronger position than did Chiang Kai-shek.

The authors devoted many pages to the methods used by the victorious Communists to grind down the Chinese citizenry. Of course Mao insisted on absolute control. To achieve it he employed the techniques developed by the Communists in the Soviet Union. These are the gulag, detention centers, torture, prisons, executions (public if the effect was needed), mass rallies, public trials and confessions, and other methods that Douglas could not comprehend.

Douglas found Chapter 31, *Totalitarian State, Extravagant Lifestyle*, to be informative. In it, the authors contrast the arduous conditions under which the people were forced to live with Mao's life of luxury. The authors say, speaking of Mao, that "…his subjects were utterly shorn of legal protection." A sentence that chilled Douglas read, "…courts were replaced by Party committees." The inference was that the body of law that had governed China over the centuries was thrown out and learned judges were replaced with party functionaries. It was as though, Douglas surmised, the Common Law and the entire body of law of the United States were tossed out, along with judges, to be replaced by doctrines advanced by the party of a newly-elected president. Citizens of the Western world were accustomed to receiving fair treatment in their courts, and indeed they turned to their courts in expectation of receiving it. In Mao's system, the courts became another instrument of the state, set up to shape and control society.

Mao went after the remains of the Nationalist Party, those who had served in its army and government and those who had worked in the intelligence service. The authors write that in the land reform program as many as three million people perished. It is suggested that a greater number of people might have been killed except for the need of labor in the gulags.

The authors describe a program that they call "typically Maoist," in which people are placed under surveillance. They could not have committed serious errors because their punishment would have been far more severe. It was sufficient that they might deviate in the future. Douglas wondered whether Mao and his police apparatus determined that a percentage of the people, irrespective of their conduct, would be placed under surveillance in order to keep the population as a whole on its toes.

Those rights that Americans refer to as their First Amendment Rights vanished. Citizens were better off having no opinions and being careful of which books they owned. They could not relocate at will to a new job with a new address. Their place of employment was chosen for them. Spying, citizen on citizen, became the order of the day.

In contrast, Mao lived the life of emperors. His lodgings, modes of transportation, creature comforts, and foods were the best available. It was only in the matter of clothing that he kept the common touch. Clothing did not interest him.

Douglas knew that a piece of the puzzle was escaping him. Dictators were brutal. They were killers. Those that he was reading about had a program, which they insisted on forcing upon their populace. Was there a connection between the willingness to kill and the need to force a program on to one's citizens? Did they always go together?

Douglas imagined that Mao could have awakened the Chinese people, dragged them from feudalism, redistributed land, and industrialized the nation without any killing at all. Did the populace need to be completely regimented in order to launch five year plans and increase agricultural output? Perhaps the heart of the matter was that dictators took no chances on being removed from power, and for that they were required to terrorize their citizenry. Douglas concluded that dictatorships are much alike, differing in degree. The safeguard against the formation of a dictatorship, he reasoned, was the distribution of power. If it can be concentrated, there will come along a rascal who, with a handful of accomplices, will manage to seize power.

*　　*　　*

Before Douglas ended his examination of Mao's politics, he thought he should read some or all of *Quotations from Chairman Mao Tse-tung.* The text was known also as *The Little Red Book,* for obvious reasons. The American publisher followed tradition and published a 4" X 5" book, complete with red cover.

The sayings are divided into thirty-three categories such as The Communist Party, Class and Class Struggle, and Socialism and Communism, which are the first three categories. For the most part, the sayings are excerpts from speeches and writings. While they describe the plan that Mao and others worked from, they omit the details. There is no mention of the oppression required to execute the various steps in achieving results. The sayings are benign and a reader cannot fathom from reading them the treatment of the population required to bring about Communism. Douglas hoped that he would have better success investigating Confucius so that he could find out whether this sage was responsible for implanting feudalism into Chinese society. He knew where to start: Volume 1 of The Story of Civilization by Will Durant. It has as its second title, Our Oriental Heritage. Surely Confucius' teachings would be discussed in detail. The book was in his mother's library at home in Seattle. He would ask for the copy at his local library.

Feudalism, which Mao wanted to remove from Chinese culture, roots and all, had a great deal to do with the ownership of land. The original propertied class had little to own except land. In European society, these men would be barons and earls and other titled people. Their tenant farmers paid rent to the land owners using a portion of their crops and farm animals. Coins were scarce. As a dedicated Communist, Mao was intent on ending the practice of private ownership of land. The land would be the property of the state.

Mao saw that a modern China would need to substitute the sciences and mathematics in place of memorizing the Chinese classics. He recognized that two-thirds of the population was tied to the land and in order to break up the system of agriculture then in use in China, he had to abolish the landlord class and substitute mechanized collectives. The feudal approach would not serve a modern technical economy. The teachings of Confucius represented stagnation. They had no place in a modern society that was moving toward being a manufacturing and military power of the first rank.

Mao had long been an advocate of women receiving equal pay for equal work. That was a break in tradition. Confucius believed that women owed obedience to men. Women were second-class citizens, as it is said now. On the subject of women's place in society, Will Durant writes, concerning a peasant husband's view of his wife, that, "he admires her not for her beauty or her culture, but for her fertility, her industry and her obedience." Perhaps this was a view held by Confucius that Mao wanted to eradicate.

FIDEL CASTRO

AN EXAMINATION OF Castro, Douglas sensed, would yield different results from his reading up on Lenin, Stalin and Mao. One of the differences, not an important one, he knew, was that Castro still held office while the others had died decades earlier. Castro, in fact, had come to rule over Cuba five years before he, Douglas, was born. Castro was a household name. Douglas had been reading about him all his life. Most recently, being an ill man, Castro had retired and turned over the presidency of Cuba to his brother, Raul.

It seemed that Castro had been motivated primarily by the depravity of the senior officials in the Cuban government. Corruption was rampant. One could amass wealth by becoming president or finding a niche as a minister. In Castro's early years, the president had been Fulgencio Batista, who came into office by staging a *coup d'état* in 1952. He had held the office legitimately from 1940 to 1944. Castro had a second reason to involve himself completely in the politics of his country, and that was his dislike for the unnecessary influence of the United States in Cuban affairs and Cuban life in general. At least Castro viewed the influence as unnecessary.

The United States had driven Spain out of Cuba in 1898, ending four hundred years of colonial rule. With the Spaniards gone, the American government asserted its influence, and American commercial interests in agriculture and manufacturing invested in the Cuban economy. One of the largest American companies to invest was United Fruit.

An important venture in need of foreign capital was the manufacture of sugar from sugar cane, requiring over one hundred factories to be built.

Before the fall of the Batista government and its replacement by Castro in 1959, Castro's additional complaint against the U.S. was over the continued sale of weapons to the Batista regime. Castro made the point that he was doing his best to unseat Batista in a guerrilla war for the betterment of the Cuban people while the U.S. kept Batista supplied with arms. The U.S. government was motivated by Batista's anti-communism while Castro was suspected of wishing to bring Communism to the Island. The Cold War was in full swing and the U.S. government was at one of the two poles. Castro denied the accusation at the onset that he had Communist leanings but once firmly installed in office in 1961, he declared his allegiance to Marxism-Leninism.

Cuba is too small to have permitted Castro a Long March, as Mao had organized for his army. Castro had to be satisfied with starting his civil war in the eastern portion of the country, using the Sierra Maestra as a staging ground. This mountain range is remote and inaccessible and situated at the eastern end of the island. It was at the foot of these mountains that Castro landed with a small band of armed men in December 1955. They had come from Mexico in a yacht, purchased for the mission from its American owner. The vessel brought a band of eighty-three revolutionaries nearly a thousand miles across the Caribbean Sea.

Douglas, along with many others, wondered at Castro's transition from an advocate of democracy to becoming a Communist dictator. There is little question that the Cuban people were tired of corrupt politics. They were in favor of the rule of law and democratically elected officials. They were against military coups, which were usually followed by arbitrary rule without benefit of a constitution.

As long as Castro advocated a return to democracy he was on safe ground, Douglas concluded, but after his victory when he opted for a socialist government without elections, then he had gone against his word, changing the rules in the middle of his game. Douglas guessed that Castro had been a Communist all along and advocated democracy only as a step in obtaining power. The particular style of his politics, however, was not important to him as long as he was in charge.

As far as obtaining the correct books at the library, Douglas thought he had found a pattern that worked. The librarians who staffed the reference desk were knowledgeable in many ways. Most of them held a master's degree in library science. As part of their training, they had become experts at delving into the recesses of the Internet. On this particular day, in the early evening hours, the reference desk was manned by Helen, with whom he had spoken before. He wondered if she was the only employee for this position. Her first words to him were, "You're back, Lieutenant. Finished with Mao?"

He answered, "Yes, and now it's on to Castro." He went over in his mind once more the matter of her age. In a previous conversation she had mentioned a trip north to visit a ten-year old grandchild. If she had had a child at twenty and that child had married and produced an offspring at twenty and the offspring was now the ten-year old grandchild, then Helen could be fifty. She looked thirty-five. She was wearing a pants and blouse outfit that featured horizontal stripes of many colors. She looked wonderful. Douglas could not account for this affliction, this powerful, consuming interest in women. Perhaps all men were that way.

He gathered his thoughts and said to Helen, "I'm particularly interested in Castro's change in orientation from democracy to Communism." Helen answered that she did not have material devoted specifically to that topic. She said, "Here's a guess. Read *Havana Dream*. It's by Wendy Gimbel. It's the story of a Cuban family, aristocratic, I would say, covering four generations. Fidel and a woman named Naty, a part of the second of the four generations covered in this book, had an affair, which produced a daughter. Naty's full name is Natalia. You might get an inkling of his politics from that text."

"Sounds interesting," Douglas said. He enjoyed reading books laden with romance. "And read *Fidel, A Critical Portrait*. It's by Tad Szulc, the *New York Times* reporter. They tell me it's definitive. That's the adjective they drag out for books that hit the mark."

The book, *Havana Dreams,* did not take up Douglas' question: why did Castro switch from democracy to Communism, with its attendant repressions. Perhaps no one but Castro's brother Raúl knows the answer. The book introduced Natalia Revuelta, born in 1925, and Fidel Castro, born the year following. They met briefly at the University of

Havana. Both were married at the time, Naty to a doctor by whom she had a daughter. Naty aided Castro in his early revolutionary attempt when he and a small group attacked the army barracks in the town of Moncada on 26 July 1953. Those not killed were captured. When Fidel was captured, he was sent to the civilian authorities, which fortunate accident saved his life. He was convicted and given a fifteen year sentence. Those captured who were sent to the military authorities were executed.

Naty and Fidel did not become lovers, but they did fall in love through correspondence. Many of their letters, his from prison, hers from her home in Havana, were published in the book. Both Fidel and Naty wrote affectionate and provocative letters to one another when he was in prison. They professed love for one another.

When an amnesty was declared, Fidel was released from prison after serving about two years of his sentence. It was then that they consummated the relationship and their daughter resulted. Fidel neither legitimized his daughter by giving her his name nor did he ask Naty to leave her husband and marry him. Natalia's husband reacted differently. He took their older child with him into exile in the U.S. Natalia remained in Cuba with her daughter by Castro. Eventually the daughter of Fidel and Natalia grew up and married and had a child. With faked passports and clever make-up, this daughter of Castro and Naty left Cuba for Spain, making arrangements for her daughter to follow her. They both ended up in the U.S.

Soon after the birth of this daughter, Castro left for Mexico where he organized a group that would invade Cuba. Castro's mind was never far from rebellion. Leading a revolutionary movement was in the forefront of his mind and guided his activities. Marrying Naty could have been a distraction from his principal pursuit. Of course, there were other women in his life. It is reported that after Naty he fathered five sons with another woman, without benefit of marriage.

For an answer to the question of why Castro switched to Communism, Douglas returned to the reference desk at his branch library. The person on duty was not Helen, but a young man. Douglas posed his question again. The young man thought for a moment, "You say Helen could not find anything in our collection. Let's try an inter-library loan. There might be something out there."

The librarian typed a question into his computer. He scanned the terminal. "Bingo. How about *The Early Fidel: Roots of Castro's Communism*. It's by Lionel Martin. The title looks propitious."

Douglas checked the library every second day and in a week the book had arrived, traveling the short distance from the University of Miami. It should tell him in detail why one dictator, at least, had adopted Communism and rejected democracy. Douglas guessed that reading the book would alter many of his former views.

It appeared that Castro was influenced for the remainder of his life by the children he played with as a boy. They were dirt poor kids from farming families, living on the lowest rung of society. Castro's father had migrated from Spain and purchased farm land. He ran the farm successfully. There was enough money to send young Fidel to a Catholic school in Havana and upon graduation to the University of Havana where Castro studied law and received his degree. Castro came to appreciate money and privilege but never overlooked the disparity between the peasant-children of his childhood and himself and those richer than he.

Once at the University, Castro gravitated to student politics, which in Havana leads to involvement in national politics. If the University had been located in a city far removed from Havana, the recent history of the country could be different. Cuban politicians, nearly without exception (that was Castro's view), operated beyond the law. Graft, gain by illegal means, was the term that came to mind for Douglas. Tax receipts arrived at the National Treasury. Money was then appropriated by Congress. Castro could and did document occasions when money was siphoned off into the pockets of politicians. On one occasion he went to court and sued the president of the nation at the time over illicit gains. There was no question that Castro was incorruptible and fearless.

During the years following his graduation with a law degree, Castro joined a law firm from which he provided legal services for the poor. Perhaps a great deal of it was pro bono work. In 1952, he ran for a seat in the lower house and might have won except that the election was canceled when Fulgencio Batista staged his coup to become president. He had been president previously from 1940 to 1944. It may have been the coup d'état which prompted Castro to say that he preferred action over parliament as a means of solving Cuba's problems. That may have been an off-the-cuff remark or it could have represented his convictions. In his view, the systems were corrupted, poverty was imbedded, and wealth was not distributed properly. These three situations prompted Castro to think and say that the classes in Cuban society needed adjustment. There needed to be leveling. That led to his anti-American position.

The position's origins are not discussed in the text but it seemed logical to Douglas that rich Americans and American corporations would search for opportunities in Cuba. Land would be acquired and factories constructed. Cuban governments might or might not have welcomed these investments but they were not in violation of Cuban law. In the matter of manufacturing facilities to process sugar cane into sugar for sale internationally, capital not otherwise available came from American investors. Douglas surmised that no more than prevailing wages were paid to farmers who worked on land acquired by Americans and American firms. The wages were pitiful but cheap labor is frequently an incentive to invest. It appeared to Douglas from the reading he was doing that Castro grouped Cuban politicians with American investors, neither group held in high esteem. Bribes could have been paid by Americans to Cubans to obtain the necessary permits for conducting business. Douglas did not know. When his chances came, Castro would eliminate the existing political class in Cuba by substituting one of his making and he would expropriate or nationalize without payment the Cuban assets of Americans and American firms. The assets held by Cubans in the U.S. were left undisturbed by the U.S. government.

The author, Lionel Martin, reported that Castro had read Marx and was particularly impressed by the *Communist Manifesto*. Because Douglas had read it and had identified omissions (managerial labor has no value, managers appear by magic from among untrained proletariats, as examples) he supposed Castro had not spotted these omissions or had not wished to. Douglas thought that by chance he had stumbled on a partial definition of a Communist: a person who thinks he can construct an advanced technical society without capital and without educated, accomplished people.

Douglas guessed that reading texts on economics and politics might have reinforced Castro's existing views but these views would not have originated with reading another man's writings. They would have come from what he learned as a child and from what he witnessed of Cuba's politics as a young man at the University in Havana. His past made him predisposed to search for a system of governance on which the leader can enforce his will.

In *The Early Years: The Roots of Castro's Communism,* the author elaborates on Castro's personality and a guiding principle in his conduct of politics. The descriptive terms that Douglas gathered were: excellent orator, powerful memory, natural leader, fearless and vastly intelligent. On his own, perhaps through study, Castro came to obey a rule of politics that told him not to get ahead of the people. He may have wanted to clean up Cuban society from top to bottom, reorganizing it along socialist lines, but he never said those words or words similar to them at the beginning. It was enough to tell the Cuban people that their leaders were corrupt and needed to be replaced. Even though he was the leader of his movement and sensed that he would become the leader of the nation, he recognized that it was ineffectual politically to get ahead of the people: having Batista as a punching bag served Castro's purposes. It reminded Douglas of reading Mao's oft-stated remark that he, Mao, could not have brought Communism to all of China without the struggle with the Japanese army. After Castro came to power he was free to discuss his ambitions and over time put many of them into effect.

Castro has been a masterful politician, in the Sierra Maestra and to this day. He was able to maintain his position of leadership and his popularity with the Cuban people. He used existing organizations such as the Communist Party without joining them and at the same time without losing their backing. Douglas was in sympathy with much of what Castro did and wanted to do. It's legitimate to curb corruption. It's admirable to solve the problems of the very poor. It's correct to introduce health care and education to those who have access to neither. As Douglas read along, he saw, perhaps inevitably, that under Castro, the blood started to flow.

The first sign demonstrating that Castro could be casual about the lives of others came during his triumphal march from the Sierra Maestra to Havana in 1959. The enforcers of Batista, many with questionable records as policemen, were executed summarily by crowds when Batista's army crumbled and could no longer offer protection. There may have been five hundred men executed. Castro's excuse for permitting this violence (or not lifting a hand to prevent it) was that if his not-yet-in-office government had attempted to stop these vengeful acts, the crowds would still have acted as they did. It was better, Castro said, to allow the Cuban people to vent their hatred.

Douglas didn't care for Castro's reasoning. If one of the intentions of the revolution had been to restore the rule of law, then the slow, cumbersome custom of trial by jury should have been used against the accused. Inasmuch as Cuba used Napoleonic Law rather than the Common Law, it would have been trial by judges (not by jury) in which the accused must prove his innocence. In any event, Castro should have insisted on due process rather than give in to mob rule. Douglas thought that the first time someone in authority crossed the line and imprisoned a person for holding an unorthodox belief was the moment that he became a dictator. It was that moment which Lord Acton referred to when he said, "Absolute power corrupts absolutely." Siphoning off public funds only to make them appear in one's bank account was a corrupt act. Lord Acton was correct on that score. He went further. The casual incarceration of a person without cause, except for holding a different opinion, was absolute corruption. Castro engaged in this activity along with Lenin, Stalin and Mao. Douglas wondered whether dictators, as well as being corrupt, were insane. What view of life is it that sets one at the top of a pyramid composed of killers, torturers, interrogation officers, firing squads, prison guards, dishonest prosecutors, and bought-off judges, all perched on top of twelve million citizens frightened into submission?

There have been a sufficient number of dictators over the centuries that a term had to be set aside to describe their behavior. Douglas thought that megalomania fit the bill.

When Castro came to power in 1959, he also came to a fork in the road. If he took the right fork he would have welcomed all Cubans to stay and rebuild their country. Nations have only the accumulated savings of their citizens to invest. Castro might have suggested that the Cuban gold in mattresses at home and abroad be put to work in local projects. Cuba needed the rich, educated, talented sections of her society. If he took the left fork in the road, he would scare off the most valuable Cubans. Their money, skills and work ethic would migrate to other countries. If he confiscated the assets left behind and if he expropriated the assets of Americans, he would receive a one-time windfall, but it would be killing the goose. All the capital Cuba needed was ninety miles away in Florida but after expropriation it was out of reach. Castro took the left fork in the road, of course. The cream of Cuban society left, taking their wealth and skills with them. Castro called them worms. The poorer, less skilled segments of society remained, under-equipped to rebuild their nation. Castro called them real revolutionaries. The ten percent of the population that left Cuba did so to live their lives without the excesses of a dictatorial government. Many left to hold on to their wealth. Later on, perhaps in 1961, or 1962, citizens could no longer leave. That would be a double indictment: a mass exodus as long as leaving was possible followed by an enforced imprisonment when it appeared that anyone who could leave would avail himself of the opportunity.

Marx was wrong. Countries need capital in private hands, generated internally or raised externally, and they need skilled individuals if the people are to improve their lot. Communism aggregates all wealth to the state and the top members of the Party, leaving nothing for the individual except an impoverished security. The incentives to improve one's capabilities and the ability to decide what's in one's best interest evaporate.

Douglas knew that he was not an economist. He knew what he had learned about colonization in one of his two courses on world history. He wished Caroline were with him to discuss the steps Castro took and those he might have taken. Castro had promised a return to the 1940 Cuban Constitution. The populace had been enthusiastic over the idea. Douglas read that Constitution. Article 1 states, "Cuba is . . . organized as a unitary and democratic Republic for the enjoyment of political freedom, social justice, individual and collective welfare, and human solidarity." That sounded like First Amendment Rights to Douglas.

If Caroline were with him she would suggest that property rights and the rule of law should be observed. On corruption, Douglas thought, she would say it could be brought under control by shining a bright light into dark corners. As far as having peasants who wished to do so farm their own land, Douglas thought that experts in finance could calculate means for legal transfer of property in which present owners would be compensated. He knew he was over his head in writing out the details.

Perhaps all that Castro had to ask himself was what could he accomplish without use of force?

Admiral Stevens, during one of their semi-weekly meetings, asked Douglas for a progress report. At the end of it, when Douglas was standing to leave the Admiral's office, he said, "On Castro, Nielsen, can you let me have a page or two? You can write it in your office during working hours. And give me the titles of any books you've read. Anyone in my job needs to know more about Castro than he knows about himself."

"Aye, aye, Sir," Douglas answered. "Would forty-eight hours be soon enough?"

The return letter from Elena had arrived. It contained three photographs that Douglas looked at before reading what she had to say. The first photograph showed her in a bikini flanked by her parents. On the back was written, "Mon and Dad, Cape Cod." The date told him that they had been on vacation three summers ago. The second was of her taken in white shorts and blue T-shirt, leaning up against a car, presumably hers. The third photograph was of Elena sitting alone on a sofa. She had turned her head to the right and had taken the time to pose. Her mouth was open a bit, telling him that he had remembered correctly, her upper lip was thin and the lower lip average. He'd loved kissing her mouth and holding her face in his hands.

She addressed him as "Dear Douglas" and signed off with, "Warm hugs to my member of the Armed Forces stationed east of the Continental Divide." It was a bit long, Douglas thought, but original. There was her telephone number at home, with a notice that he should call anytime. There was a paragraph devoted to her having selected a professional photographer who would produce the most beautiful portrait of her that was possible, "limited by the material we are working with." She said he would receive it in a couple of weeks. She ended the paragraph by writing, "I don't have a photograph of you, handsome."

Douglas picked up where he had left off in Hawaii. He found a one-bedroom apartment with only a view of the neighborhood. It was furnished and he liked that it came with a large desk, a large table really, for his computer and for taking notes as he read on Communism. To that end, he had been filling a notebook holding a hundred pages of lined paper. As was his custom, he wrote down the titles and the authors of the books he read. He would add the list to the report he was preparing for Admiral Stevens. Douglas also bought a used car. It was the same model he had owned in Honolulu. He knew where the knobs and switches were.

Douglas and Elena started telephoning one another, which they did on Monday evenings. There wasn't a great deal to talk about but they always ended on a note of missing their time together. This led one evening to Douglas' asking where they might visit, in Miami or Seattle. Douglas also advanced the notion that they could meet in Mexico on the Pacific Coast. "That would work but whatever time we have we should live together," Elena said. Douglas couldn't think of anything to say to Elena's suggestion. She continued. "From the way we've been talking it seems that we are heading for a test period. How would it work between us? That's what we want to know. If you come to Seattle you'll stay with your mother and Frank and we'll go out on dates. If we meet in Mexico it will be in a hotel room. But if I come to Miami for a week we'll be living in your place and we'll get to know whether we have a fit."

"That's most direct," Douglas said.

"Well, we can't play games at this distance."

Douglas thought for a moment, and then he said, "It promises to be a warm winter here. We could plan on some time when it's too bleak to stay in Seattle any longer and you need to see sunshine."

"The first week in February; that's what you are describing. Do you plan on taking any time at Christmas?" Elena asked

"I have leave saved up. You use up two days flying back and forth but I should be able to scare up three or four days around Christmastime."

That was the tentative plan. It became the hoped-for plan and then became the plan. Before Christmas Douglas was off to Mexico, not to see Elena but on business. The purpose was to study the sea routes that drug traffickers might use. There were several ports, the largest of them Vera Cruz. Douglas devoted two weeks to this trip during which he met with Mexican police and navy personnel. They were most accommodating to an American who spoke flawless Spanish. By time he returned to Miami his promotion had arrived. He was now a lieutenant commander. He met with the Admiral immediately and promised that he would have a written report finished in two days at his desk. He said that he had blocked it out in the evenings while in Mexico.

"We ought to go through a little champagne over your promotion, Nielsen," Admiral Stevens said.

When Douglas presented his thirty-two page bound report on Mexico to the Admiral and others, the invitation was extended. "If you are free next Thursday evening, you might have dinner with my family. I want you to meet my wife. My son and I have the same birthday. He'll be coming from Atlanta with his wife and six-year old daughter. By the way, I think we should wear our uniforms."

"Yes, sir. I take it your son is not in the navy."

"That's correct. He's a graduate of the Naval Academy but had other ideas after five years. He teaches physics at Georgia Tech."

"And your granddaughter's my date for the evening?"

"That's also correct. She'll have a crush on you. Party dresses do that to girls."

Douglas visited the offices of the two Cuban-American associations he had contacted. They had sent him pamphlets, which he had digested. The material made several points. One dealt with the length of time properties in Cuba had been in the hands of Cubans who had stayed. Because several decades had passed, these organizations and the people they represented did not expect that those properties would be returned to the Cubans who went into exile. The idea was to forgive the past. When the ailing Castro died, the argument went, there will be a new deal between those who left and those who stayed, and the deal won't include the return of property. Douglas thought that the parties who had written the aims were evenhanded. Those who came and had been granted U.S. citizenship probably would keep their new status. A few might decide to return to Cuba to the land that had been their home.

Douglas and the higher-ups in the organizations discussed the number of people who were leaving Cuba in whatever conveyance they could find and the number of these who managed to get a foot on dry land in the U.S. They were still coming in spite of efforts by Castro's regime to make it impossible.

The framed photograph arrived from Elena. She had signed it, "For Douglas, Love, Elena." He appreciated that she had posed in a strapless evening gown. The top of a white dress was in view as were her bare shoulders and neck. This time the mass of black hair was pulled back to reveal all her face. She wore no jewelry. He thought of Caroline and Joanne. They were both lovely women and Douglas guessed that Elena's attraction was so powerful because they were already talking about a life together. He hadn't felt the need as strongly before. He wondered how it would have turned out between them if they had known one another when they were younger. As he held the photograph, Douglas knew he wanted Elena right there in front of him. There was no question that he would make the necessary plans.

The Admiral's dinner took place at the officers' club. There were birthdays to toast followed by a toast to Douglas' promotion. It was Admiral Stevens' wife who turned to him and asked whether he was planning a forty-year career. "I don't have to tell you, Mrs. Stevens, that there's precious little room at the top. I think I'll stop when it's apparent that I've had my final promotion."

The Admiral had been listening. He joined the conversation. "We decided on forty years when we married. I've been out of the Academy for thirty-seven years and we've been married thirty-six. You're right in a way, though. If I had been passed over for admiral I might have stopped."

"What was your previous assignment, sir?" Douglas asked.'

"I was in charge of a task force in the Gulf. This may be my last job but you never know. The navy could need an officer next month with my experience to be in charge of the Sixth Fleet, or some other fleet, and yank me out of Miami. I do what the top brass asks."

The Admiral's son explained to Douglas that he had left the navy after five years because he couldn't look forward to being without his wife and daughter. "It didn't make sense to live without them," he concluded.

The Admiral then turned to Douglas and said, "Continue doing the high quality work that you turn out and you'll have no problems."

Coming from the person who would review his progress reports,

Douglas thought that the Admiral was saying in effect that the navy needed people with his qualifications who could turn out first-rate work. The Admiral added, "Nielsen, I read with care the biographical material you gave me on Castro. You write well, by the way." The table fell silent and then the Admiral's wife looked at Douglas and asked, "Is there anyone special in your life that we'll meet sooner or later?"

Douglas smiled. "There have been special ladies but I wasn't able to pull off anything. There's a new special lady and I hope we can find our way to the altar." Douglas was surprised to hear himself utter these words. Those at the table fell silent again to digest this declaration.

The Admiral said, "Nielsen, you wrote that Castro declared himself to be a Marxist-Leninist in 1961. Would you write up two hundred words giving me a definition? I wouldn't know a Marxist-Leninist if I were introduced to him."

"I'll be glad to, sir. It will take a little research on my part to find the correct terms."

ELENA AND DOUGLAS

PART 12:

DOUGLAS DIDN'T PICK up the framed photograph of Elena, as he had done so often. This time, sitting at his desk, he leaned forward and studied the arrangement of her hair. If that mass of black hair was not in view then it had to be wound into a bun and held close to the back of her head. He had been searching for a more formal word than bun, knowing there to be one. Yesterday in his office it came to him. It was chignon, of course a French word, but it had made it into the English dictionary on his desk.

What a lovely woman, he thought. He wanted her so badly. He recalled having seen a chignon worn by the Greek women who graced museums as marble statues. Venus de Milo might be one. He couldn't recall. Thanksgiving had passed and on Monday Douglas would go to Personnel and check up on leave at Christmastime. He was told that the possibility existed but that he should check with Commander Sullivan.

Douglas walked down the hall to the Commander's office and introduced himself. Commander Sullivan said, "How do you do, Nielsen? I've seen you around here for about eight weeks. Been here that long?"

"Yes, I have, Commander. Why did Personnel send me to see you?"

"Because you and I will be the duty officers in the first week of January, including New Year's Day. I was about to contact you.

We should meet before the fifteenth of December and get our act together."

"What does the job consist of, Commander?"

"We're in charge of all the communications that flow in and out of the District and anything unusual that comes up, revolutions, hurricanes, that sort of thing. Where will you be going for Christmas?"

"I hope to go to Seattle."

"Book your return flight for the twenty-ninth so you have forty-eight hours to squander on cancelled flights and terrible weather."

"I'll do that, sir, and I'll leave off a copy of my itinerary."

Douglas felt that he was coming to the end of his study of Fidel Castro and the Cuban version of implementing Communism. He needed data on the number of Cubans liquidated by the regime but he thought that in the meantime he could start studying Allende and perhaps look into President Ortega of Nicaragua. Salvador Allende was born early in the twentieth century, in 1908, and elected president of Chile in 1970. Douglas knew that there had been a coup staged by the military chiefs in 1973, one of whom was General Augusto Pinochet who became head of state. The one-day coup forced Allende to commit suicide. There are those who say that he was gunned down. Concerning these matters, Douglas wanted to find out what manner of Socialist Allende was. He had managed to get elected to the presidency and had not staged a revolution as Lenin and the Bolsheviks had. And then, how much of a Socialist-Communist program was he advocating for Chile? Would it be all-encompassing as in the case with Castro? And finally, rumors notwithstanding, could the CIA have been responsible for originating the coup that did away with Allende after his three years in office? Could the CIA have instructed the military of Chile to overthrow the elected government of Salvador Allende? Douglas doubted it, but he would delay making up his mind until he had read the material available to him.

After overthrowing the regime of Allende, the military men who took office, it was reputed, killed a fair number of Chileans. These were people of the Left, Douglas knew, but he viewed all murders for political reasons as repugnant and probably avoidable. How dangerous were these people of the Left once they were out of office? Why throw them out of helicopters, as the rumor ran, rather than forcing them into exile or denying them the right to play any part in the politics of the country? Why was the solution so often death?

Daniel Ortega was younger than Allende. He was born in 1945 and elected president of Nicaragua in 1985. He failed in his bid for re-election in 1990. Douglas was forced to conclude that Ortega was of a different breed from Stalin and Mao. If Stalin permitted elections, he would make certain to receive at least ninety-nine percent of the votes cast. Ortega was opposed by Violeta Chamorro in the election of 1990 and lost. What kind of Communist dictator is it that permits himself to lose an election? Perhaps Communism was exhausting itself, and fewer and fewer people were being captivated by the empty promises. In the Americas, the secret might be out that Communist revolutions are staged for the benefit of the plotters. Those for whom the revolution was intended, the workers and the peasants, received short rations and brutality, along with a few social benefits, admittedly. Douglas had read that health care delivered under Communism in Cuba was at least as good as the health care in the 1950s, before the Communists arrived.

Douglas could sense, as he started his inspection of Chile, that its situation would resemble Spain's. In 1931, Spain elected a Leftist government. It was not a Communist government but the leadership focused on the poverty in the country, which was more extensive than in neighboring nations. The Soviet Union had only been in place for a decade and important Communists there subscribed to the idea of world revolution. Spain spelled opportunity. The Spanish military, speaking as guardians of the nation, blocked the spread of Communism into the Iberian Peninsula. Civil war commenced over the issue in 1936, with General Francisco Franco in charge of what became known as the rebel forces.

In 1970, Salvador Allende was elected president of Chile. He was an avowed Socialist. In the election the votes were divided. Allende received but 36.2% of the total. The Chilean laws did not require that the winner in a presidential election receive at least half the vote. There was no run-off.

The Allende government was accused of not enforcing the laws. Farmers would seize land from owners, which illegal conduct would not be corrected by the government. If a law was broken that brought an advantage to the poor segment of the population, the government tended to avoid enforcement. On another matter, the government was alleged to have brought on inflation by printing scads of money. Douglas would have to look into these allegations to satisfy himself and obtain a balanced view of matters.

As with Spain, the military, billing itself as the defender of the nation's honor, orchestrated a coup to oust the government. Allende was guaranteed safe passage out of the country by plane, along with his family, in exchange for immediate, unconditional surrender. He chose to fight, and in a one-sided affair that lasted a day, 11 September 1973, he elected to take on the army. The scene was the Presidential Palace in Santiago. By mid-afternoon, Allende was dead.

Douglas had been examining Communist regimes in chronological order but in his new post he realized the advantages to studying Nicaragua before Chile. Were he to adopt that sequence, though, Douglas thought it would increase the chance of leaving out Chile altogether. It might never seem convenient. Stick with the plan, he told himself. He wanted to visit both countries and he realized that he would be sent on a tour of Nicaragua sooner or later. Perhaps Elena and he would go to Chile on their wedding trip. They had been introduced in the cathedral, had one dinner date, and had exchanged letters, photographs, and telephone conversations. That was the extent of it, yet he found himself imagining a wedding trip. It startled him that he could make so much progress on his own based on only a few experiences. Perhaps Elena was contributing with her interest.

Douglas would not forget the Admiral's request for the definition of a Marxist-Leninist. He had the Admiral's permission to work on the assignment in his office. It was not a simple task because the Leninist part was ill-defined. It would be easy enough to write an excerpt from the Communist Manifesto to locate Marx's contributions.

Douglas purchased his round trip ticket to Seattle on-line and printed an extra copy of his itinerary for Commander Sullivan. The arrangements gave him six complete days in Seattle. Elena would be home from work for a few of those days, Christmas Day at least.

Douglas' mother met him in Baggage Claim at SeaTac. "In the future, you shouldn't come, Mom. I can take the bus and you can meet me downtown," he said.

"I wasn't busy. Frank went to work, as usual. And anyway I enjoy driving by Boeing Field to see what's on the runway there."

When they were in the car, Amelia moved right to the topic of Elena. "We see her at church. She tells me you talk on the phone Monday nights."

"We don't have a great deal to talk about as the history between us is short," Douglas said.

"I suppose her positive outlook and good humor come through," Amelia said. Douglas thought that his mother was on a fishing expedition. "You're right. We both put on our best manners for those conversations. It wouldn't do to say something upsetting. It's so difficult to right a wrong that's been committed over the phone."

"I hope it's in your schedule to break away after dinner tonight. Frank will be at home promptly. He wants to see you, of course."

"As I do him," Douglas said.

"With no children of his own, he's taken up our family. My grandchildren have started calling him 'Grandpa,' which he enjoys enormously. He refers to them collectively as 'the grandchildren.' Soon enough it will be 'our grandchildren.' I'm so glad for all of us."

Frank left work at closing time. The three of them assembled around the table in the living room with the view of the Bay. Frank was interested in Douglas' reading accomplishments and in Southern Florida, which he had not visited. "It's never been on my way to any place I was headed for and I never considered it a destination, so I've not been," Frank said. Douglas told them about the city of Miami and surrounding places such as Palm Beach. He went into the Latino atmosphere that pervaded the area. He had no report on Key West. He knew he was saving that part of the state for Elena. He described his work, leaving out the sensitive aspects.

"Of course Elena talks about you every Sunday. Wants any details she doesn't have," Frank said.

"I would be the topic you have in common. You wouldn't want to talk to her about the weather," Douglas answered.

"Is she expecting you this evening?" Frank asked.

"Yes. Why don't I call her at her work and firm up the time?"

Douglas had rehearsed the drive several times in his mind and he made no mistakes on the turns to take. Elena wore a suit and Douglas assumed that she had not changed on coming home. They embraced and kissed and Douglas felt slightly embarrassed that he and Elena had seen so little of one another and yet were behaving as a couple who had been together for a year.

"Did you bring a uniform?" she asked.

"Yes. Blues. I want you to see me wearing two-and-a-half stripes."

"I'm so pleased. Men look their best in a tuxedo but the naval uniform runs a close second."

Douglas knew he was searching for the correct tone to launch their conversation. He guessed Elena was doing the same. She asked, "What would you enjoy doing while you are here?"

"One of each: movie, play, opera, dinner and concert," he answered.

"That makes five. We have six nights. Tomorrow I could cook dinner for us. Would that be acceptable?"

"Wonderful, but I expect there will be one night at home with the entire family. You will be on display. Do you object to that?"

"No, of course not. You're saying, 'Well, here she is. Let me know what you think.' It's a challenge for any woman to be the only stranger in the room. But I want to win them all over."

They were sitting on the sofa. He leaned over and kissed her. In no time they were in each other's arms. After a few moments, Douglas held Elena a short distance away from him. He said, "This is madness, very enjoyable madness but madness nonetheless. We haven't scratched the surface but we're acting like people who have known each other forever."

"Don't think I haven't been through the whole matter many times, particularly how we should act toward one another," Elena said.

"The trouble comes from distance. We can be intimate over the phone and in our letters, but it's difficult to translate that to the appropriate acts face to face," Douglas said.

"As you indicate, it's the distance. If you lived and worked in Seattle we could proceed at a leisurely pace, but as it is we have accomplished more per encounter than the average couple."

"You're telling me. We've left the average couple in the dust. Have you concluded anything?" Douglas asked.

"Do you suppose these difficulties happen mostly in the military?" Elena asked.

"I've seen plenty of it," Douglas answered. He was thinking of Joanne, his second flame in Hawaii, who deserved far better, left by her husband, the chief petty officer. "In fact, I've seen plenty of it," he said, repeating himself. "Two people find one another. They've both reached the stage when a serious commitment is called for. They know they have to cut short the slow-paced experimentation others go through."

"We might try to break down a few barriers during your stay. At least go to new places in conversation."

They had moved a foot apart. His arms were around her. He brought her close to him. They kissed and then started talking about the work they were doing, and about their hobbies. Douglas told Elena about his interest in reading on the introduction of Communism into various countries. She asked, "Where did that interest come from?"

Douglas thought for a moment then said, "I think left-leaning women made me ask myself why that particular form of government could hold any interest except for the very few who were at the top."

"That's our topic of conversation for dinner tomorrow night. We may as well know one another's leanings -- get that out of the way."

"Will this be painful?" Douglas asked.

"It promises to be mildly disturbing," Elena answered. "There is a political center. I'll guess you're a little to the right of it and I'm a little to the left."

As Douglas drove home he thought about the desirability of their becoming lovers. It might be awkward to have it happen on the last night they were together. Best plan to have it happen on the day previous. It would be a Sunday and they could make a late afternoon of it. He knew most everything there was to know about Elena in these matters. She had sent him the photograph wearing a bikini. There were no mysteries about her body. He had held her closely and they had joined their bodies together when saying goodnight in her apartment. The remaining piece was her attitude. Would she be stand-offish? Or would she consider being in bed together a natural and normal expression of their feelings? He was certain that he would make the event happen before flying east.

Within a minute of six-thirty the following evening, Douglas rang Elena's door bell. She asked him in, wearing a slight smile, as though nothing were out of the ordinary. She was wearing a white robe buttoned over a white nightgown. Douglas thought first that she had purchased the combination for a trousseau and wedding trip that never materialized. Then he thought she might have come up with this outfit in anticipation of his visit. He guessed she would tell him if she felt a need.

They kissed and then she said, "The dinner is prepared and in the refrigerator."

He studied her for a minute and said, "That's a very fetching outfit you're wearing. I hope it doesn't mean you're exhausted from work."

"No. In fact, we're tearing down a barrier before dinner." He followed her into her bedroom. The lights were on and Douglas knew she had left them on for a reason. He admitted that he was surprised by the direction the evening was taking, although intrigued by it. She removed her robe. Douglas could see that she wore only a nightgown.

She woke him gently about an hour later and said, "Time for me to put supper on the table." She dressed in front of him in the semi-darkness, putting on slacks, a blouse and sweater. He reached up for her and pulled her down. "I love you, Elena. That's the emotion, none other."

"It's the perfect thing to say, Douglas. We can say plenty more on that subject later. Time to get up, get dressed and let me feed you and give you drink. Come open the bottle."

It took no time to steer the conversation to an examination of their political leanings. Douglas said, "I think we could vote for many of the same people, although for different reasons."

"How so?" she asked.

"We might want the same results but think of different ways of paying for it."

"The only way to pay for anything is through taxes, I think," Elena said.

"Yes, but the tax code can take many forms and the size of the programs can vary," Douglas answered. "I'm against all the spending we do. We need to cut back and balance the budget. Of course, that reduces the size of the social programs that can be delivered."

"You know, I'm a safety net person," Elena answered. "Perhaps I'm willing to pay for a bigger one than you are."

"Paid for by increased taxes on you?" Douglas asked.

"Yes. Tax us a bit more. Spread it around to those in need. I can live on less than I take home. If we all gave a little more we could help the homeless, the unemployed, the uninsured, you name it. We could even fix the roads and bridges."

"I think you've isolated the difference between us. It's not insurmountable," Douglas said. "I have to admit that I have a built-in problem being a conservative as I'm completely supported by our taxpayers. The navy's bases, ships, planes, salaries, everything, comes from the generosity of American citizens."

They changed the topic to Douglas' interest in Communism. He gave Elena a résumé of what he had learned so far and told her that he had a few more countries to read up on before finishing.

Elena was silent. She studied Douglas' face and hands. "You're a nice-looking man," she said.

"My desire for you is rekindled, Elena. Do you think the dinner did that?"

"We'll never know." She reached for his hand and said, "The dishes can wait."

They walked hand in hand to her bedroom. He sat on the foot of the bed and brought her to him and held her close. She was still standing. He thought about how much their relationship had changed since he had arrived a few hours previously. She had taken the initiative three days before he had planned to. Douglas thought she was making several statements. The first was that she was his. He could assume correctly that she wanted to give herself to him. Second, that he fit the bill. He was the type of man she had been looking for. And third, that she wanted to change her life and change it through him. Were they a combination that sought out marriage?

He pulled her gently onto the bed and started to undress her. He said, "I watched closely when you were dressing and I'm just doing the reverse." He was careful and affectionate and felt fortunate to be close to her.

It was the following morning. Douglas thought he could spend most of the day profitably re-reading the *Communist Manifesto* and starting on his homework for Admiral Stevens. He borrowed Frank's copy and dove in. When he was through he thought about his presentation. This was not a formal assignment and he concluded that he could write his reflections without creating a document that started with To, From, and Subject. These were his introductory remarks:

Communism came to Russia, China and Cuba by force. It was held in place in Eastern Europe by the Soviet Army. When the opportunities came to rid themselves of the Communist system, people availed themselves and moved on to forms of government more democratic. Communist governments (Socialist, if you wish) were installed by vote in Chile (1970) and Nicaragua (1985). The first was overthrown by the military. We will never know whether it would have survived a second election. Nicaraguans voted out Daniel Ortega's regime in 1990.

The element of force reduces the credibility of any government. That element must start with the belief on the part of leaders that they, the few of them, know better than the mass of people what's good for the nation. They feel that their vision for the future of their country is correct and people who do not agree with them will be dealt with appropriately. It's interesting, by contrast, that leaders in democratic societies do not have gulags, prisons, and other holding pens for those of their citizens who want to express an opinion about the system they are living under. All are free to vote their preference on Election Day. The unwillingness of dictators to allow their citizens free access to regularly scheduled elections undermines any legitimacy the dictators might claim.

The class system, which Communists spend a great deal of time writing and speaking about, has lost its authority in Capitalistic, Democratic societies. Vast numbers of individuals in all fields of endeavor have risen in one lifetime from humble beginnings to the top, all because of their merit. These individuals are not held back by class actions. The old landed aristocracy has been replaced in the modern world by highly educated, ambitious, capable individuals. There is no need for class warfare. The matter has taken care of itself because industrial and technical societies offer unlimited opportunities in many fields. Communism has made the fatal error (fatal to many millions) in assuming that the bourgeoisie had to be destroyed so that it no longer would be there to press its collective foot on the necks of the proletariat. Those same Communist leaders had only to bring education, opportunity and the vote to those they called the oppressed masses. They could have achieved the results they hoped for speedily and without terror.

If indeed Communists wished to destroy the bourgeoisie so that their wealth could be distributed to workers and peasants, they found out too late that when the bourgeoisie was destroyed their wealth vanished with them. Wealth is crated and renewed by industrious individuals who can operate enterprises profitably. When operators of enterprises vanish, their enterprises vanish. Communists cannot admit that individuals left to their own devices can generate wealth. They cannot admit that the state is often an impediment to the creation of wealth.

Douglas stopped at that point. He would suggest to the Admiral that he read the *Manifesto* to draw his own conclusions. Lenin interpreted Marx as he expressed himself in *Das Kapital*. Lenin became a theoretician. Of Lenin's actions, Douglas had the following to say.

It appears that Marx's principal belief had to do with this question: who owned the profits stored in manufactured goods? Marx maintained that all the value in manufactured goods belonged to the workers who had contributed their labor. The managers, this bourgeois element, were simply skimming off as much of the profit as they could. The bourgeoisie, the capitalists, owned the machinery used to produce goods. They owned real estate and the means of transportation and all the systems of trade. Little wonder that they could demand a share of the profits. Marx's solution was to eliminate private property -- eliminate the bourgeoisie and place their property in the hands of the state. Now all the profits would be available for distribution to the proletariat.

There are two obvious errors in Marx's thinking. First, not to recognize that the state consumed all the profits that the leadership had hoped to distribute to the workers and the peasants, leaving nothing for those whom the revolution was intended to benefit. Second, not understanding that without the motivation that comes from the opportunity to enrich one's self, the production from all levels of society is diminished. The mystery is why those Communist leaders who came after Stalin and Mao wasted their time building a society that would fail.

Marx misjudged also. He held that societies would progress through Capitalism before reaching Socialism. He maintained that Socialism was the logical resting place for governments and that they could get there by being victims of the excesses of Capitalism. The contrary has proved to be the case. Capitalistic countries reach a stable state because the wealth created is for distribution among all classes to enjoy and because Capitalism comes with constitutional governments and universal access to the voting booth.

Lenin may have believed Marx concerning the detour through capitalism. Lenin, who had been plotting revolution all his adult life, was too impatient to wait for Russia to pass through several decades of Capitalism before his chances came to foment a revolution with himself at the head of it.

As proof, Lenin reverted to an aspect of Capitalism when his revolution brought starvation to Russia. He allowed peasants to sell their products freely into the market and retain those profits not taxed away. This reversion to Capitalism ended the famine within two years. Stalin, being a more severe Communist than Lenin, collectivized the farms and killed off many kulaks (excessively wealthy peasants).

Douglas' plan was to hand these few words to Admiral Stevens and at the same time to suggest that he read both texts, the *Manifesto* certainly in full and *Das Kapital* selectively. If the Admiral wanted more details he would ask for them.

Elena worked three of the complete days that were available to them. She did not take off more time as she was saving up for her trip to Miami. "Do you still want me to come?" she asked one evening.

"Of course, I do. If we hit the weather right, we can swim in the ocean and you can return with a tan."

The evening after Christmas, on Boxing Day, the family gathered as they always did. Neckties were worn by the men and fancy clothes by the women and children. Elena wore a dress with subdued red and green colors. The dress had no sleeves and Elena compensated by wearing a white silk blouse under it. It had a fancy collar that contrasted with the black hair, which she wore in one long braid. Douglas noted that she gave ample time to the children, speaking to them individually. As promised, Douglas wore his blues with two-and-a-half stripes freshly sewn on. He had collected a few ribbons but did not wear them on the basis that the Military had become ribbon-happy. He was careful to change out of his uniform before driving Elena home. As an explanation he told her that he couldn't change a tire with his uniform on. In fact, in the event of an unforeseen accident, he did not wish to have his name and rank in the newspaper, a situation that he would report to headquarters even though it may not have been called for.

It appeared to Douglas that he and Elena did not need to court any longer. It was established, he thought, that there were no barriers to surmount. Both wanted to live in the company of the other. The conversational exchanges were easy. They enjoyed exploring points of view to determine where they differed. They relished the intimate moments. They adjusted their schedules to leave unhurried time.

Douglas thought he could have a successful marriage with Caroline, Joanne or Elena. The results would vary, of course. But Elena was in front of him. He couldn't let her get away. If they didn't succeed in making it to the altar they would both be bruised and it might take quite some time for the black and blue marks to disappear. He concluded that he had to bring up the topic for discussion before leaving. There might be such an arrangement as a partial, conditional engagement. He felt that if he married Elena tomorrow they could circumvent the problems that would arise. The major one was the matter of career. Would he leave the navy and bank on being able to find work in a new field or would she leave her company and move to Miami? It would be wise to get to the heart of the matter to settle that important issue.

They were in her living room, drinking coffee on returning to her apartment after seeing a play. "Fewer than forty-eight hours," he said.

"And you'll be on the plane."

"Yes, and I don't see you until I pick you up at the airport in Miami. That's five weeks from now."

"I hope it goes quickly," Elena said.

"Me too. I'm surprised that in such a short time you've come to occupy me completely."

"If you mean that I'm on your mind a fair amount of time, then I can claim the same condition. I enjoy it, having you to think about," Elena said.

"What would happen if I told you that you couldn't get away, that you had to be the center of my life?" Douglas asked.

"It's thought provoking. For that to happen we would be required to make two moves, one concerning an address and the other, our marital status."

"The marital status is simpler than the change of address, I think," Douglas said.

"I hope I can welcome change," Elena said. "I've been in and around this neighborhood all my life. Of course I've thought of this eventuality. I can't tell you how proud of you and your naval career I am. You've expressed some misgivings about promotions coming your way but I think every lieutenant commander must have those moments of uncertainty."

"I suppose so, and not much one can do about it," Douglas said.

"You've been very flattering to me, but you've never told me I'm clever," Elena said.

"There's something slightly derogatory about that adjective," Douglas said.

"You're competing with all the other lieutenant commanders. I'd like to think that I'm clever enough to bring you a few advantages."

"I'm certain you would. Which brings up the matter of careers. For the privilege of living with you, I'm prepared to give up the navy and return to the Northwest," Douglas said.

"Not on your life," Elena answered. "My talents are transferable. I can do research and teach in Florida. There's really nothing to discuss."

Douglas had not expected that answer. He thought for a moment and asked, "Will you marry me, Elena?"

"Yes, I will, with pleasure." They kissed before Elena said, "We could marry in Miami. We can tell them later. I'll come back, give up my job, close my apartment, and see how fast I can get back to my husband." Douglas surmised she had evaluated all the possibilities previously.

Douglas realized the advantage to him of marrying in Miami, an elopement of sorts. He would not be required to make another trip across the country and attend the functions that their families would insist upon. There were different advantages for Elena. Before she gave notice at her company, and before she took steps to dismantle her apartment and pack that part of her life she would be taking to Miami, she would be married. Should either get cold feet, it would be too late.

After Elena had accepted his proposal she held his hands and said a few things that he thought he would remember the balance of his life -- not the exact words, but the sense of them.

"When I shook your hand at the cathedral, that first time, I experienced a marvelous sensation. I wanted to take the other hand as well. The hand I was holding was firm, strong and flexible. That describes you. They were the hands I wanted to hold on a walk. They were the hands I wanted giving me a few directions. I'm not certain what that means. They were the hands I wanted exploring and caressing my body. That I understand. I'm glad you happened when you did. I might not have been able to wait much longer."

In their last half-hour together, Elena did her best to sum up her feelings. "I recall that there were men in my earlier life. Some were a better fit than others. I was waiting for you; I suppose worried that you might not exist. At the family gathering I felt my life come together. I can't describe it better than that. To tell you I love you is the smallest part. I'll act it out day by day living with you."

"I feel badly that we only had a short visit with your parents," Douglas said. "We owe them and the balance of your family and friends the chance to see us together for more than a fleeting moment."

"Why don't we arrange a vacation in the Northwest?" Elena said. Five weeks would pass and they would be together again in Miami.

MORE ON ELENA

PART 13:

WEATHER WAS NOT an impediment. Douglas arrived in Miami on schedule two days before New Year's Day. He reached Elena at home for a brief talk, just to say that he had made it to the apartment and that he missed her a great deal. In the first week of January, as well as being Commander Sullivan's assistant duty officer, Douglas telephoned the Cuban-American organizations whom he had contacted previously and who had sent him materials through the mails. He explained that the information they had sent him did not contain the figure that he was interested in: the number of Cubans that had been killed by the Castro regime since 1959. The three individuals to whom he spoke gave him approximately the same answer, to the effect that the figure was unknown. Perhaps when the Castro regime fell, the records would be opened and data would become available. In the meantime, those living outside Cuba, and most living on the Island, would be forced to rely on educated guesses. One individual did venture a number: a half-million deaths attributable to Castro's government. He asked that his organization not be identified and he said that he would deny taking part in this conversation if he were quoted. He noted that the causes were firing squads, and deaths due to malnourishment and neglect while in prison. To that he added those who perished at sea when their vessels sank or when they were gunned down from the sea or the air as they attempted to flee. The speaker made the point that his half-million estimate covered several decades. He said also that other individuals in the field had their own estimates.

Douglas condensed this data into a short paragraph which he forwarded to Admiral Stevens. The Admiral had not asked for this information but Douglas knew from the Admiral's questions that he would welcome having it.

Douglas did note that the organizations he spoke to kept track of political prisoners currently incarcerated. They were known by name, political crime, length of sentence, location of prison, and general condition. Douglas surmised that publicizing these prisoners individually gave them notoriety that humanitarian organizations could use to shorten their sentences or to ameliorate their situations in another fashion.

The week following his stint as duty officer, Douglas told the Admiral about his wedding plans. "Sir, at dinner, Mrs. Stevens asked me if there was a special person in my life and I indicated there was. Her name is Elena Kelly. She's coming to Miami and we plan to marry on the first Saturday in February."

"Well, that's good news, Nielsen. I'll tell Mrs. Stevens about it."

"Should you and Mrs. Stevens have a free moment when Elena is here, I'd like it very much if you would meet her."

"I think that can be arranged. Who will be your best man?"

"I'll have to ask one of the officers I've met recently."

"Did you and Sullivan get along well?"

"Yes Sir, we did."

"Well, there's your man, then. If your Elena isn't arriving with a maid or matron of honor you might think of Sullivan's wife, Susan. Great, really a great woman." The Admiral continued. "Will you be asking for time off?"

"No, Sir. We'll be married that Saturday then for Elena it's back to Seattle to give notice at her company and pack up her things. She could return in three weeks."

"Your next assignment will be Venezuela. There are obvious indications that portions of Columbia's drug production flow through there on their way here and to Europe. If we set it for mid-February your Elena will not be rushed to get back."

Douglas could not tell whether the Admiral had set the date based on Elena's schedule. In any event, it would give Elena more time to break down her apartment and pack the items she would ship. In a brief conversation the day after his proposal of marriage she suggested that they find a larger apartment and that her furniture should be shipped. A larger apartment in the building he was occupying might be a satisfactory solution, she said.

For his study of Chile, Douglas started by reading Isabel Allende's, *My Invented Country: A Nostalgic Tour of Chile*. Douglas had not read any of the works by this celebrated author and was glad to study this text written in the first person. The author was born in Peru and lived in Chile, Venezuela and the United States. Isabel Allende wrote that Salvador Allende and her father were cousins. If they were first cousins and therefore of the same generation, then Isabel Allende would be a first cousin once removed from the Chilean president. She writes at length about the period of Allende's presidency. Douglas knew that he should corroborate Isabel Allende's opinions by finding similar conclusions in other texts.

Allende won 36.2% of the vote in the presidential election of 1970. According to the constitution of Chile, the senate must validate the election by declaring a winner. Isabel Allende wrote that the CIA attempted to alter the vote (deny Allende the presidency) by bribing Chilean senators. No names or amounts are given. The attempt, actual or fictional, failed and Allende took office. Douglas had only heard in the past that the CIA had involved itself, but now he had a few details. Isabel Allende went on to report that the plot (fomented by the CIA? Douglas did not know) called for a second election later in 1970 in which there would be but two candidates. Surely Allende would lose this second election between two candidates, he being one and a conservative the other. As far as Douglas could tell, such a second election was blocked by the constitution of Chile.

Allende had run unsuccessfully for president previously. He did not organize a coup d'état to take over the country. As Socialists go, he was not from the same mold as Lenin. He did not stage a revolution but came to power by legal means. He nationalized private enterprises, banks and copper mines, some owned by North American interests. Douglas could not tell whether all private property went to the state, as was the case in the Soviet Union. Douglas would conduct his research until he knew the answers to the following questions: how committed a Socialist was Allende; the reasons that the Chilean military had used in order to force Allende from office in 1973; and the level of brutality, indeed if there was any brutality, imposed on the citizens by the Allende regime.

Douglas did not discount the influence of Castro on the policy makers in the United States. Castro had been in power eleven years when Allende took office. Most American politicians were ready to expend considerable effort and some treasure to prevent Communist takeovers in this hemisphere. The Chilean victory by parties of the Left could have been viewed as the first of many. A Communist South America, in the view of American officials, spelled disaster for Central and North America. Communism could creep north. With policy makers in Washington holding those points of view, there was ample reason to appreciate their intolerance of Communists or Socialists, elected or not.

Douglas picked up the phone. He recognized Elena's voice immediately. "Do you still want me to come?" she asked.

They had been separated for two weeks or so and spoken over the phone five or six times.

"Of course," Douglas answered. "And by the way, you've asked that question before. What's up?"

"My knees shake a lot."

"You gave notice at work, didn't you?"

"Not quite yet. I'll do it tomorrow." She paused for a moment. "We hardly know one another."

"Let me tell you where I stand on that. We want to be together, I think that's correct. The three thousand miles of separation can only be bridged with marriage. I think we both concluded as much."

"You'll have to supply courage for both of us," Elena said.

"I have a best man and his wife is ready to be your maid of honor -- good people. I've signed up the assistant at the church I attend, looked into a license and been by a jeweler. I have the rings picked out."

"You have no hesitancy?" Elena asked.

"No, none. I'm looking forward to being married to you and living together."

"The closets are full, as is every dresser drawer, every shelf, and every possible storage place in the kitchen. It's overwhelming," Elena said.

"I wish I were there to help you. Can you hire a moving firm and simply supervise?"

It was the first time Elena had shown any hesitancy. Douglas thought she had been sure of herself during their time together at Christmas. She had mentioned other men in her life and Douglas assumed that they were near-misses. And he assumed as well that she wanted to marry and get past the times of uncertainty that young people go through. He felt that by marrying Elena they could move to the next stage of life, from experimenters to being part of a family unit, and soon enough parents.

Douglas wondered about his mother and the balance of the family. They all knew that he and Elena had just met, yet none suggested that they move slowly. "It's time he married. She's a fine woman. Let it happen. We want him married." Douglas could hear various ones of them repeating these words. He went back to a saying he had heard long ago. "Marry in haste. Repent at leisure." He wondered who had uttered these words first and the experiences that brought them on. He could not recall a source. Perhaps the saying had become a proverb. He telephoned back in a few minutes and suggested to Elena that they talk every evening. "You can't lose your nerve. We're too good together," he said as he signed off.

The meeting went on longer than Douglas had expected. Admiral Stevens, a captain, a commander and he were reviewing the situation in the Caribbean, paying attention to the marine traffic. Douglas would glance at his watch from time to time. He had explained to Elena that he might be late fetching her.

When the meeting broke up, Douglas excused himself and drove to the airport, just over the speed limit. He found a parking place and made his way to the luminous panel that would tell him whether her plane had landed.

He saw her in the middle distance. She was concentrating on finding her bags on the carousel. The black hair was up in a bun. She was wearing a dark blue pant suit and Douglas guessed that she had not calculated on the eighty degree weather in Miami. He thought she would end up carrying her jacket to the car. She had held herself together during the nightly telephone conversations, but not by a wide margin. "I should be a happy person, off to marry into the navy and start a new life. Instead I'm apprehensive." That was her report on one occasion. He would ask her what she had to be apprehensive about and she would answer that everything would be new. The explanation came in various forms but that was the gist of it.

He came up behind her. "Elena," he said softly. She spun around and threw her arms around his neck. They hugged for a moment and then kissed. After the expected questions about her condition and the flight, she asked, "It's beach weather. Can you take me to the ocean?" There were two suitcases. Douglas pointed to the larger and asked, "Wedding dress?" She looked at him and said, "No, bikini collection."

When they made it to his apartment and he had lugged her baggage up a flight of stairs, they entered and she examined the rooms, starting with the bedroom, commenting on the twin beds. "I think it's an inconvenient arrangement," she said. He shrugged. "With furnished apartments you take what they give you."

"I want to show you the wedding dress," Elena said as she opened the larger suitcase. It was made of off-white material, slightly peach-colored. The jacket had three buttons down the front. "Do you wear a blouse under this?" he asked.

"No, it's the severe look. I think you'll like it. How do you feel about my wearing the outfit occasionally after we're married?"

"Sounds wonderful. Brings back the moment, they say."

She showed him the high-heeled shoes that went with the suit. He thought the shoes were covered with nearly the same material, if not exactly the same material as the suit was made from. She unpacked both suitcases. Douglas had made room in a closet and cleaned out two drawers in a dresser.

When Elena came into the small living room, she was wearing shorts, a T-shirt, and sneakers. "Do you think you can take me to the beach?" she asked.

They drove toward the water, he pointing out a few features on the way. They walked along the water's edge in bare feet. "Warm enough for a swim tomorrow," he said. They outlined the necessary duties to tend to, such as rings and a marriage license. "Tomorrow, we're meeting the Sullivans, who, as you know, are standing up for us. Late Friday afternoon rehearsal at church followed by dinner at the officers' club. I would call it the smallest rehearsal dinner on record. The Admiral knows you will be there and he and his wife may put in an appearance to meet you. Saturday, the main event. We'll go out afterwards. I've chosen a place. Sunday morning some of your stuff gets packed but you can leave everything you won't need. Then it's off to the airport."

"All thought through," Elena said. "I'm glad you've been in charge. I might have dithered."

When they returned to his apartment, Elena went into the kitchen. "White wine in the refrigerator?" she asked. "Yes. Uncorked but otherwise not tampered with. Glasses on the counter, as you can see," he answered.

She came out of the kitchen and handed him a glass and reached up to undo the top two buttons of his shirt. "Nature, or God, or some intelligent spirit, invented this means of communicating between two people. It's been bumpy for a while but now it feels as though I'm on sound footing. That's the message I'm conveying."

"When you started showing uncertainty over the phone I thought it was just a matter of being together and everything would right itself," Douglas said.

She reached over and undid another button on his shirt

"Your T-shirt has no buttons," he said.

"I'll put my hands in the air and you can pull the T-shirt up over my head," she said.

"In the bedroom?" he asked.

"No. Where ever. The couch, the floor. Nice rug. Why don't you pull the shades?"

A few hours later, they were in a restaurant finishing dinner and drinking coffee. She was quiet for a moment, reflecting. "You know, I've been the one with the willies. Usually it's the man. I'm settled now. Saturday afternoon we'll be an old married couple. Just think of that!"

"I am thinking of that. You're so beautiful, by the way," he said. He was examining the black hair, contrasting it with the white skin. He wondered about the color of her skin when exposed to the sun. She had not worn a hat nor applied lotion when on the beach these last two days.

Elena was holding her coffee cup in both hands, looking into the coffee as she gathered her thoughts. "There's more that I want to say about my behavior. When I took you to bed in my apartment, it was a matter of getting beyond something. I thought I could make it easy for us. I don't know that I did. I didn't let you develop the moment. I didn't let you participate the way you might have wanted to. I feel I should apologize for all that."

"We managed to get it done, Elena."

"And earlier this evening, it was the same performance. I didn't want bedtime to arrive and face a forced effort. I want to moment to be spontaneous. That must be why I move early and turn the moment into a farce, perhaps a circus. Maybe the word I'm looking for is mockery. I wish I could let you take the initiative."

"Don't be too hard on yourself. These are not easy times for either of us," Douglas said. "My sense of it is that our relationship will flow easily with time."

"I hope you're right. Let's see what a few months of marriage bring us."

The week that Elena spent in Miami went off as planned. When she was with other people, her hesitations faded. She charmed people easily by engaging them in direct conversation. She would comment on their observations and pleasantries, answer their questions, and limit herself to talking half as much as the people she was with. Douglas felt proud of having won a woman at once lovely and intelligent. She would cut short her answers to questions and ask twice as many questions as the questioners had asked her. People who met her wanted to know whether she would pursue her career, to which she said that her skills and knowledge were in demand and that she was thinking of starting by canvassing the local universities.

Admiral and Mrs. Stevens appeared at the officers' club the night prior to the marriage ceremony. It was indeed a small rehearsal dinner. Douglas introduced them to Elena. The Admiral said, "We won't be able to call you Miss Kelly much longer. When you return from Seattle to stay with us, you'll find my wife to be the other half of this operation. I want you to get to know one another."

Mrs. Stevens asked, "How long have you been engaged?"

"All of eight weeks, Mrs. Stevens. That is, eight weeks since we met. I don't know when we became engaged."

"That is fast, but why so fast?"

"We didn't discuss it beyond saying that it was quick. Speaking for myself, it was evident that we wanted to be attached. I didn't want to lose him. Maybe Douglas has another reason."

"The long engagements are no better indication of survival than the short engagements," the Admiral added.

The wedding went off as planned. Without changing clothes, Elena and Douglas went off to the restaurant he had chosen. He had invited the Sullivans to make it a party of four. They ended with champagne and cake. The uneaten portion of the cake was boxed for the trip to Seattle. "My family will want it," Elena said.

Douglas thought his wife had got past her uncertainties. She seemed to lead the conversations, finding humorous passages, interesting observations, and, as he had noticed, the instinct and ability to feature the ideas of those to whom she was speaking. He knew that he, or rather his mother, had found an outstanding mate.

The librarian on the reference desk, the impossibly young-looking grandmother named Helen, found a collection of papers written by learned political scientists. They were contained in a book titled, *Development and Cultural Change: Cross-Cultural Perspectives.* It was edited by Ilpyong J. Kim. Because it was published in 1986, the two articles on Chile had the advantage of being written toward the end of the Pinochet regime in Chile, close to the events being discussed. The first article was titled, *Development Strategies in Chile, 1964-1983: The Lessons of Failure.* It was written by Paul E. Sigmund, who was at the time, and may still be, a professor at Princeton.

In the article, the economic strategies discussed cover the years 1964-1970, when Eduardo Frei was president of Chile; the years 1970 – 1973, when Salvador Allende was in office; and the years 1973-1983, during the first two-thirds of General Pinochet's tenure.

It struck Douglas right away that Chile suffered from an imbalance in the distribution of wealth. It didn't matter that there were very rich people. It did matter that there were large numbers of poor people. In any country, if one attempts to distribute the wealth of the rich, there isn't enough wealth to bring up the level of the poor. The idea, Douglas thought, was to leave the rich alone while creating new wealth to be owned by the poor. The rich, most of them, do not sit on their money.

They invest much of it to build larger empires than they already have. Taking the wealth away from the rich and distributing it to the poor in a society destroys the wealth-producing enterprises that the rich own and operate. Leave the rich alone, that was Douglas' instinct. Douglas thought that in the United States education was available to those who understood its value, and opportunities abounded for those who wished to put to use the talents learned at school. In poor countries, education was not as readily available, nor were opportunities. For various reasons, some social and other economic, opportunity was not available to the poor on many occasions. Douglas was thinking of young Africans who had migrated, perhaps illegally, to Europe.

Literacy was high in Chile but opportunity to educate young people in professional schools was lacking. The country had a long tradition of democracy, which suggested to Douglas that the missing link, the element that kept Chileans from creating wealth and thereby eliminating poverty, would be difficult to isolate. He would have to wait until he visited Chile on his wedding trip with Elena to discuss the point with willing Chileans. Douglas didn't think that confiscating land from large landowners and distributing it to the poor was the solution. That plan may help 100,000 fortunate peasant-farmers but it would do nothing for the remaining millions of poor people.

A large segment of Chile's population consisted of poor peasants. Many in search of work had migrated to Santiago, the capital, bringing the population of the city to about five million individuals, a quarter of the country's total.

Allende, a declared Socialist, pitched his campaign of 1970 to the poor workers and peasants. He would abolish Capitalism. As Dr. Sigmund wrote, Allende would, "destroy large land holdings, take over banks and credit, and nationalize mines and industries." One of the principal targets was Chile's copper mines, owned principally by U.S. interests.

The article immediately following Dr. Sigmund's was a commentary on Sigmund's, written by Dr. Takao Fukuchi at the University of Tokyo. In it, Fukuchi identifies the errors in judgment made by the politicians of Latin America as they attempt to solve the problems into which their countries have become ensnared. If politicians make the same errors in country after country, irrespective of the continent where the country is located, then, as Douglas concluded, the economic model they selected was wrong. Certainly Communism was wrong. It had never solved the problem of poverty. Wide-open Capitalism can be followed in advanced societies where there are few poor people but wide-open Capitalism may not work in developing countries. Perhaps a limited form of Capitalism was the correct model. Douglas knew he was not a student of these matters but it occurred to him as he read Dr. Fukuchi's article that he had seen this litany of errors played out several times in the past.

The story went like this: a country with a sizable segment of poor people turns to the International Monetary Fund (IMF) to borrow money in order to execute a plan of industrialization. The plan is not carried out properly and unforeseen difficulties arise so that targets are not met. The loan from the IMF is in dollars and the Fund expects to be repaid in dollars. The country receiving the loan may inflate its currency (print more money than is warranted by the hard currency reserves that it holds) in order to pay for social programs that it finds desirable. The inflation destroys the value of the local currency along with many of the country's savings. Not necessarily because of the inflation, the country finds that it cannot export in sufficient volume to earn the dollars needed to meet its schedule of payments at the IMF. The country defaults and asks the IMF to reschedule its loan.

Douglas had read this scenario several times and he wondered why politicians in various countries did not try a new model that had a chance of success. No need to follow the path to certain failure.

As he speculated about this field of international development, about which he knew precious little, Douglas wondered if earlier in life, at a university, he could have mastered the intricacies of all the data and theories that had to be dealt with to arrive at valid conclusions. At the same time he wondered whether the current practitioners in the field of international development could have become effective naval officers. The talents at work were markedly different.

Douglas felt strongly that countries who wished to become richer should take some of the following steps. The first would be to examine the growth of their population. If the population is growing too rapidly then any increase in national wealth must be divided by that many more people, negating results. Mexico came to Douglas' mind. About ten million Mexicans had migrated north over twenty years. It seemed obvious to Douglas that Mexico was creating babies faster that it was creating jobs. If the country could have created ten million more jobs than it did over those twenty years, the young people, instead of migrating north, could have remained in their own culture.

Another step would be to examine the food supply. Is the country self-sufficient? Can it feed itself? A third step would be to evaluate the ability to export. Are there natural resources, manufactured goods and agricultural products that could find markets abroad in order to earn foreign exchange? A country must export in order to import, unless it is willing to be owned by foreign interests. And fourth, how will these programs be run in order to achieve the social and economic goals that a majority of the citizens agree on?

Concerning stabilizing the population, Douglas had read that the certain way to accomplish that goal was to educate the female half of the population to the same extent that the males were, so that the females enter the work force, preferably at all levels. Encourage them to be teachers, doctors, lawyers, architects and engineers. Women grow accustomed to and value their earnings, and the independence that comes with a paycheck. They postpone marriage and childbirth. The growth in population decreases. The formula has worked and continues to work wherever it is in use.

Douglas didn't list this as a step to take, along with the other four, but he thought that countries that wished to develop should stay away from borrowed money, whether it came from the IMF of from private interests abroad. Borrowed money must be repaid. When private interests abroad wish to invest in a country, there invariably will be the creation of new jobs and associated economic activity -- good news for the short run. Some of the profits from operations may be re-invested for expansion -- more good news. Sooner or later, however, there will be a call to repatriate profits to the home country. The country where the investments have been made feels colonized. Occasionally those sentiments trigger the nationalization or expropriation of assets, the later being confiscation without compensation. Yes, stay away from borrowed money. If there is foreign investment, part of the bargain must be that over time the host country is to regain ownership of the entire enterprise. Let profits remain where they are earned.

ALLENDE OF CHILE

ELENA AND DOUGLAS were in touch every evening. Neither could speak at great length. It was not in their make-up. She gave him progress reports on her accomplishments after work: selecting the pieces of furniture that were destined for the moving van. He told her that he would be on his way to Venezuela shortly, to return before she flew back to him. He had telephoned his mother and Frank and surprised them with news of the marriage. "I laid siege to your mother for thirteen months and you pull it off in eight weeks. I take my hat off to you," Frank said. Elena went to her family and started by showing them the rings on her finger. "You've only met him once, I know. Trust me, it was the correct move," Elena announced.

The librarians continued to be productive. To learn about Allende, a thin volume had been dug up. It came on loan from Occidental College in Eagle Rock, California. Eagle Rock is a small town bolted to the southwest corner of Pasadena, and therefore in Los Angeles County. The title was, *Salvador Allende: English and Spanish texts of his political platform, the program of the Popular Front, and his biography.* The text was prepared by Squirrel Publications, in Washington, D.C.

The platfom is divided into two parts, the first being "THE FOR-TY MEASURES WITH WHICH THE POPULAR GOVERN-MENT WILL BEGIN," and the second, "BASIC GOVERNMENT PROGRAM OF THE POPULAR FRONT (UNIDAD POPULAR), UNANIMOUSLY APPROVED BY ALL PARTIES SUPPORTING

THE PRESIDENTIAL CANDIDACY OF SALVADOR ALLENDE."
There was no question in Douglas' mind that these documents were
for use in the presidential campaign, and therefore were written pri-
or to the election held in the fall of 1970. The assertion that comes
through in both documents is that democratic institutions will remain
in the event of a victory by Allende. There are Communistic features
to the governing methods he advocates but this does not include the
end of Democracy, as in abolishing parliament. The forty points that
will guide a victorious Allende regime would make interesting reading,
Douglas thought. Here they are:

1. ABOLITION OF FABULOUS SALARIES.
We shall limit the high salaries earned by all trustworthy officials.
We shall end the accumulation of posts and salaries. (Advisory posts,
Directors' jobs, Representatives). We shall finish with administrative
managers and political wheeler-dealers.

2. MORE ADVISORS? NO!
Every official will be paid according to the regular scale, and none
will be paid more than that provided for in the Administrative Law.
There will be no more ADVISORS in Chile.

3. GOVERNMENT HONESTY
We shall put an end to favoritism and the skipping of grades in
the Public Administration. There will be a freeze on the mobility of
public officials. No one shall be persecuted because of his religious
or political ideas; government officials will be supervised so that they
attain efficiency, honest and good relations with the people.

4. NO MORE EXTRAVAGANT FOREIGN TRIPS.
We shall cancel all foreign travel by government officials, unless it
is indispensable for the best interests of the State.

5. NO MORE USE OF PUBLIC MONEY FOR AMUSEMENT.
Under no circumstances will official cars be used as private ones. All
available cars will be used to fill public needs, such as to transport school
children, carry the sick from remote towns, or for police business.

6. THE NATIONAL TREASURY WILL NOT PRODUCE
NEW RICH MEN.

We shall establish adequate control over the income and property of high public officials. The government will cease to be a factory for turning out new rich men.

7. EQUIRABLE PENSIONS, NOT MILLIONS.

We shall end millionaire pensions, either for members of congress or for other officials of the private or public sectors, and we shall use these resources to improve lower-income pensions.

8. EQUITABLE AND TIMELY RETIREMENT.

We will grant the right to retirement to all people past 60 years of age, who have not been able to retire because of the lack of adequate tax provision.

9. PROVIDING FOR EVERYONE.

We will include within the social security system all small and moderate-scale business men, industrialists and farmers, independent workers, craftsmen, fishermen, small-scale miners, and housewives.

10. IMMEDIATE AND TOTAL PAYMENT OF RETIREMENT AND PENSIONS.

We will readjust with one payment pensions due to Armed Forces personnel and we will see to the prompt payment of all pensions by the Social Security Service.

11. PROTECTING THE FAMILY.

We shall create a Ministry for the Protection of the Family.

12. EQUALIZING FAMILY EXEMPTIONS

We will equalize all family exemptions at the same level.

13. CHILDREN ARE BORN FOR HAPPINESS.

We will grant all children free registration, books, notebooks, and supplies in the elementary schools.

14. IMPROVEMENT IN FOOD FOR CHILDREN.

We shall serve breakfast to all elementary level children and lunch to all children, whose parents cannot provide it for them.

15. MILK FOR ALL CHILEAN CHILDREN.

We will assure half a liter of milk daily for all Chilean children.

16. MATERNITY CLINICS IN SMALL TOWNS.
We shall establish maternity clinics in all small towns.

17. TRUE VACATIONS FOR ALL STUDENTS.
The best elementary grade students, selected from all over the country, will be invited to visit the Presidential Palace in Viña del Mar.

18. CONTROL OF ALCOHOLISM.
We will fight alcoholism not through repressive measures, but through the improvement of living standards, and we shall suppress moonlighting (clandestinaje).

19. HOMES, ELECTRICITY AND DRINKING WATER FOR EVERYONE.
We shall create an emergency plan for the immediate construction of homes, and we shall guarantee a water supply by blocks of houses, and electric lights.

20. NO MORE READJUSTMENT FEES FOR CORVI (the government housing agency -- the editor)
We will cancel readjustments of dividends and debts to CORVI.

21. FIXED RATES FOR RENTS.
We will establish a maximum of 10% of family income as payment for rents and interests. Immediate suppression of the right to hold keys.

22. UNCULTIVATED LANDS, NO!
We shall turn over all uncultivated public, semi-public or municipal lands for construction.

23. TAXATION ONLY FOR MANSIONS.
We will free of taxation all homes up to a maximum of 80 square meters, where the owner lives permanently, and if it is not used as a luxury or leisure home. (80 square meters is equivalent to 861 square feet - author).

24. A TRUE AGRARIAN REFORM
We will deepen and extend Agrarian Reform in order to benefit

medium and small farmers, small landholders, middlemen, employees and suburbanites. We shall expand agricultural credit. We shall secure a market for all agricultural products.

25. MEDICAL ASSISTANCE WITHOUT RED TAPE.
We shall put an end to all bureaucratic and administrative red tape which prevents taxpayers and the unemployed from receiving adequate medical attention.

26. FREE MEDICINE IN THE HOSPITALS
We shall cancel payments for drugs and medical examinations in hospitals.

27. NO MORE FRAUDULENT DRUG PRICES.
We shall lower drastically the price of drugs by reducing import taxes on their raw materials.

28. STUDENT SCHOLARSHIPS.
We shall establish the right to scholarships for all students in good standing at elementary, intermediate, and university-level schools, in accordance with their individual family needs.

29. PHYSICAL EDUCATION AND POPULAR TOURISM.
We shall develop physical education and we shall establish recreation areas in schools and towns. Every school and town will have its own soccer field. We shall organize and promote popular tourism.

30. A NEW ECONOMY, AN END TO INFLATION.
We shall increase the manufacture of products for popular consumption, control prices, and we shall stop inflation by applying new economic measures.

31. NO MORE TIES WITH THE INTERNATIONAL MONETARY FUND.
We shall disavow all agreements with the International Monetary Fund, and we shall put an end to the aggravating devaluations of the escudo.

32. NO MORE TAXATION ON FOOD.
We shall end increases in taxes on primary foodstuffs.

33. AN END TO TAXES ON BUYING AND SELLING.

We shall cancel taxes on buying and selling, and replace them with a better and more equitable system.

34. AN END TO SPECULATION.

Economic crimes will be severely punished.

35. AN END TO UNEMPLOYMENT.

We shall assure the right of employment for all Chileans and we shall stop dismissals.

36. JOBS FOR EVERYONE.

We shall immediately create new sources of jobs through the development of Public Works and Housing, with the establishment of new industries and with the implementation of our development plans.

37. DISSOLUTION OF THE MOBILE GROUP.

We shall guarantee order in the barrios and towns, and security for the individual. Carabineros and Investigators will be primarily fulfilling a police function against common delinquency. We shall do away with the Mobile Group, and its members will reinforce the police.

38. END TO CLASS JUSTICE.

We shall create a fast legal procedure, free of charge, with the cooperation of Neighborhood Juntas, which will study and solve special cases, like fights, killings, home abandonment, and disturbances of the peace within the Community.

39. LEGAL COUNSELING IN THE TOWNS.

We shall establish offices for legal counseling in all the towns.

40. ESTABLISHSMENT OF A NATIONAL INSTITUTE OF ART AND CULTURE.

We shall create a National Institute of Art and Culture, and schools for artistic training in all communities.

Douglas thought that the forty items listed above were reasonable. All were aimed at constructing a just and equitable society. Inevitably there would be a number of Chileans who would be asked to sacrifice by losing their property, or a portion of it. That was in the nature of Socialism and Communism. Douglas enjoyed reading the specific points of Allende's platform over the generalities that one found often in the literature. The following is a further discourse on Allende's plans for his country. This section gives the government program and is titled: BASIC GOVERNMENT PROGRAM OF THE POPULAR FRONT (UNIDAD POPULAR), UNANIMOUSLY APPROVED BY ALL PARTIES SUPPORTING THE PRESIDENTIAL CANDIDACY OF SALVADOR ALLENDE.

Introduction.

All parties and groups belonging to the Coordinating Committee of the Popular Front (Unidad Popular), without prejudice to the maintenance of each one's own philosophy and political ideas, fully agree with the presentation of the national reality, as is expressed hereafter, and in the programmed proposals which will form the basis of our common action and which is submitted here for consideration by the people.

1. Chile is living through a deep crisis which manifests itself in the economic and social stagnation of the country, in the poverty, in the backwardness, which is suffered by laborers, farmers, and other exploited classes, as well as in the increasing difficulties facing employees, professionals, small and medium-scale entrepreneurs and in the very minimal opportunities open to women and young people.

Chile's problems can be solved. Our country has great riches, like copper and other minerals, a great hydroelectric potential, and vast expanses of forest, a long coastline rich in fish species, more-than-adequate agricultural land, etc., and can count besides on the will to work and the progressiveness of Chileans, their technical and professional skills. Where then is the failure?

Chile's failure is in having a system which does not correspond to the needs of our time. Chile is a capitalistic country, dependent on imperialism, dominated by bourgeois sectors which are tied to foreign capital, which cannot solve the fundamental problems of the country, precisely because the problems are derived from their own class privileges which they will never voluntarily renounce.

Moreover, as a consequence of the development of world capitalism, the handing over (of our country) by the national monopolistic bourgeoisie to imperialism is increasingly and progressively accelerated, and this (trend) more and more accentuates the dependency of the bourgeois and its role as junior partner with foreign capital.

For a few, the daily sale of a piece of Chile is big business. Deciding for everybody else is what they do, day in, day out.

For the majority, on the other hand, the daily sale of effort, intelligence and labor is the worst kind of business, and deciding their own destinies is a privilege of which most of them are deprived.

2. In Chile, all the "reform" and "development" recipes stimulated by the Alliance for Progress and adopted by the Frei government have not succeeded in altering anything. Fundamentally, it has been a new bourgeois government at the service of national and foreign capitalism, whose weak attempts at social change have been shipwrecked without pain or glory on the shoals of economic stagnation, high prices, and violent repression against the people. This has demonstrated once again that reformism is not equal to the task of solving the country's problems.

3. The development of monopolistic capitalism denies the expansion of democracy and exacerbates unpopular violence.

The increase in the intensity of the people's struggle, as reformism fails, hardens the position of the more reactionary sectors of the ruling classes, which in the end have no other resource but force.

The brutal forms of violence of the present State, such as the actions of the Mobile Group, the thrashing of farmers and students, the killings of citizens and miners, are inseparable from other no-less-brutal crimes affecting all Chileans.

For a state of violence exists wherever there are those who live in luxurious homes, while a majority of the population lives in unhealthy quarters, with some who do not even have a place to squat; violence exists when some throw away food and others have nothing to eat.

4. Imperialistic exploitations of backward economies is carried out in many ways: through investments in mining (copper, iron, etc.), in

trade, banking and industrial activities, through technological control which obliges us to pay enormous sums for equipment, licenses, and patents; through usurious American loans which we are obliged to spend in the U.S., with the added obligation of having to use American ships to transport the purchased products, etc.

To give just one example. From 1952 to the present, the United States has invested $7 billion in Latin America, and taken out in return $16 billion.

Imperialism has taken from Chile enormous resources, equivalent to double the amount invested during a long history

North American monopolies in complicity with the bourgeois governments have succeeded in taking over almost all of our copper, iron and salt mines. They control foreign trade and dictate the political policy, through the International Monetary Fund and other organizations. They dominate important industrial enterprises and services; they enjoy privileged statutes, while at the same time imposing monetary devaluations, decreasing salaries and wages and distorting our agricultural sector by means of their agricultural surpluses.

They also intervene in education, culture, and in the communication media. Taking advantage of military and political treaties, they seek to infiltrate the Armed Forces.

The ruling classes, partners in this situation and incapable of self-help, have intensified Chile's indebtedness abroad in the last ten years.

They said that loans and agreements with international bankers could produce greater economic development. However, their only achievement is that today Chile holds the distinction of being one of the most indebted countries in the world, relative to the size of its population.

5. In Chile government and the law favor the few, the great capitalists and their accomplices, the companies that dominate our economy and the landholders whose power goes unchallenged.

The owners of capital are always interested in making more money and they are not concerned with the needs of the Chilean people. If the manufacture and import of high-priced cars, for example, is a good business, valuable resources of our economy are diverted along that route without considering that only a small percentage of the Chilean population is able to acquire cars, and that there are more urgent needs that require attention, some of them in the same sector, such as the development of collective means of transportation, and the obtaining of farm machinery, etc.

The managerial group which controls the economy, the press and other communications media; the political system which threatens the State when it attempts to intervene or refuses to grant favors cost all Chileans very dearly.

For (Chileans) to be considered worthy of "working," for only (the privileged few) can provide them with the luxury of work, it is necessary for them:

--- to give them (the rich) all kinds of aid. The large investors can crush the State by threatening that there will be no private investment, if the guarantees and help requested by them are not granted.

--- let them produce whatever they want to with Chilean money, instead of manufacturing the products which are needed by the majority.

--- let them take their profits out, to put them in accounts in foreign banks.

--- let them discharge employees when they ask for better salaries.

--- leave them in charge of distributing foods, so that they can stock them and raise prices when the people are in want, so that they can multiply their riches at the cost of the public.

In the meantime, those who are producing effectively are experiencing a difficult time:

--- Half a million families lack homes and many other live under terrible conditions due to the lack of sewers, drinking water, light, and health services.

--- The people's needs in the fields of education and health are not adequately met.

--- More than half of Chile's workers receive inadequate salaries, not enough to cover their minimum living needs. Each family suffers from unemployment and the uncertainty of having a job. Opportunities for employment are very difficult to come by and instable for many young people.

Imperialist capital and a group of the privileged few, which does not number more than 10% of the population, monopolize half of the national income. This means that for every one hundred <u>escudos</u>, 50 stay in the pockets of the wealthy and the other 50 are distributed among 90% of the Chileans belonging to the lower and middle classes.

6. The high cost of living makes a hell of the homes of the people and especially for the housewife. In the last 10 years, according to official data, living costs have risen almost a thousand per cent.

This means that every day a part of the Chilean's salary is being robed from him. The same thing happens to retired people, the independent worker, the craftsman, the small manufacturer, whose small incomes are daily being cut by inflation.

Alessandri and Frei have assured us that they would put an end to inflation. The results are easy to see. The facts prove that inflation in Chile is due to deep-seated causes related to the capitalistic structure of our society, and not related to salary increases as several governments have attempted to make us believe to justify the continuance of the system and decrease the workers' salaries. The great capitalist, on the other hand, defends himself from inflation, and even more, benefits from it. His property and capital are appraised, his construction contracts with the National Treasury are readjusted and the prices for his products grow higher, always keeping them ahead of salary increases.

7. A great many of Chileans suffer from malnutrition. According to official statistics, 50% of the children, 15 years of age or younger, are not well fed. Malnutrition affects their growth and limits their learning ability.

This demonstrates that the economy in general, and especially the agricultural sector, is unequal to the task of feeding the Chilean population even though Chile at this time could feed 30 million people, or three times the present population.

But on the contrary, we have to import hundreds of thousands of dollars worth of food every year.

The large landholder is the big culprit in the food problems of all Chileans, and is responsible for the backwardness and misery in the countryside. The figures on child and adult deaths, on those who can not read or write, on the lack of homes, on the lack of health services are higher in the rural zones than they are in the cities. The

Christian Democrat government with its inadequate Agrarian Reform program, has been unable to solve these problems. Only a fighting rural population, with everyone's support, can resolve them. Its present fight for land and an end to the landholding system is opening new perspectives for the popular Chilean movement.

8. The growth of our economy is minimal. In recent periods we have had an average growth rate of scarcely 2% per year per capita; and since 1967 we have not advanced at all, we have retrograded, according to government statistics (ODEPLAN). This means that in 1966 every Chilean had a larger quantity of goods than he has now. This explains why the majority is discontented and is looking for an alternative for our country.

9. The only truly popular alternative, and therefore the fundamental job of Government of the People, is to end imperialistic domination, monopolies, landholding oligarchs, and to begin the building of Socialism in Chile.

There is a great deal more to the document quoted here, but Douglas thought he had extracted the flavor with the quotations taken. Douglas, after reading the first nine points of Allende's Government Platform, concluded that the United Front (assuming that a committee had written the document, and not Allende himself) could always find people to blame. He thought that it was the duty of individuals and their government to assume responsibility for their conditions and to make plans that addressed the problems. Allende blamed the bourgeoisie, imperialists, and capitalists for Chile's condition. No tangible solutions were offered.

On the matter of the imperialists taking over Chile's riches, Douglas had this thought. When copper was discovered in Chile, and there was a world-wide demand for the products manufactured from copper, there was at the same time insufficient capital in the country to develop the mines. Needed were earth-moving equipment, trains to move the ore to a harbor, a working port, trained personnel, and all the small pieces that go to transform an idea into a going enterprise. Chileans could have decided to wait and calculate how to put together a pool of capital in order to pay for the extraction of copper ore from their mines. They chose instead either to borrow the money necessary or to allow a foreign company to do the work. In either case, Chile would have jobs and income much quicker than if they waited to form their own pool of capital. Most people borrow to buy a house. Most people borrow to buy a car. They are free to save their money and pay all cash for their purchases but they must delay the time of purchase and forsake comfort and utility that would come with the ownership of a house and car.

Douglas could see the other side of the argument. The terms and conditions for extracting ore from Chile's mountains had been settled decades earlier. Had not the companies and the lenders made enough money on their investments? On one hand the Leftists writing this document wanted to honor contracts while on the other hand they were asking: are there not conclusions to these arrangements? Would it go on forever? Couldn't Chile recover ownership of its patrimony?

Inflation is not a complicated phenomenon. Money is a commodity and the value of other commodities is determined by the amount of money in circulation compared to the amount of money needed to manage the financial transactions that require money to complete. If there is inflation, it is certain that there is too much money in circulation. Douglas recalled reading that during the times of the Weimar Republic, which would be Germany's government after World War I, a valuable tool was a wheelbarrow into which one could put the billions of paper marks required to buy a loaf of bread. Allende would find out that his government could not fund social programs by turning on the printing presses at the Treasury. He did print too much money. Inflation rose to 360% in the third year of his presidency.

Douglas read on to the end. Several paragraphs were included that caught Douglas' attention. They were written in that empty style that conveys some emotion but no facts. He had heard thoughts expressed in this fashion from men and women he knew and to himself he termed these statements, "Left-wing boiler plate." Here are three paragraphs illustrating that manner of thinking and speaking, taken from the same document.

"The imperialist and ruling classes of the country will fight against popular unity and will try to deceive the people once more. They will say that liberty is in danger, that violence is taking over the country, etc. But the popular masses place less and less faith in their lies. Their social movement grows daily, and is stimulated by the unity of left wing forces.

In order to stimulate and guide the mobilization of the Chilean people in the conquest of power, we will establish Popular Unity Committees everywhere, in each factory, land establishment, town, office or school, comprising militants and left wing parties and integrated by that multitude of the Chilean citizenry which stands for fundamental change.

The Popular Unity Committees will not be political bodies only. They will interpret and fight for the vindication of the masses, and will be prepared to exercise Popular Power."

Douglas didn't understand these and other paragraphs written in the same fashion. He wished that he had taken the time to sound out Elena more deeply than he had so that he could know with certainty that she would not utter paragraphs similar to these three. His marriage would be in shambles and he would be required to re-educate her politically, a process that could take a year or more, generating a great deal of friction. He admitted to himself that he might fail at the task. Douglas thought that much of the document outlining Allende's Government Program contained questionable material and he despaired for Allende that his handlers and fellow politicians were devoid of sensible plans. One should be able to understand a political platform, Douglas thought.

So much for Allende's forty points and his Government Program. The first text that Douglas read concerning Chile in the times of Allende was *How Allende Fell*. The authors were James Petras and Morris M. Morley. The publishing house is the Bertrand Russell Peace Foundation Ltd., (Spokesman Books), located in Nottingham, U.K., and dated 1974. Douglas assumed that the authors were experts in Latin American affairs and had been inspired to write this book because of the recent (at the time) coup staged by Chile's military in 1973.

Douglas guessed from the title that the final chapter would describe the excesses of Allende's government, which were too far left for General Pinochet and company to stand, resulting in the military uprising, Allende's death and a new government. The authors did not write the story as Douglas had expected. They gave one short paragraph to the phenomena which could have triggered the coup in 1973. The authors' words on the matter are on page 107. "The Party's governing council issued an official statement which asserted that the Allende government 'was preparing to stage a violent coup … in order to install a Communist dictatorship.' Everything indicates that the armed forces did nothing more than to respond to this immediate risk."

The bulk of the writing consists of financial arrangements between the governments of Chile (under various presidents) and governmental banks such as the International Monetary Fund (IMF) and commercial banks (not limited to American banks), and multinational corporations (mostly in the business of mining and exporting copper ore). Douglas concluded that it was a simple tale of a country consuming more than it produced with the result that its economy had to be sustained by a never-ending infusions of cash from foreign governments and foreign banks.

It surprised Douglas that bankers, whether governmental or commercial, would lend Chile so much money when the chance of timely repayment on loans was remote. It was as though Chile needed fresh loans to be used partly to pay interest and principal on last year's loans. Douglas concluded that there was an entire field -- international banking -- that he did not understand. The operations of these banks violated Douglas' view of the exercise of common sense.

Allende, ever the good Socialist, vowed that Chile would take over the ownership of the major copper mines. These were owned by U.S. interests. Anaconda Corporation came to Douglas' mind. The mines were expropriated, that is to say they became the property of the Chilean government, but no schedule of payment in exchange for the taking of the assets had been arranged. The United States government and various lending agencies would not arrange new loans or extend additional credits to Chile as long as good-faith efforts to compensate Anaconda were not in place. Douglas read elsewhere that the Chilean Government ultimately paid Anaconda $250,000,000. This transaction might have occurred after the book was published.

The results were predictable. The government of Chile, now the operator of the mines, no longer had sufficient cash on hand to purchase spare parts and equipment to operate the mines, thereby reducing further the ability of Chile to earn foreign exchange. Without exports of its most profitable commodity the country would slowly slip into insolvency.

The authors made the point that the American government could exercise great influence over the military of Chile by promising the restoration of loans and credits if Allende's regime was overthrown. Douglas suspected that American policy makers might put this inducement to work. In General Pinochet and other top brass of Chile the policy makers in the U.S. had attentive listeners. The flow of money that came after the coup supported this theory.

The next text that Douglas studied had the title, *Marxism and Democracy in Chile: From 1932 to the Fall of Allende.* It was written by Julio Faúndez and published by the Yale University Press in 1988. In it, Douglas found the answer to his first question: what style of Socialist was Allende? Douglas thought the answer was that Allende was a theoretical Socialist, one who practiced the teaching of Marx without use of force. It must be noted that Allende was voted into office and subsequently kept the government largely as he found it. The elected Congress remained in place as did the constitution. Allende's government submitted its desires to Congress where the necessary legislation was enacted. Allende did not have a clear majority in the Congress but between his party and a few members of the Christian Democrat Party he usually could prevail.

Lenin would not have understood Allende. Lenin's concept was that the Communist Party held all power, all property and all assets. The Party owned the means of production. Not only that, but also the Party owned the allegiance of all citizens, and any deviation in support of the Party could be and was punished by one of several means: execution, a prison term, or a decade in a gulag, where one was sent frequently with no hope of return.

Douglas could find no mention in this text of a secret police for enforcement of beliefs. He assumed that the Allende government had not practiced absolute control and the fact that the Congress was allowed to remain supported that position. In fact the rights of the individual were guaranteed and liberty could only be denied by a change in the law, requiring legislation from Congress.

In the matter of nationalization of farms and manufacturing firms, the government exercised restraint. Only large land holdings were taken by the government. The land in excess of eighty hectares (200 acres) was nationalized but the farm machinery was left to the owner along with the eighty hectares not taken. Douglas imagined that the government ran up large expenses re-supplying these new holdings of land with the necessary agricultural equipment. Terms of compensation were not discussed.

Concerning the nationalization of manufacturing firms, the total number of firms brought under control and the level of assets which would trigger a takeover varied over time. The debate went on so that the number of firms to be nationalized changed month by month, sometimes less frequently. About one hundred large firms were nationalized.

There were six political parties that made up the coalition of the Left. The group called itself the Popular Unity. The two parties with the largest membership were the Communists and the Socialists. Debates were common among the six parties, showing once again that Allende had a democratic side to him. Stalin and Mao, after they had established themselves, did not tolerate dissent. There may have been free discussions at the level of the Politburo but it was foolhardy for members to disagree with the chairman while not falling into agreement with him before the session ended. Stalin and Mao had long memories and any marked differences in points of view would be rewarded in the end with a penalty that ran from demotion to execution.

Douglas could not identify a prime cause for the military's coup in September 1973. He guessed there were several reasons. The first might be the talk from many quarters that the Left would replace the Congress (both houses) with a Popular Assembly, also elected. The military leaders may have viewed this move as a first step toward a Communist dictatorship. This proposal, however, did not get beyond the talking stage.

The economic situation of the country needed addressing, particularly the rate of inflation. Constant upward adjustments in wages were called for to maintain the individual's purchasing power. The lack of the ability to purchase from abroad due to insufficient foreign exchange made it difficult to maintain the manufacturing levels of those items that could be exported. There was always need for spare parts and new machinery.

The arrival of Allende's government proved to be a signal for industrial workers to organize so that they might press for higher wages and better working conditions. The number of strikes per year and the time workers stayed out on strike went up. One of the effects was to reduce the nation's production of goods, manufactured and agricultural. Indeed, the military was called in to end one particularly long and costly strike.

Douglas wished that Allende had been allowed to finish his term in office, which was set to expire in 1976. Perhaps the Leftist Alliance would have been voted out of office over their inability to operate the economy successfully.

To get an answer to his question of whether the Allende government used a secret police to enforce its will, Douglas would wait for his trip to Chile with Elena when he would ask the question of people he met who had lived through the times. Without the opportunity for a wedding trip soon after they were married, Douglas had felt that when both their schedules permitted it, Elena and he would head for South America. Chile seemed the ideal destination.

HUGO CHAVEZ

PART 15:   HUGO CHAVEZ

FOR HIS UPCOMING trip, Douglas wanted to be conversant on the president of Venezuela, Hugo Chavez. He had read the newspaper accounts over the years and was not certain that Chavez was a Communist at heart. Indeed he had orchestrated a military coup to oust the president in 1992, which effort failed. He and other conspirators spent a couple of years in jail and were pardoned. Perhaps the coup attempt is a frequently-enough occurring event in Venezuela and other Latin American countries that a government subjected to a failed coup remains lenient towards the perpetrators. Alter all, the next attempts might succeed and clemency would be expected in turn.

After his two years in jail, Chavez came out to discover elective politics. He captured the presidency in 1998 and was inaugurated 2 February 1999. As would be expected, a *coup d'état* was attempted against him in 2002. This coup succeeded, but only for forty-eight hours. In addition, there was a recall election late in 2002, but it did not manage to remove him from office.

Douglas concluded that Chavez was a not dedicated Communist, in spite of his having said that he wanted to establish a government in Venezuela that resembled Castro's regime in Cuba. His ambition was to be president of his country and his politics have always been to align himself with the poor, the have-nots.

Douglas armed himself with two biographies of Chavez, the first being titled simply, *Hugo Chavez*. It was written by Cristina Marcano and Alberto Barrera Tyszka and published by Random House. Douglas read as much of Venezuela's history and about the current president as he could before he left on his ten-day trip. He flew into Caracas and then followed the tour determined for him by the security forces of the country. One half of Venezuela's border (excluding the border on the Caribbean) is along Columbia's east side. Great amounts of illegal drugs come across that border, originating in Columbia, making their way through Venezuela, and then by sea to North America and Europe. Douglas wanted to learn about the routes taken and the conveyances used. The Venezuelan police and armed services were very helpful as they divulged what they knew. Douglas realized that the drug problem was not theirs. It was driven by the demand. The largest market for these products was probably the United States. The inhabitants of Venezuela were not great users of the drugs that crossed through their borders and therefore the military and the police were not pressed to treat the matter as a national disaster.

Douglas impressed the officials he met with his knowledge of Simon Bolivar, the country's liberator. Venezuela had been on its own since 1821, ending Spain's colonial rule in that year. Douglas impressed them as well with his ability in their language and in the scattered information he held of the country. Concerning the current president, Hugo Chavez, he had nothing to say. If any of his hosts wished to venture an opinion, perhaps to draw him out, he would deflect with an innocuous remark.

Douglas knew a portion of Chavez's history. He was born in 1954 and therefore was a young politician of the post-war variety. Chavez attended the Venezuelan Military Academy, graduating as a second lieutenant in 1975. As part of receiving his commission, Chavez must have taken an oath to defend the constitution and his country. Whether or not he took such an oath, he entered into and led a conspiracy to topple the government. The coup was planned for 4 February 1992. It failed. Chavez surrendered and was incarcerated.

Douglas had no patience with a man who took an oath to defend the constitution of his country only to attempt to overthrow the government and seize power. Why do this? The prize is always power. Henry Kissinger had said that power was the ultimate aphrodisiac. You get to hear your own voice over the radio. Your words and photographs of you are in the newspapers. The television channels carry your every step. Power is a beautiful thing. You get to put your plans in place and that is as it should be because you are always correct in all matters while others in the political class are wrong once in a while or even most of the time. They disagree with you and you must find time to debate the issues, which is particularly annoying when you are right anyway.

What comes with power? The presidential palace, a fleet of cars and airplanes as needed, the best of menus with chefs to prepare meals, the best Cognac and wines, cigars from Havana, servants, uniforms, tailor-made suits, a military which will bow and scrape, a subservient media, and finally women to suit your tastes. Ibn Saud fathered 300 sons. He must have gone through life horizontally.

What comes with power? You can kill with impunity although Hugo Chavez does not permit himself this activity. There are no political prisoners in Venezuela. To the old style dictators, such as Mao and Stalin, killing was at first a small cloud far away, but they knew that they had to have killed for their revolutions to succeed. Mao and Stalin rounded up the villains: the bourgeoisie, the landed aristocracy, and the anti-communists. In Chavez's case, the villains were the corrupt politicians and the oligarchy, and the rich who had not stripped themselves of their wealth and given it to the poor. Chavez has left the rich alone except to identify them as enemies of humanity. Douglas hoped that Chavez never used killing as part of his political process. He hadn't yet.

And why would one see a need for a coup? Obviously to gain power. The principal reason that Chavez has given is that active politicians were corrupt. The second reason given is that there is a small group that runs the country for its own purposes. This group is referred to as the oligarchy. Also among the despised groups are the elites, which members are rich, educated, and influential. They are not necessarily corrupt but they deserve to be despised and singled out because they fly to Miami and Europe on shopping sprees.

Those three groups, the corrupt politicians, the oligarchy, and the elites, needed to be identified to the poor as the villains by Chavez and as the reasons for his coup against the government in 1992. The more poor there are to support the populist movement of a coup leader, the better the chance for a coup to succeed.

Douglas also knew from his reading that Venezuela had desperate poverty and hunger and unemployment while it had enormous wealth in oil. How could the phenomenon of poverty exist side by side with a practically unlimited flow of money into the national treasury earned from the exportation of oil? Where did all the money go if not to alleviate poverty? Douglas hoped to find out, certainly not on this ten-day journey, but over time, through reading and studying.

Douglas' journey started with a flight to the Lake Maracaibo region in the western part of the country, near Columbia. It continued by covering several towns along the Orinoco River, which comes to the sea in the eastern section of Venezuela. Certainly tons of cocaine had come down the Orinoco on various vessels. Douglas had seen the ports and had met the policemen in the upper echelons with whom he would stay in contact.

The biography he was reading gave an account of Chavez's life, but did not supply, in detail, the efforts made by Chavez's administration to tackle poverty in his country. After all, he had identified himself with the impoverished segment of the population and based the success of his presidency on uplifting the poor. The biography did indicate that programs had been established in education, food distribution and unemployment. Details were not given. He would have to find them elsewhere. Of interest is a program in which Venezuela ships oil to Cuba and in exchange the Cuban government dispatches medical doctors to bring health services to needy districts of Venezuela.

In the middle of the biography Douglas was reading, mention was made of a profile of Hugo Chavez by Jon Lee Anderson that appeared in the 10 September 2001 issue of The New Yorker. The profile was titled, "The Revolutionary." After finishing reading the biography, Douglas repaired to the library he used and read the article in question. The author stated that 80% of Venezuela's population lived in poverty. The demarcation between poor and middle class is not made but the statistic was outstanding nonetheless. What an enormous challenge faced the government of Venezuela!

Chavez's governing style interested Douglas. All the levers of power were in his hands and he ran the country as one would a town of five thousand inhabitants, this in a country of twenty-seven million souls. It is well-know that Chavez responds to supplications made directly to him, usually in the form of letters handed to him or to attendants who accompany him when in public.

In the middle of the profile, the author quotes Chavez as saying that he reads all this correspondence, selecting the worthy requests from among them, and noting actions to be taken. It does wonders for one's ego to right a wrong in the life of a destitute citizen, but it is more effective to build institutions that have a chance to improve the lives of millions. The profile was written in 2001. Perhaps the government has been modernized since then.

Chavez's blood is a mixture of Spanish, Indian and African. His facial construction reveals just that. Douglas wondered about the social demarcations in Venezuela. Certainly money and education made a great difference. How important was race? he asked himself. The profile stated that a quarter of a million wealthy persons had left Venezuela since Chavez came to power, "taking their money with them." Would they be white? Was it fear of Communism? They have migrated to Europe and North America. Douglas knew the social demarcations in the United States. Money and education counted, as did race and lineage. The division into classes may not have been very different between the two countries. Something is made in the profile of the fact that Chavez's second wife is white, blonde and blue-eyed.

Because the profile is titled, "The Revolutionary," Douglas hoped that the revolution Chavez was leading would be defined. What were the several parts? Unfortunately there was no itemized list of the component parts of this revolution. Douglas tried to make his own list. The first part was that Chavez must not alienate a large section of his population. He could say that he wanted to bring Castro's style of government to Venezuela but he knew that he could not do it. It would not be possible politically. The odds were that if he tried to bring Communism to his country there would be another coup, this one staged against him by the military, and it would be successful. Because the most important element of his life was to remain president as long as he wished, he would display only the revolutionary zeal required to keep the affection of his base without breaking faith with the remainder of the citizenry. Do what it takes to stay in power; that is Chavez's religion. As part of the program, pull Uncle Sam's whiskers; cozy up to Fidel; make friends with Evo Morales, the new president of Bolivia; and befriend Daniel Ortega, the returned president of Nicaragua. All that posturing satisfies a deep-seated need to be thought of as a politician on the international stage. Douglas thought it wasn't worth a hill of beans. Better to show tangible results in population control, education, job creation, building an infrastructure, and all those pieces of running a country. Douglas would continue searching for a definition of Chavez's revolution. No, he wasn't a Communist dictator of the old school. He was and is a popularly elected leader who has managed to suppress dictatorial tendencies in his makeup, to the extent they ever existed.

Douglas started on the second biography of Chavez. This one was titled *HUGO!,* by Bart Jones. It was published by the Steerforth Press, Hanover, New Hampshire in 2007. After reading the first chapter, Douglas was impressed that the same material he had read in the first biography could be written in a different tone. The authors of the first biography came down hard on Chavez. In the second, the author, Bart Jones, gave a sympathetic presentation of Chavez, showing him to be a man of the people and the first president of Venezuela to rise from the have-nots to the highest political office. The author accounts for Chavez's rise to power because of these traits in his personality: intelligence, willingness to work hard, unwillingness to be corrupted, dedicated to solving the problems of the poor, ending poverty, and finding a cure for corruption, the national malaise, which siphons off much of the oil riches into the pockets and bank accounts of many members of the wealthy class.

The two authors of the biography that Douglas read first tell of Chavez's preference for certain types of clothes and wrist watches, and discuss his trade-in of the old Boeing 737 that had ferried Venezuelan presidents for a decade or two, and Chavez's ordering of a new Airbus plane. Perhaps the upgrade could be justified on its merits.

Douglas thought that many Latin Americans and their leaders did not view the diplomacy practiced by the governments of the United States over the decades as just and fair. The starting point could have occurred in 1898, when the U.S. expelled Spain from Cuba and for years to come made itself a substitute for Spain. The U.S. seized land to build the Panama Canal. Marines landed at Vera Cruz, Mexico. The Nicaraguan governments of Somoza, father and sons, were given their start by the U.S. under the guise of stability. Douglas remembered reading a remark made by Franklin Roosevelt about Somoza Senior in answer to a question from a person in the State Department. "Yes, he is a son of a bitch, but he's our son of a bitch."

More recently the complaints against the U.S have covered the range from blaming the CIA for anything not easily explained otherwise, to financing a war against the Sandinistas of Nicaragua, to fomenting civil war in El Salvador. Chavez has played and continues to play the anti-U.S. card on an as-needed basis and he may well be correct some of the time. Douglas didn't know. It's handy to have someone to blame when things go wrong. When the accused is far away and can only respond with diplomatic notes, then blaming the U.S. turns into a habit.

Douglas thought that the essence of Hugo Chavez was captured in this quote from page 83 of the biography, *HUGO!* This is Chavez speaking: "We knew the enemies of Venezuela were hunger, corruption, misery, unemployment, and the handing over of the nation's immense abundance of riches." Chavez did not mention the lack of education, health care, and appropriate nutrition for much of the population, but then one quote is not meant to represent a complete political statement. The heart of Chavez's appeal was and is that he was willing to devote his life to finding solutions to the problems of the poor. There was money at hand (oil exports) to pay for the necessary programs. Previous presidents had not understood the problems faced by most of their countrymen and in any event were not willing to use significant portions of the oil revenue to finance programs that would alleviate suffering among the poor. Chavez not only understood the problems but also he was willing to find solutions to them.

It was not as though Chavez won the presidency, was sworn in 2 February 1999, and started working immediately on the pressing issues. It appeared to Douglas that Chavez was the victorious candidate who asks on the first day, "What should we do now?" There was a coup attempt against Chavez in April 2002, which could have cost him not only the presidency but also his life. The coup lasted two days, and then failed. This was followed by a referendum, conducted in accordance with the new constitution, which asked the question, "Shall we replace the sitting president?" Chavez won this challenge with nearly 60% of the votes cast. Between the coup and the referendum, opponents of Chavez staged a strike centered on disrupting the oil industry. The strike nearly toppled the government but Chavez prevailed in the end by finding solutions to the shortages of food and gasoline.

It was not until after victory in the referendum that Chavez concentrated on putting systems in place to conquer the afflictions of poverty. In chapter 24, The Social Missions, the author, Bart Jones, lists the programs put in place by Chavez and his administration. It's an impressive list, which suggested to Douglas that Chavez had his heart in the right place. Heading the list was healthcare, which, along with the obvious services, offered newly-built hospitals and repaired old ones. In the trade with Cuba of oil for doctors, as many as 14,000 doctors arrived from Cuba to practice medicine among the poor, many of whom had never been attended to. Dentistry was provided, also to many for the first time.

The second concentration was in eradicating illiteracy and allowing those who had not graduated from high school it to complete their education. While the program was criticized as over-ambitious, it did provide skills in the three Rs that many people lacked. Chavez founded an institute of higher learning for the poor that he housed in a large downtown building in Caracas formerly used by functionaries of the state oil company. Chavez had let go half the staff of this bloated government-run corporation, with the result that the building was emptied. It appeared to have found a different and better use.

Chavez ameliorated the dietary problem of the poor by creating subsidized food markets where the staples of the Venezuelan diet could be purchased at large discounts. He decided on opening factories to manufacture shoes and basic garments.

Venezuela's citizenry carries an identification card and it is necessary to have one to complete several transactions. Many of these ID cards are lost and all expire with time. The aggravation of confronting the Venezuelan bureaucracy kept many, especially among the poor, from renewing their ID cards. Chavez broke the logjam and included voter registration with the program.

Another of his administrative successes was to grant titles to land when deserved. Many poor had simply migrated to untitled land. Some had built small houses. Others had grown crops.

Douglas viewed the list as a set of significant accomplishments. Federal money to bring about these results was money well spent. No man is without his faults and Douglas thought it would be appropriate to make a list of those in order to balance them against Chavez's fine traits. At the head of the list would be his willingness to bad-mouth people. The activity of name-calling may provide an accurate description of the victim but it implicates the accuser as being vulgar, quick to judgment, and a bully. Chavez has no compunction about singling out individuals, groups and entire populations. He suffers from the affliction of name-calling and unfortunately many of the people he names feel forced to return the insult. Turning the other cheek, the advice handed out by Jesus to victims of this form of bad behavior, has not taken hold so that those insulted by Chavez feel forced to respond in kind. Douglas understood that all sides should be quiet for a while so that they might tend to important business.

Another fault of Chavez's, Douglas thought, was that the president was slowly being consumed by his ego. Chavez was correct to identify the social problems that had not been attended to in his country. He was correct to put programs in place to cure these problems. As it happens, however, Chavez was starting to think of himself as the leader of the Latin American Left. The other presidents of the region who shared Chavez's vision were supposed to be followers of Chavez. They may not have realized it. On a grander scale, Chavez was said to have international ambitions, to be seen as the guide for the politics of second and third world countries who wished to break away from the grasp of the imperialists (first world countries).

This brand of thinking led Douglas to his third objections to Chavez's behavior and beliefs, that while it was permissible to accept investments that increased employment and the gross domestic product of Venezuela, and while it was beneficial to accept loans from the International Monetary Fund (IMF) and the World Bank, it was no great sin to fail to obey to the letter the repayment schedules that these arrangements called for. Douglas was only aware that the United States was involved in many of these transactions, particularly as the World Bank and the IMF were located in Washington. Douglas thought that the World Bank might be relocated to Buenos Aires, the capital of Argentina, and the IMF to Madrid. It may be a problem for Chavez to bad-mouth the employees of these institutions in their common language. Douglas returned to the conclusions that Chavez cared for the poor, took actions to improve their lot, was not corrupt, and was making a best effort to clean up corruption in his country. He held no political prisoners. He could win at the poles. He wanted to be president for life.

In December 2006, Chavez took the presidential election with 63% of the vote. Without a coup that ends his presidency, he will be in office through 2012. He will have ample time to decide whether to remain on the current path of democracy or attempt to introduce Communism into his method of governing. By a vote of the people, Chavez has had removed the prohibition of running for the presidency as long as he wishes. Term limits have ceased to exist.

*   *   *

Douglas was disappointed that he could not identify a set of circumstances in a young person's life that would be necessary to produce a Communist in adulthood. Abject poverty might be the catalyst, but then Lenin and Castro enjoyed a good measure of comfort in their early years.

Daniel Ortega, born in 1945, and his brother, Humberto, born in 1947, suffered from poverty. There were six children, the first two dying of illnesses that might have been cured with a standard medical treatment. There was no money for these services. Of the remaining four children, Daniel was the oldest and Humberto next in line.

The formative influence in the lives of many Nicaraguans was the presence of the Somoza family who dominated the politics of the country from 1933, when Anastasio Somoza became the commander of the National Guard, to 1979, when the Sandinistas took over the government.

The Somozas, the father followed by his two sons, were presidents of Nicaragua, which they treated as their fiefdom, aggregating to themselves vast riches in land and businesses. It would be correct to say that the Somoza family pilfered much of what there was to be had in Nicaragua.

The U.S. Marines had a long involvement with the country of Nicaragua, starting in 1853. At the time, the government of Nicaragua, which had ceased being a colony of Spain, and finally a nation separate from Mexico in 1838, did not have a sufficiently sophisticated government to grasp the implications of foreign investments and foreign businessmen operating in their country. Both Britain and the U.S. had commercial interests in Nicaragua. A few of these enterprises concentrated on creating a crossing of the country by ship in order to connect the two oceans. A plan that Douglas found in a 1933 atlas had a canal starting on the Atlantic side, moving inland near or in the San Juan River, at the border that separates Nicaragua from Costa Rica. Ships would continue by crossing the southern end of Lake Nicaragua, and finally a second canal would be dug, perhaps ten miles long, from the western edge of the Lake to the Pacific. The discovery of gold in California encouraged the movement of goods and people from the east coast to the west coast of the U.S. Nicaragua was long considered to have the most practical route, but in the end, Panama was selected as the site for the ocean-to-ocean canal.

The Marines first came to Nicaragua in 1853 to protect the lives and possessions of U.S. citizens. A few Americans had been killed, fewer than ten, and some buildings burned. One of the owners of the damaged property was Commodore Vanderbilt, who was exploring means of reaching the Pacific. The Marines debarked from U.S. warships, suffered no casualties, inflicted no damage, stayed all of two days and finished their peace-keeping mission.

Nicaragua was not noted for stability. Early on, the two principal political factions, the Conservatives and the Liberals, fought it out for supremacy. Elections were often violent. In 1909, as warfare continued between the two sides, two Americans who had been involved in the conflict as fighters for one side, were captured by the other side and executed. In 1910, American-owned property was damaged. The president at the time, William Howard Taft, sent in the Marines. An important issue was whether loans to the Nicaraguan government and to various businesses could be repaid. The fear among bankers was that their loans would be non-performing. To that end, the Nicaraguan and U.S. governments worked out a system for collecting import duties, which would be deposited into a fund used to repay the loans. This purpose was served and the Nicaraguan government was provided a secure source of income as well.

The number of Marines stationed in Nicaragua varied from 100 to 2,000. When in the smaller number, they acted as guards to the legation in Managua. At 2,000 strong, the Marines were active, fighting against rebels, mostly in the north of the country. The rebels seemed to oppose the government of the moment, or simply opposed Marines.

The Marines and enlisted personnel of the U.S. Navy served an unusual function. They supervised several presidential elections, occurring each four years, 1924, 1928, etc. In the 1928 election there were 432 polling places in the country, each manned by either a Marine or a sailor. The election was peaceful and said to be honest. In 1927, President Diaz asked the U.S. to train a new National Guard. The purpose of the Guard was to disarm the political factions in the country and bring law and order to the population. By September 1929, there were 1,800 men in the National Guard, with an American officer in charge.

At the time of the departure of the Marines in 1933, the American officials felt that the electoral system and the National Guard were their two best contributions to the lives of Nicaraguans. Unfortunately neither lasted long in their original configurations.

Anastasio Somoza, who had been made chief of the National Guard, held the presidency from 1936 to 1956. If he was not the president in fact, the office would be held by a person subservient to him. He was assassinated in 1956, taking four bullets from a gunman who died immediately at the hands of Somoza's bodyguards. He was succeeded by one son, then the other.

The American military involvement, even though it was sanctioned by one or the other political parties, certainly by the party in office, was viewed by many Latin Americans as imperialist domination. There can be no question that the Marines fought against and killed Nicaraguans, who, for their own reasons, wished to bring about the fall of those in power. The Americans viewed their contribution as bringing peace to the country. It would be difficult to foretell that the National Guard, meant to be an element of stability, turned out, in the hands of Somoza, to be a force of repression. As far as Nicaraguans living after Somoza, the details disappear but the impression remains of military intersession on the part of the Americans.

Enter Augusto César Sandino (1895 – 1934), an important political person in the history of Nicaragua. He was a man of the Left, but he is principally identified as being opposed to the American military's presence in Nicaragua. He wanted to make the campaigns of the Marines so costly in lives that they would be forced to leave. That result never came but the two sides, Sandino on one, and the National Guard fighting with the Marines on the other, campaigned against one another for a few years until the Marines left in 1933. After Sandino's capture in 1934, his execution was ordered by Somoza, at the time commanding officer of the National Guard, but not yet president.

Sandino favored a coalescing of Central American countries for the purpose of reducing the influence of the Unites States, which he called the "Colossus of the North." Sandino could not be described as a Communist. He may have tended in that direction but never having achieved political power in Nicaragua there exists no record of how he might have governed. He was honored about 1959 in having the organization that would topple the Somoza family named after him. The Sandinistas, they were to be called. The organization is known officially as Sandinista Front of National Liberation, the FSLN.

The struggle between warring factions reached a climax on 17 July 1979, when the second son of the original Somoza was driven from office by the FSNL. Somoza relocated to Florida. On one side of the contest were the forces of Somoza, principally the National Guard, and on the other side the army of the FSLN (Fronte Sandinista Liberacion Nacional). By this time, Daniel Ortega, though not a founding member of the FSNL (he was too young), had risen to become one of the leaders of the movement. It was he who pulled together the factions to create a cohesive, successful force. He went on to win the presidential election of 1984 and governed until 1990 when he was defeated for a second term by Violeta Chamorro. Douglas knew that Ortega had returned to office as president, winning the election of 2006.

Because it was felt, and probably was the case, that some leaders among the FSNL were Communists, that group earned the hostility of American policy makers. The United States would not have Communist countries in this hemisphere if it could be helped. Their record in the matter of human rights was poor and to have Communism establish itself as a going concern was unacceptable. Douglas agreed with this point of view. Communism, as it has been practiced, is a brutal form of government, which does its best to expand the territory it covers and to increase the number of people under its supervision. At least under Democracy, voters have a chance to throw out the rascals now and again on a regular, predictable schedule. But Allende, Ortega, and Chavez, although leaning to the Left, have arrived by election, and in the case of Ortega, arrived, departed and returned, all by means of elections. These are not dictators of the Lenin and Stalin stripe.

Historical events cast long shadows. The dislike for Communism brought the United States once again into the affairs of Nicaragua. As the Sandinistas were forcing the last Somoza out of office, members at the top split into two factions, those favoring Marxism, and those opposed. Daniel and Humberto Ortega were in the first group. The members of the faction that broke off, anti-Marxists, called themselves the *Contras*. The United States, with money and personnel, lent a hand to this rebellious group that chose southern Honduras as a base of operations. The warfare may have been intermittent but it lasted approximately from 1981 to 1988. One unfortunate result was the need for the Nicaraguan government to divert assets from social programs to fending off the Contras. A second unfortunate result was the death of combatants and civilians along with atrocities probably committed by both sides. A third unfortunate result was drawing the United States into a struggle that could easily be viewed by people in all corners of the globe as another imperialist thrust, the far larger country inserting itself into the political life of a small neighbor. Douglas guessed that interventions of that nature would only end when activities in one country did not appear to threaten its neighbor.

When the Somoza family and those close to them left their country, their possessions (the large, immobile ones) remained behind. In an unseemly orgy, the upper echelon of the FSNL helped itself to what it needed. The Ortega brothers, and others, occupied sumptuous houses without the formality of a purchase. The rationale was that all this property belonged to the people, and that ownership was not being transferred to the new occupants. These properties remained in the hands of the people and were only being used by the new occupants. Douglas and millions of others had heard the expression, "To the victors go the spoils." Douglas went to his Bartlett's and found that William Learned Marcy (1786 – 1857) had said the following in 1832 while a senator from New York. "There is nothing wrong in the rule that to the victor belong the spoils of the enemy." Henceforth, Douglas titled this

Marcy's Law and it seemed to apply to Marxists as well as to common criminals.

Douglas' reading to educate himself on Nicaraguan affairs included two texts. The first was one of a series on world leaders published by Chelsea House Publishers, New York, in 1991. The title, obviously, is *Daniel Ortega*. It is by James D. Cockcroft. The second is, *The Civil War in Nicaragua: Inside the Sandinistas,* by Roger Miranda and William Ratliff. This text is from Transaction Publishers, New Brunswick, New Jersey. It came out in 1993.

Douglas reacted as he had when reading the two biographies on Chavez, to the effect that based on presentation and emphasis, the same material can leave different impressions. In *Daniel Ortega*, the author, James D. Cockcroft, blames the United States for many of Nicaragua's troubles, while the two authors of *The Civil War in Nicaragua* scarcely mention that influence. Indeed in the second book there is Part III titled "The Enemy of Humanity" with the sole chapter in the section called, "The Gringo Imperialists." In it the two authors analyze the interactions between the Nicaraguans and the U.S. government, placing the blame where it belongs (some on either side) depending on the actions taken.

As he was growing up, Douglas' father emphasized a distinction between taking responsibility and assessing blame. When your life is moving along nicely, he would say, it's a simple matter to take responsibility for the fine outcomes, and of course as there are no problems there is no one to blame. When the situation reverses, and successes are no longer rolling in, it's an easy matter to deny any responsibility and to find others to blame. Douglas' father, Carl Nielsen, counseled his three children that it was the wise course to accept 100% responsibility for all events that entered your life. It was often difficult to do, but it was the wise course. As far as blaming others, go easy on them. After serious examination, it usually turns out that those you wish to blame have only contributed minor amounts to your discomfort; and for the most part you brought your troubles on yourself.

In examining the actions of the Ortega brothers, Douglas wondered about the blame they heaped on the United States for the four decades of the rule under the three members of the Somoza family. Those three dictators did not accomplish the stripping of Nicaragua by themselves.

There must have been thousands of accomplices, all Nicaraguans, and when their turn came, the Sandinistas at the top recreated the seizure of assets that had taken place under the Somozas. The Ortega brothers occupied real estate left empty when previous owners skedaddled to Miami, or other safe harbors. Douglas wondered whether the top Sandinistas had stashed loot abroad against the eventuality that they would be forced to leave. Because it was a popular activity among leaders, Douglas guessed that those bank accounts away from home existed.

The United States did have a hand in the ascent of the Somoza family, but the responsibility does not rest there in its entirety. It would have been a better example for their countrymen if the Ortega brothers and others had led a more monastic life than they did after coming to power in 1979.

In another area, that of political coloration, the Sandinistas who remained in Nicaragua, holding the reins of power, declared themselves allied to Marxism. As well, they deepened contacts with the Soviet Union, Cuba and the revolutionaries in El Salvador. These actions were taken as though it would be acceptable to the United States, which as in the cases of Cuba and Chile, had shown that it would react to the importation of Marxism anywhere into the Americas. The long revolution fought by the Sandinistas to bring down the Somoza regime was for purposes of ending corruption, improving the infrastructure, providing health care and education, and working on what might be their greatest problem, poverty.

The introduction of ideology into the affairs of state was irresponsible on the part of the Ortegas. Douglas thought that they should be held 100% responsible for the conflict between the Contras and the United States on one side and the Sandinistas on the other. That decade-long tragedy could have been avoided by the Ortegas had they only stuck to repairing their country without wandering into the underbrush and the thickets of international power politics tinged with Marxism.

A satisfaction that Douglas realized in reading this second biography was that one of the co-authors, Roger Miranda, having been an important figure in the FSLN for several years, was present at many events that he described. He worked primarily with Humberto Ortega, who held the position of Defense Minister. Miranda attended important meetings and met, in Cuba and in Nicaragua, the influential politicians and military people. His reporting of the events stands a better chance of being accurate than most authors can hope for.

Being swayed by Marxism, the upper echelon of the Sandinistas brought on state control of the economy, with the expected disasters. Inflation ran out of control. Basic necessities became unavailable. Gross Domestic Produce per inhabitant fell to $300 per year, an amount equal to that of the residents of Haiti.

Because of the government's attempt to build the largest military force in Central American history, a draft had to be instituted for men between the ages of eighteen and twenty-five, and approximately half of the national budget devoted to military affairs.

Miranda made the point that the Contras did not consist exclusively of former members of Somoza's National Guard. A few hundred of the Contras could claim that as an origin, but the bulk of the Contras consisted of people of the country who wanted neither Somoza nor any form of dictatorship.

The Sandinistas paid a high price for being driven by ideology. In the first eighteen months after they had removed Somoza, the United States had come forth with $118 million in aid to Nicaragua. Naturally that source dried up once the Sandinistas adopted Communism. Douglas looked for the numbers of Nicaraguans who were put in prisons, tortured or executed, but even though these activities took place, no totals were offered.

ELENA AND DOUGLAS, A FAMILY

ELENA ARRIVED FIRST, followed by her furniture, cooking apparatus, books, clothes, and artwork. In preparation, Douglas had managed the move of one floor upwards, to a two-bedroom, two-bathroom apartment. The view was not an improvement but then ocean-front housing is not easy to come by.

The reaction by both to settling down to married life was slight shock. They understood that they had taken on a permanent arrangement that did not provide the excitement that comes with dating. They spoke about it and decided that spontaneity had given away to planning. These two objectives, or operations, were the opposite of one another, they concluded. Lovers make spontaneous moves. The moments can be exciting. Married people rarely act on the spur of the moment. They plan their lives together to achieve goals that have been decided upon, spoken or understood. Some of the thrills are gone but the satisfaction of having assembled a family unit and knowing what takes place the next day is often ample compensation.

Elena put a Florida driver's license at the top of her list. She opened a checking account and made a date for Saturday to have Douglas and her sign on both accounts. She made other financial transactions and spent any time available converting the goods that had arrived from Seattle into comfortable living space. Douglas, on surveying the finished product said, "I wish we had married earlier."

Elena interviewed the heads of the biology department at two universities. She had never taught but one of the universities offered her two sections of biology lab, which would occupy Tuesday and Thursday afternoons. The semester was starting soon. The laboratories would require setting up and the lab reports would need grading. The same department head all but promised that a teaching position would open up in freshman biology in the following semester. The laboratory work carried the title of lecturer while teaching biology was performed by an assistant professor. The head of the department was impressed by Elena's work in industry and her broad knowledge in the field of microbiology. He asked for a copy of her doctoral dissertation.

"You're newly married. I suppose that means babies are on the way," the department head said toward the end of the interview.

"We'll try for two and have them arrive in the summer for minimum disruption," Elena answered.

"And your husband is in the navy. That could mean a change of address," the head of the department continued.

"Yes, that's the wild card. My husband just made lieutenant commander. He may stay at this assignment four years and then be transferred."

"I hope you take the job offer. It appears we need one another," the head of the department said.

Elena and Douglas discussed details. She was anxious to accept the offer. "It's a miracle, when you think about it," she said. Elena was able to give more time than the position required and expressed an interest in substituting for teachers who fell ill or were otherwise indisposed. These would be among the teachers of the class she hoped to have assigned to her in the fall.

There was Florida to explore, from the beaches on the panhandle that fronted on the Gulf of Mexico to Key West jutting into the Caribbean Sea. They cared most for the saltwater swimming and did not get over the fact that good weather made this a year- round activity.

The frequency of their swims forced Elena to conclude that her abundant supply of hair would need trimming. She discussed the matter with Douglas who agreed reluctantly. "You're right on the merits," he granted. She promised to bring home a large sample and keep it available for examination.

Douglas was sent on his work to additional countries in the

Caribbean basin. Elena worked diligently at supervising her students in the labs, and longed for the following semester when teaching might come along. Prior to that there would be summer when she and Douglas would be off to Chile on their wedding trip.

Douglas was anticipating meeting the four people that had been selected by a member of the Cuban-American community that he had met. This person had taken an advanced degree in Cambridge, Massachusetts, and subsequently had been invited to teach at the University of Chile in Santiago. He had lived there in the era of Allende, before, during and after the years of Allende's presidency, 1970-1973. It was from the people that this professor had befriended while in Chile that Douglas would get his advanced education in the politics of this South American country.

This Cuban-American friend told Douglas that the four former colleagues he would meet varied in political point of view from out-and-out Communist to laissez-faire right wingers. Douglas was not told which person he met would wear which label. Douglas' task was to form his opinion based on the interviews.

Elena and Douglas flew into Santiago from Miami and after paying the reciprocal duty to enter the country (the United States charges Chileans to fill out a visa request) they moved through perfunctory immigration and customs inspections, then by a six-passenger bus to their hotel downtown. "It's a bit lavish," Douglas conceded, "but if you play your cards right you only get one wedding trip in your lifetime."

It was midday and they embarked on a walk around the center of the city. The main avenue is called the Alameda, but the name of the avenue includes that of Bernardo O'Higgins, whom the Chileans call the liberator as he was instrumental in ending the Spanish rule in 1818. The principal government building, no longer the largest, is La Moneda (the mint), which houses the offices of the presidency, although not the living quarters. The Alameda separates the Moneda from a statue of O'Higgins on horseback. The Moneda and the statue of O'Higgins form a large square. There is ample open space for anyone wishing to mount a coup to amass armored vehicles and battalions of armed men. Douglas was interested in walking around this building because it was here that Allende was surrounded by units of the army on 11 September 1973. Two of the people whom Douglas interviewed said that without doubt Allende had committed suicide. He was not killed in a shoot-out with men in the army. The man to whom Douglas talked about the matter said he knew a friend of the pathologist who had performed the autopsy. A woman he spoke to said that new data turned up recently confirmed that Allende had taken his life.

Douglas had two important questions to be answered on this trip. The first was to ascertain how powerful a Leftist Allende was (Lenin, Douglas had concluded, being the gold standard for extreme Leftism) and the second, was there any particular event that led the armed forces to stage their coup.

To the first question, Douglas concluded that Allende was a middle of the road Socialist who came to power through an election and who in his three years in office kept to the parliamentary system, that is, ruling through both houses of congress.

Allende's political platform had a Socialist ring but the reforms he advocated were much in need by the large section of the population that was impoverished. Allende neither took nor held political prisoners, nor was it a crime in his times to speak out against government policies and actions.

The man whose friend knew the performer of the autopsy had this to say, to the effect that it was one thing to give an excellent speech, as Allende could and did, and another to run an economy, which Allende could not. One of Allende's campaign promises was that he would bring inflation under control. He learned to his and the country's dismay that he could not finance all the social programs that he thought vital while keeping the currency's purchasing power stable.

The same friend, showing his colors, remarked that Socialists and others who try to change the ways of an entire nation feel that they know the way to do it and can do no wrong. No one knows better than they. How better to disabuse them of this notion except to have their plans fail! This friend went on to say brilliant men could apply to be Pope. What did it matter if they are not Catholic? They were brilliant!

Another individual Elena and Douglas conferred with told them that people of the Left, not all of them, are able to postulate without proof; that is, they can fabricate axioms when it suits their purposes. One of these was that Chile's industry did not work to capacity, thereby making it difficult for the country to have sufficient quantity of the basics. Never mind that there had been no investigation into this matter. It was declared to be the truth. A second postulate held that under Socialism a new man would be created. When the ownership of personal property is removed and all workers produce for the benefit of society as a whole then this new Socialistic man will appear.

The events that took place, however, were different. Companies that produced the basics of daily life, sensing that they might be nationalized, produced less than they might have. Many owners of these companies cashed out and left the country. The citizens who could afford to do so started to hoard necessities. Those who could not afford to hoard faced living with shortages. The result was protest marches by housewives holding a pot or pan in one hand and a wooden spoon in the other. New Socialistic man never arrived. People change slowly. People living through any of the 5,000 years of recorded history have lived their lives pretty much the same way others have.

As an additional disaster, farmers, fearing the taking of some of their land, planted less than they might. A few who were able to moved their farm machinery and farm animals to the east, into Argentina. This activity took place in the south of Chile where the borders are porous. Perhaps the guards at the frontier were susceptible to being bribed.

Those that Elena and Douglas spoke to thought that Chileans in general were satisfied with Allende's programs to help the poor until shortages of basics materialized. From then on he could do little right. When the coup came, General Pinochet and others in the military, not schooled in running an economy, reverted to market forces. They found economists who had graduated from the University of Chicago Business School. These so-called "Chicago Boys" stabilized the country's economy. Douglas thought the country as he saw it now was prosperous but he admitted to himself that he was examining a small portion of a country 2,400 miles in length. It is the case, he was told, that the export of copper still accounted for half of the country's income earned abroad.

On the question of whether there was one act on the part of the Allende regime that triggered the coup, none of the people Elena and Douglas spoke to could identify such an event. They thought it was the accumulation of failures, demonstrating that while Socialism reads well for some people, it is difficult for government leaders to operate an economy based on Socialist precepts. Market forces prevail in the end and attempts at creating the new Socialist man have always failed. How rapidly Russian, Chinese and Central European populations reverted to economies that gave them choices when the yoke of Communism was lifted!

At dinner one evening, nearing the end of their stay, Douglas turned to Elena and asked, "Well, what do you think?" Elena had participated in all the conversations and had taken notes as well as writing a summary of her thoughts when they were in their hotel room.

"What we heard speaks for itself, I would say," she answered. And then she added, "There's a strong sentimental attachment for Allende but not for his way of governing. Our visit to the museum in his honor on the Avenida Republica spoke volumes on those matters."

Douglas was silent for a moment, reflecting on Elena's observations. He thought he would pursue the topic. "What do you think of Socialism and Communism now that we have had a look at them?"

"At heart, I think that history has had societies move toward the Left, a constant drift in that direction, with the speed varying over the decades," Elena answered. She held up her hand, indicating that she had a few words to add. "If society as a whole doesn't agree on a decent division of political power and wealth, then the have-nots will rearrange the social contract for the entire society."

Douglas shook his head slowly, indicating that he agreed with the insight of her remark. Then he asked, "Do you suppose we'll come to a situation at home in which no further drift to the Left is required?"

"The future is not that clear. Communism as practiced by the brutal dictators, Lenin, Stalin, Mao and Castro, to name four, was overkill, if you'll pardon the expression. The Soviet Union became Russia again, and China is becoming a capitalistic society. When the Castros die off, Cuba will once again become a democracy with a constitution, perhaps a Left-leaning democracy. So when it's overdone, a reaction sets in to restore equilibrium."

"It's interesting to me," Douglas said, "that in the case of these Latin American dictators, Allende, Ortega and Chavez, that they used elections to achieve power, although Chavez has not been afraid to stage a coup."

"It tells me that citizens in these nations are insisting on elections. They don't mind experiments to the Left, but they want to retain the power to end the experiment if in their judgment it is failing."

"Elena, you're a keen observer. You didn't let on that you have thought considerably about politics. At home, do we have a greater distance to travel toward the Left?"

"The obvious answer is that we have not solved how to pay for universal health care. Any solution will be done at the cost of additional distribution of wealth from the rich toward the remainder of society," Elena answered.

"Yes, I suppose so. I don't think there's another way but of course if we raise taxes there might be a reduced income to the Treasury," Douglas said.

"I'm aware of that outcome," Elena said. "I don't know that doctrinaire Leftists are aware of it, and I don't know that it's convenient for them to admit to it."

"Are you having a nice time?" Douglas asked.

"Yes, and I hope for more trips like this one. There are too few stamps on my passport. But there's another matter. We've talked about having two children. If I get pregnant in October, then the baby will arrive early in July, the best time as far as my teaching job is concerned. Have you heard of a woman's best six days to get pregnant?"

"No, I didn't know there was such a phenomenon," Douglas said.

"The six days are three days on either side of the moment the egg appears. If a man cooperates for those six days, pregnancy is almost guaranteed."

"It sounds like great fun."

"Young mothers I've talked to in Seattle reported to me that their men all thought that the experience would be delightful but after the fourth night they were ready to check into a motel."

"Elena, I look forward to challenges. I'll do my level best."

APPENDIX A

ST. PETERSBURG HAS had its name changed several times since its founding in 1703. Czar Peter the Great seized lands that were a Swedish outpost on the Baltic Sea and built a city there, starting in May 1703. He named the city after his patron saint and made it the capital of Russia in 1712, the seat of government having been Moscow. The Bolsheviks made Moscow the capital once again in 1918.

At the start of World War I, the government felt that St. Petersburg sounded excessively Germanic. The name of the city was changed to Petrograd in 1914. When Lenin died in 1924, the city's name was changed once again to Leningrad.

After the Soviet Union went out of existence, the populace voted to determine whether the name should be changed back to the original. Fifty-four percent of voters wanted the change and the city has been St. Petersburg since 1991.

APPENDIX B

IN READING ABOUT the events of 1917, particularly about the arrival of Communism in Russia, one runs across the expression, "Sealed Train." It refers to the railroad car used by Lenin and thirty-two others (one publication records as many as thirty-eight people) in their ride north from Switzerland in April 1917. Lenin and other important Communists were on their way from Switzerland to Russia and they asked the German government to seal the car they were occupying so that at some later date they could not be accused of cutting deals with the German government during the trip.

Of course Lenin had already cut his deals with the Germans. If he could take Russia out of the war then Germany could move many of its troops on their eastern front to the western front where these new forces, combined with those troops already fighting there, might have a chance of defeating the British, French and Americans. Vast sums of money were transferred from the German government to the Bolshevik movement so that a propaganda campaign could be mounted, a campaign featuring peace between the two countries.

There are several sources for information on the route taken by the sealed train. "Lenin, A new Autobiography," by General Dmitri Volkogonov (The Free Press, 1994) provides details. Lenin lived in Zurich. He travelled by train north via Berlin to the Baltic Sea, where he took a ferry for Trelleborg in the south of Sweden. He proceeded by train to Malmö and on to Stockholm. He continued by train north along the east coast of Sweden to the northernmost point of the Gulf of Bothnia. He crossed to Finland in a sled and went by train to Petrograd, arriving in April 1917. The Sealed Train travel is just that portion of the trip through Germany.

Lenin left Russia in July as the government of Kerensky had issued arrest warrants for him. He back-tracked to Helsinki and safety. He made it back to Petrograd in October 1917.

The start of the revolution is given two dates: 25 October and 6 November 1917. On that date, the Bolsheviks staged their revolution and ended the government of Kerensky. One could say that the change in governments did not take place in one day. Perhaps two weeks were required for the new group to replace the previous administration. The reason for the two dates, one in October and one in November, is that the Russians were among the last to accommodate the order of Pope Gregory XIII, who stipulated in 1582 that about ten days would be sacrificed in order to bring the calendar (The Julian Calendar) in synchronization with the solar calendar. When Pope Gregory XIII issued his order, the Catholic countries took action right away. The United Kingdom and its colonies waited until 1752 and the Russians not until early in the 20th Century.

The reason the calendar fell out of whack was that Julius Caesar, in 46BC, had set the year to be 365.25 days in duration. In fact it is nearer to 365.2422 days, a small difference taken into account by Gregory XIII's changes. By using Pope Gregory's duration, the vernal equinox, for instance, falls behind or moves ahead of solar time gradually. The proper application of leap years is required, which phenomenon Caesar and his astronomer recognized. They recognized that a leap year was required each four years, but could not measure the small errors that could build up over the centuries if one did not do something at the end of a century, as we do currently.

Credit goes to Julius Caesar for arriving at 365.25 days per year. There was no particular system in place for keeping track of the seasons of the year until he made his adjustments. It was asking too much of science in the time of Caesar to get closer than 365.25 days. Pope Gregory XIII did very well to arrive at 365.2422.

A volume titled "Sealed Train," by Michael Pearson (G.P. Putnam's Sons, 1975) gives additional details. A map shows the itinerary. The train left Zurich and went to Frankfurt and Berlin before arriving at Sassnitz, the ferry port on the Baltic Sea. The ferry crossed to Trelleborg, in Sweden, and the party proceeded north as noted. The border town in Finland is Tornio and the tracks take Lenin to Petrograd by a route north and east of Helsinki, which is on the Baltic Sea. The trip from Zurich to Petrograd spanned one week.

The author Michael Pearson gives the date for the arrival of Lenin at Petrograd as 18 April 1917, but he does not say whether this is by the old or new calendar. He does instruct us that by "sealed train" we are not to think of a locked passenger car. We should think of a white chalk mark on the floor of the car, which demarks the start of Lenin's section that he occupied with his wife.

It is correct that the Bolsheviks set the date for their armed uprising as 6 November 1917. It was confined to the area of Petrograd. Mr. Pearson writes that they had achieved their aim and replaced the Kerensky government by 8 November. Some time must have passed before the Bolsheviks had gained complete control of all Russia.

BIBLIOGRAPHY

Alexandrov, Victor. The Tukhachevsky Affair. Englewood Cliffs, NJ: Prentice-Hall, 1962.

Allende, Isabel. My Invented Country: A Nostalgic Journey Through Chile. New York: Harper Collins, 2003.

Anderson, Jon Lee. "The Revolutionary," The New Yorker 10 Sept. 2001: pp. 60 – 79.

Carson, Clarence B. Basic Communism: Its Rise, Spread and Debacle in the 20th Century. Wadley, AL: American Textbook Committee, 1990.

Chang, Jung, and Jon Halliday. Mao, The Unknown Story. New York: Knopf, 2005

Cockcroft, James D. Daniel Ortega. New York: Chelsea House, 1991.

Creighton, Louise. Life and Letters of Mandell Creighton. London: Longmans, Green, 1904.

Davis, Daniel S. Spain's Civil War: The Last Great Cause. New York: E.P. Dutton, 1975.

DePalma, Anthony. The Man Who Invented Fidel: Cuba, Castro, and Herbert L. Matthews of the New York Times. New York: Perseus, 2006.

Droz, Jacques. Europe Between Revolutions 1815-1848. New York: Harper & Row, 1967.

Duveau, George. 1848 The Making of a Revolution. New York: Pantheon, Random House, 1967.

Engels, Friedrich and Karl Marx. The Communist Manifesto. New York: Signet, Penguin Group, 1998.

Engels, Friedrich and Karl Marx. The Communist Manifesto. New York: Verso, 1998.

Faundez, Julio. Marxism and Democracy in Chile; from 1932 to the Fall of Allende. New Haven, CT: Yale University, 1988.

Gimbel, Wendy. Havana Dreams. New York: Knopf, 1998.

Hobsbawm, E.J. The Age of Revolution: Europe 1789-1848. London: Weidenfeld and Nicolson, 1962.

Jones, Bart. !HUGO! Hanover, NH: Steerforth, 2007.

Kim, Ilpyong J., ed. Development and Cultural Change: Cross-Cultural Perspectives. New York: Paragon House, 1986.

Malia, Martin. The Soviet Tragedy, A History of Socialism in Russia, 1917 – 1991. New York: Free Press, 1994.

Marcano, Cristina, and Alberto Barrera Tyszka. Hugo Chavez. New York: Random House. 2006.

Martin, Lionel. The Early Fidel: The Roots of Castro's Communism. Secaucus, NJ: Lyle Stuart, 1978.

Marx, Karl. Das Kapital, A Critique of Political Economy. Washington, D.C.: Regnery.

---. Marx for Beginners. New York: Pantheon Books, 1975.

Meneses, Enrique. Fidel Castro. New York: Taplinger, 1966.

Miranda, Roger, and William Ratliff. The Civil War in Nicaragua; Inside the Sandinistas. New Brunswick, NJ: Transaction, 1993.

Morley, Morris M., and James F. Petras. "How Allende Fell." A Study in U.S.-Chilean Relations. Nottingham, UK: Bertrand Russell Peace Foundation, 1974.

Payne, Robert. The Rise and Fall of Stalin. New York: Simon & Schuster, 1965.

Preston, Paul. Franco. New York: Basic Books, 1994.

Quirk, Robert E. Fidel Castro: The Full Story of his Rise to Power. New York: W.W. Norton, 1993.

Quotations From Chairman Mao Tse-tung. San Francisco: Chinese Books and Periodicals.

Short, Philip. Mao, A Life. New York: Holt, 1999.

Simons, Geoff. Cuba: From Conquistador to Castro. New York: St. Martin's, 1996

Snow, Edgar. Red Star Over China. New York: Grove Press, 1938.

Snow, Lois Wheeler. Edgar Snow's China. New York: Random House, 1981.

Spence, Jonathan. Mao Zedong. New York: Viking Book, 1999.

Szulc, Tad. Fidel: A Critical Portrait. New York: Morrow, 1986.

"The Program of the Popular Front, and His Biography." Salvador Allende, His Political Platform. Washington, D.C.: Squirrel Publications.

Valladares, Armando. Against All Hope: The Prison Memoirs. New York: Knopf, 1986.

Volkogonov, Dmitri. Lenin, A New Biography. New York: Free Press, 1994.

Wilson, Edmund. To The Finland Station. Garden City, NY: Doubleday, 1940.

ABOUT THE AUTHOR

Fred Weekes lives in Lakewood, Washington, a city forty-five miles south of Seattle on the I-5 corridor. After a career in business and engineering he retired to writing on topics that interested him: World War II aviation, general reference, and love stories. Some of these titles are available through iUniverse. He enjoys writing romances. They may be his favorites. This is a study of the history of Communism as understood by a young naval officer. Naturally there will be romantic interludes added to this examination.

The room that Weekes writes in has a fine view of a lake. Water fowl are in abundance and an occasional heron and eagle come by.

Weekes holds degrees from the University of Pennsylvania and Catholic University of America. He prizes these as he sees no chance of earning additional degrees.